Learning to Fly

Also by April Henry

Circles of Confusion
Square in the Face
Heart-Shaped Box

Learning to Fly

APRIL HENRY

THOMAS DUNNE BOOKS / ST. MARTIN'S MINOTAUR
New York

THOMAS DUNNE BOOKS.
An imprint of St. Martin's Press.

www.minotaurbooks.com

Book design by Heidi Eriksen

Library of Congress Cataloging-in-Publication Data

Henry, April.
    Learning to fly / April Henry.
        p.   cm.
    ISBN 0-312-29052-7
    1. Traffic accidents—Fiction. 2. Mistaken identity—Fiction. 3. Drug
traffic—Fiction. 4. Young women—Fiction. I. Title.

PS3558.E4969 L43   2002
813'.54—dc21
                                                                    2001058549

10 9 8 7 6 5 4 3 2

This book is for Nora,
who liked the idea from the start.

Acknowledgments

Sergeant Master Criminalist Ken Jones came to my burglarized house to take fingerprints and ended up patiently answering my questions about what a criminalist does and why it's important. Val Humble graciously shared his experience with alopecia. Kevin Beckstrom answered my questions about traffic accidents. When I needed to know if an AK-15 has a shiny or a matte surface, among other things, I turned to Joe Collins, Keith Gipson, Lee Hadaway, and Fred Rea. Any errors are my own.

Don Cannon let me borrow his name, but there the resemblance to the real Don ends. Folks on DorothyL have provided me with advice and a long list of great books to read. And Jan Bellis-Squires's support—as well as that of dozens of other Kaiser Permanente staff—has been invaluable.

Wendy Schmalz continues to be a friend, cheerleader, and fairy godmother all rolled into one. Julie Sullivan is a delight to work with. And when I grow up, I want to be just like Ruth Cavin.

I'm learning to fly, but I ain't got wings
Coming down is the hardest thing

   —"Learning to Fly" by Tom Petty and Jeff Lynne

Warning: Cape does not enable user to fly.

                —label from a Batman costume

Learning
to
Fly

One

Saturday, OCTOBER 14, 5:20 P.M.

The moment before Free Meeker drove into the dust storm, the sky was a clear bleached blue. The next day Free would read in *The Oregonian* about how a farmer plowing his fields, eleven weeks without rain, and a wind clocked at eighty-four miles an hour had combined to cause a fifty-two-car chain-reaction accident. The same story would also list Free among the dead.

But when everything began, all Free knew was that suddenly she couldn't see a damn thing outside her car's windshield. The Impala had suddenly been enveloped in a brown fog.

"Hang on!" Free screamed at Lydia. She put her foot on the brakes and began to pump. Frantically, she tried to recall the configuration of cars that had been around them before the dirt dropped like a curtain. Outside their windows nothing but boiling brown. She couldn't see three feet in any direction. What had been ahead of them, behind them, to either side? A pack of cars, that was all she could remember. Her eyes darted from the windshield to the sideview mirror to the rearview mirror. Nothing back there but darkness. Wait—did the mirror show headlights a few feet behind them, piercing the gloom?

Ease up on the brakes, she told herself. If they stopped

abruptly, they'd get rear-ended. Turning on her own lights, Free leaned forward to peer through the windshield.

A hundred feet ahead of her, a sudden patch of clarity in the wall of dust opened up. Occupied by a fat white motor home. At a dead stop, angled across both westbound lanes. Old man's face in the driver's side window. Mouth open. Eyes wide behind black-framed glasses. Free was going to T-bone him for sure. Already knowing it was too late, she jerked the Impala's steering wheel hard to the left.

A red pickup loomed up beside her, close enough that if her window had been open, Free could have reached out and touched the yellow flames painted on the side. Could she squeeze through the rapidly narrowing gap between the pickup and the motor home? Even as she formed the thought, Free knew there was no-where to go.

But then the red pickup bucked as an invisible blow from behind sent it angling away from her, creating a space, or at least the possibility of one. Ignoring Lydia whimpering beside her, Free steered for it, her foot once again pumping the brakes. With a long squeal, they refused to hold. The car went sliding beneath her, the road as slick as if it were coated with black ice. But this was October.

A second passed, just long enough for Free to think that the old lap belt was not going to be enough to save her from this. Long enough for her to exchange a glance with Lydia. The other woman's mouth was wide in a scream that mingled with the shriek of brakes. They were going to die next to each other, two strangers who had met an hour ago when Free picked Lydia up from the side of the road.

And then, miraculously, the Impala's brakes caught and held. The car shuddered to a stop. Close enough to the motor home that you couldn't have slipped a pack of gum between them.

For a second, the world seemed to hold its breath. A gust of wind rocked the car. And then Free heard it coming. The sound of a semi barreling down on them from behind. She didn't even have time to brace herself. The cab of the semi passed them, so close that one of the great black wheels snapped off her sideview mirror. The semi slammed into the motor home, pushing it ahead as easily as a breeze scuds a crumpled piece of paper. One trailer, then two, thundered past them. Then, like the last player in a game of crack the whip, the final trailer snapped into the front corner of the Impala, spinning it sideways. The impact so hard it knocked Free out of her Birkenstocks.

Another gust of wind rocked the car, clearing things a little. They were looking at dead yellow grass. The Impala faced the side of the freeway. And, Free realized, as she looked past Lydia's shoulder at a big gold-colored car that popped out of the swirling dust and headed straight toward them, they were back in play again.

"Oh, God," Lydia screamed. Or at least she started to. All she got out was the "guh" sound before the car slammed into them broadside. Free's head snapped against the side window as the car sloughed around. Her vision narrowed to a dark tunnel. She couldn't tell if her eyes were closed or open. Another impact, this one from behind, followed immediately by one in front. They were being knocked around like a pinball. The only way they were going to survive was to get out of the car and away from the road. Free blinked rapidly, trying to focus. The passenger's side window was gone. Lydia was slumped unmoving over the inward bulge of the door.

"Lydia, come on, we've got to get out of here before we get hit again." Lydia didn't move. Free shook her shoulder. The other woman's head bobbed on her loose neck, turning toward Free. Lydia's mouth was slack and her eyes somehow flat.

A black SUV hit them, a glancing blow that tore off the back bumper with a long shriek. Lydia fell forward, sprawling against the dash. Free leaned down and picked up her shoes. At first, she couldn't get her door open. She rammed it again and again with her shoulder, finally creating a gap. Oh God, something was still holding her back. She was trapped. Then she realized she hadn't undone her seatbelt. She pressed the latch. Ignoring the scraping of her hips, Free managed to just squeeze through the door. At the last moment, she remembered to keep her belly centered so that nothing touched it.

The air had lightened a bit. She could see about twenty feet ahead of her. It was like being in a brown fog. Grit coated her teeth, scratched her eyes. For a minute, Free couldn't think. The Impala was in the middle of a nest of cars, some with their hoods pushed up, others with their doors torn away. A few feet away, a trucker hauling the long cylinder of a tanker had managed to stop in the median strip. Looking at the warning flames painted on the back, Free was thankful it sat untouched.

In between the tanker truck and what was left of Free's Impala, a semi was shooting steam into the air. The hissing sound was punctuated by a continuing series of shrieks and bangs, as more and more cars drove into the dust with their cruise controls still set at seventy miles an hour. Free walked around the semi, then gasped in shock. A small white car was embedded in the grill of the truck's cab. The body of its owner, an elderly woman, lay stretched out over the hood of the car. Her hands still held the steering wheel, which was no longer connected to anything. Free was glad she couldn't see the woman's face.

Everything had the unreality of a dream, the vivid texture of a nightmare. Absurdly, it reminded Free of the time when she was twelve and acccidently ate one of Bob's acid tabs.

A balding man walked past her, talking on a tiny cell phone, so excited his words ran together in a single shout. "We've got people dying out here!" A small purple car popped out of the dust and hurtled toward him, bouncing him up over the hood and the top of the car before Free could even think to shout a warning. His body was thrown behind a tangle of crushed and crumpled vehicles. The wind shifted, and so did the visibility, leaving her temporarily blind. The grinding sounds of another crash, very near, made Free jump.

She wanted to stop and help the guy on the cell phone, but she had to get away before she got killed too. Free began to run up the slope, away from the accident. Dirt coated her throat. She heard a shout to her right. "Run up that hill, girls! Run!" Free saw a woman pushing two girls, about eight and ten, ahead of her. All of them dark-haired and dressed up in what Free thought of as "churchy" clothes. The four of them ran over the clumps of scrub grass, hearing the sounds behind them as more and more cars rounded the bend and drove blindly into the dust storm.

A wire fence. Free put her back against it and turned to face the way she had come. The woman and the two girls stumbled to a stop, and they, too, turned to face the scene of the accident. All of them too stunned to make any noise, or even to cry.

The air seemed to be getting lighter. Free's watch read 5:23. She spit blood and dirt into her hand, and then wiped it on the back of her jeans. Realizing she was still barefoot and holding her sandals in her left hand, she leaned over to slip them on. Dizziness pressed down on her. She stumbled sideways until she finally righted herself. The woman, with her girls' faces pressed into her soft-looking body, watched Free. Looking at the children, Free wished there was someplace she could hide.

"What happened?" Free asked.

The other woman shook her head. "It must be like the dust bowl or something. All I know is that my husband tried to pull onto the inside shoulder, but we hit something in front of us. Then we were rear-ended, and I think we might have spun around and hit another car."

Looking at the woman's face, contorted with grief and fear, Free knew enough not to ask where her husband was. The girls didn't, though. Their voices muffled by their mother's pleated paisley dress, they were beginning to cry and ask for their daddy.

The wind shifted and the open space expanded, giving Free her first overview of what had happened. To their left, dark clouds of dirt still boiled on one side of the pale blue sky, like ink spilled into a bowl of milk. Below them was the curve of the four-lane highway, bordered by weeds and split down the middle by a grassy median strip gone yellow from drought. On their right, the air was beginning to clear.

The highway was filled with dozens of cars, two lines converging in a knot that crossed the median strip. Where Free stood was just above the center of the knot. Near the ends of both lines, cars and trucks were pushed together, bumper to bumper, one vehicle having rear-ended the next to form long, snaking lines. In the center, the damage was much greater. Cars and semis sat steaming in a jumbled mess that sprawled past the boundaries of the road. There were cars jammed nose to nose, or rolled on their sides, or half climbed on top of one another, reminding Free of humping dogs. Some were completely overturned, as clumsy-looking as beetles on their backs.

The stench of scorched rubber and spilled fuel was stronger even than the smell of dirt. Near the tail end of the pileup an old Datsun 240-Z took off, weaving around wrecked cars, driving in the breakdown lane. His rear bumper dragged behind him, leaving a trail of popping sparks. Free braced herself for the explosion, but it never came.

She looked back at the main knot of accidents. Lydia was beyond help, but there must be people down there who could benefit from the little first-aid kit she kept in the trunk. From watching a Petorium training video, she even knew a bit of first aid.

If she hadn't impulsively picked Lydia up an hour ago, this wouldn't have happened. Instead of standing here with her totaled car somewhere in the mess down below, Free would have been heading home to Medford, in the southwest corner of Oregon. But she still had a few days off, and had been in no hurry to get home. Offering to take Lydia to Portland had been an impulsive act, out-of-character for Free, despite the name her parents had saddled her with. Now her good deed may well have gotten Lydia killed. If Free hadn't pulled over and Lydia had had to stand by the side of the road for twenty more minutes, she might well have been in one of the cars at the end of the line, or missed the accident altogether.

"I'm going back down," she told the woman who still held her daughters close. "Maybe I can do something. Help somebody."

The other woman nodded without speaking. Free picked her way down the hill. The first person she saw made her realize how nonsensical her task was. A young woman, obviously dead, sprawled on the ground, her legs cut off mid-thigh. Free looked away as fast as she could, already knowing it was too late, that the sight had burned itself into her brain. She hoped the woman up on the hill stayed put with her daughters.

Only a few feet away, two men stood close together, arguing with each other about whose fault the accident was, ignoring the chaos all around them. Free couldn't blame them. Everything was so overwhelming that maybe the best you could do was to focus on one thing at a time.

Heading in the direction she thought the Impala was, Free edged her way around a pile of debris, like the sweepings from God's broom. Tangled scraps of metal, curving pieces of black rubber, all of it covered by glass that glittered like diamonds. The only thing Free recognized was a door, wrenched from its hinges. The wind gusted again, pushing against her so hard Free couldn't catch her breath. She had to cup her hand over her mouth to provide a space to inhale.

A man in his forties ran up to her. "Help me!" She could barely hear his shout over the wind roaring in her ears. His face was so red she worried he would have a stroke on the spot. "My wife!" Still shouting, he slid back the door to a crumpled purple minivan, and now he climbed in. Free looked in the door. Two women, one about forty, the other about sixty, sat in the warped back seat. Free leaned in and helped him unfasten their seatbelts, already knowing it was too late. The two women sat slumped and silent, not breathing, not moving, no pulse when she rested her fingers tentatively against the sides of their throats. "I'm sorry," she said, then backed out of the van. She left the man with his head buried in his wife's lap.

As Free made her way to where she thought her car was, a man in his mid-fifties walked by. His hand was over his heart as if he were about to say the pledge of allegiance. The wind had died again, so she could hear what he was saying to himself. "My chest," he was mumbling. "My chest hurts." Bruised from the steering wheel or the first pangs of a heart attack? Either way, Free figured there was nothing she could do.

She came upon an old man, his squinting face furrowed into wrinkles. A young boy held his legs so tightly that the older man was in danger of tumbling over. "I've lost my glasses," the old man called out, his face turning blindly back and forth. "I can't see." Free walked them up the hill, taking care to angle away from the woman without any legs, and helped the old man sit down on the brittle grass. Taking the boy's hot, wet face in her hands, Free said, "You have to help your grandpa, okay? You have to stay with him and help keep him calm. Help is coming." He nodded vigorously. She thought of the man with the cell phone and pushed the thought away. Surely someone had gotten through by now.

Finally, she spotted the distinctive flat mint green of the Impala, a color that Detroit hadn't used since about 1975. The car itself was nearly unrecognizable. Looking at it, Free felt her heart squeeze within her chest. The car had been her freedom, her personal space, her one valuable possession. Now it was nothing but scrap. One of the front wheels had been turned until it was nearly parallel to the axle. Most of the front of the car was crushed backward to the firewall. The back bumper was gone. Whatever had hit the passenger side had done so with so much force that it had left its license plate behind.

Free reached through the still-open door to get her keys from the ignition. She was careful not to touch Lydia's body, which now lay draped over the center of the seat. Still, Free's groping fingers touched something unexpected, and she jerked her hand back until she saw what it was. Lydia's purse. Free never carried one, fitting everything she needed in a man's wallet tucked into the back pocket of her jeans. She picked up the purse. Even though Lydia had said she had no family, someone would want to know what had happened to her, and Free figured it was her duty to tell them.

While Free tried to fit the key into the Impala's trunk, a woman wearing a red-and-white print dress and only one red high heel walked past. She was screaming, "Gary! Gary!" without pausing for an answer. Maybe she knew there wasn't going to be one. Free's key refused to turn, and finally she gave up on the idea of getting the first-aid kit.

The wind gusted again, hard enough that it felt like she could lean into it and let go without falling forward. If only she could let go. A few yards away, a man in a white VW pickup was trying to free it from a gray Plymouth Colt. Reverse, forward, reverse, forward, rocking the wheel from side to side, trying to shake the two vehicles apart. He was oblivious to the fact that even if he succeeded, there was no place left for him to go.

"Hey, lady!" a man's voice called. "Lady, can you give me some help over here?" Part of Free was reluctant to turn, part of her was glad to think there might be something she could do with nothing but her bare hands to offer.

The speaker looked like a trucker, a short man with a lined, tanned face shaded by a black ball cap. He was kneeling beside a younger man in a red, white and blue Tommy Hilfiger shirt who lay faceup on the ground. The younger man was trying to push himself up from the ground, but Free noticed that his legs weren't moving.

"Can you help me get him to be still?" The trucker stood up and put his hand on Free's shoulder. In a low voice, he said into her ear, "I think he's paralyzed. And he's tearing himself up inside every time he moves. I can hear it." Free knelt down with him beside the younger man, setting Lydia's purse to one side.

The trucker put his hands on the younger man's shoulders and pressed him back to the ground. "Take it easy, buddy, take it easy. You're gonna hurt yourself even more if you move."

"My bag! I need my bag!" Pale blue eyes wild in his smudged face. Blood matted his short dark hair, bleached to brass on top. A tattoo circled one wrist.

"Not that bad, you don't." The older man's voice was gruff. A cigarette was perched behind his ear. "I think you got a broken back. You gotta stay still or you'll hurt yourself even more."

"What's your name?" Free leaned in.

"Jamie." Mumbled through a mouth of broken teeth. A line of blood snaked down from his left ear. This close she could see that one pupil was a pinprick, the other so wide it overwhelmed the whole iris. When she looked up, the trucker gave Free a little nod, and she knew he had seen these signs, too.

"You need to stay still." She touched Jamie's cheek for emphasis, then had to stop herself from pulling back when she felt how damp he was, clammy and cold.

"Um-mm." Shaking his head in denial, Jamie tried to rise again. "Gotta get my bag." His voice was equal parts exhaustion and determination.

She winced at the sound of something grinding inside him. Mimicking the trucker, she put her hands on his shoulders and pressed him back to the ground.

"He's right. You've got to lie still. Forget about your bag."

The word "bag" seemed to only spur Jamie on. "I need it. I've got to get it. Don'll kill me if I don't give it to him." He managed to half-sit up. Free heard something pop. The sound decided her.

"I'll get your bag, Jamie. What car is yours?"

He stopped struggling. "Brown Honda Accord." His face twisted as another spasm coursed through him. "There's a sock monkey on the rearview mirror."

"A sock monkey. Okay." Free nodded and got to her feet.

"And it's a black Nike bag. In the front seat. At least it was." He let himself fall back, apparently satisfied that someone was finally listening to him.

In the few minutes that Free had been concentrating on Jamie, she had managed to block everything else out. Jamie had presented a more-or-less manageable challenge. Now when Free stood up and confronted the totality of the wreck again, her knees sagged. It overwhelmed all her senses. Her mouth tasted of dirt and blood. Was it her imagination, or was the smell of blood now as strong as the scent of spilled fuel, a sickening, heavy, sweetish stench? The screams of the injured mingled with the cries of the newly bereaved. And finally, finally she heard the sound of sirens in the distance.

Free began to pick her way back along the line of cars, stepping over pieces of metal, keeping her head down, trying to avoid one more picture that would sear its way into her memory. She couldn't tell if she were crying, or if it was just the dust burning her eyes.

The ground was littered with what looked like square, white worms, many of them squashed. After a minute she realized that a trucker must have lost his load of frozen French fries.

Approaching her task methodically, Free forced herself to look at one car at a time. It was easier that way, to see the accident in sections. Jamie didn't look capable of walking, so the car he had been ejected from couldn't be too far off. But she didn't see it right away. Just as had happened with the Impala, the Honda must have been pushed further away from Jamie as it was hit again and again. She walked past a blue Subaru wagon, back end crumpled, but basically all right. Amazingly, its emergency flashers were still working behind shards of plastic, blinking on and off. Beyond it, was a burgundy Ford Ranger with its driver's side door torn off. Ahead of that, a white car did a handstand on its front bumper, caught between the Ranger and a pale blue Cutlass. A frail bald man hung from his seatbelt, arms dangling. Even to her untrained eye, both were fractured. Free was sure he was dead, but jumped when he moaned for help.

She reached in through the open window and touched the top of his liver-spotted head, afraid to do any more. His red-rimmed eyes pleaded with her from his upside-down face. "I'm sorry," Free said, "but I don't think I could get you out without hurting you." The sirens were closer now. She could see flashing red lights through the gloom. "Hear that? That's the ambulance. People are coming to help. I'll tell them you're here."

There was a bloody handprint on the Cutlass's open door. Ahead of it, a silver four-door sedan lay on its top, crushed down from the roof to half its normal height. And finally, the brown Honda, hood bent upward near the center. What was left of the windshield was a sheet of green glass pebbles. A sock monkey still dangled from the twisted rearview mirror. On the passenger seat, next to a pair of binoculars and a paperback birding book, was a black Nike bag. The driver's side seatbelt was fastened across the seat, the way Free's mom used to do it so that she wouldn't have to listen to the buzzer's nagging. Neither door would open, so Free leaned over the hood, carefully reached in past what was left of the windshield and plucked the bag from amid the broken glass.

She turned to walk back. Ahead of her, a man slipped a cigarette into his mouth and put his lighter to his lips, his hand shaking. All around them, shimmering underneath a coating of brown dust, were puddles of gasoline, diesel fuel, radiator fluid, oil and transmission fluid. Free ran over and grabbed the lighter from his hand before he could snap the wheel. "Are you crazy? One spark and this whole place will be on fire!"

He looked at her with dulled eyes and didn't answer. Slipping the lighter into her pocket, Free turned away and began to pick her way back through the chaos. She was glad to see that four ambulances and two firetrucks had arrived. In fact, one of the ambulances was already departing, sirens whirling. Free couldn't find Jamie, and she began to wander in ever-wider circles, searching for him. What she finally found was the trucker. He was helping another man load a gurney with a little boy on it into an ambulance. She realized that the first ambulance must have picked up Jamie.

"But I got Jamie's bag," she said stupidly, holding it up as if he might still be here to take it from her.

"That's all right. I'll give you a ride into town and you can give it to him at the hospital. It will give you a chance to get that cut taken care of."

"Cut?" Free repeated.

He reached out with gentle fingers and touched her forehead. His hand came away wet and red. Something went funny in Free's knees. She staggered and nearly fell before the trucker caught her elbow, his brown eyes full of concern. "Whoa, there." He took Jamie's bag from her and shouldered it, then put his arm around her shoulders. "Come on, I'll walk you back to my truck." They had gone about ten feet before he said, "Was there anybody with you?"

She saw that he was looking at Lydia's brown leather purse, plump and matronly, and clearly not something that went with Free's shaven head, nose ring and Birkenstocks. "She—she didn't make it."

"I'm sorry." The simple words made Free want to sit down and cry. Instead she kept walking, following the truck driver as he walked along a line of crumpled cars to a truck that sat next to them, pulled off onto the median. He said, "Here's my rig. I'm just lucky I didn't hit anyone—and I can't believe nobody hit me." He opened the passenger door and helped her up. "I'm from Tennessee. I've never seen nothing like this. My name's Casey."

"Free," Free said, bracing herself for the eyeroll or the spurt of a laugh that nearly always accompanied sharing her name.

Casey just nodded and closed her door. The squeal and thump made Free jump involuntarily. Leaning out the window, she looked at her face in the truck's huge sideview mirror. About two inches long, the cut was as neat as a seam, almost tucked into her hairline. It had nearly stopped bleeding, but the blood had washed down the left side of her face, over her temple, then fanned down her cheek to drip off her jaw. Her shirt was tacky with blood, although it didn't show much against the dark, swirling tie-dyed colors.

Casey climbed in beside her, then reached underneath the seat and handed her a white plastic box of wet wipes. He began to back up carefully, accompanied by beeping. When he reached a spot where the median strip was clear, he cut across it. Two more ambulances raced past them, headed toward the carnage.

They had driven less than a quarter of a mile when a *whump!* threw Free forward against the seatbelt. She covered her ringing ears with her hands, and then leaned forward to look in the side-view mirror. A wave of heat washed over them.

"Shit!" Casey said, looking in his rearview mirror. "I was afraid that would happen. One little spark, that was all it was going to take." The smell of burning gasoline was sickening. There were muffled popping noises as more and more cars caught fire. Behind them, the grass along the side of the road began to burn.

two

Saturday, OCTOBER 14, 5:25 P.M.

Lydia was late getting back from the grocery store. Roy looked at his watch to see exactly how much. Twenty-one minutes late.

He smiled.

He was going to have to punish her. He would make her stand in front of him, right here, in the living room. Then, at a look from him, she would slowly begin to unbutton the top buttons of her blouse. And he would check her neck, looking for the slightest redness betraying that another man's lips had lingered there.

And then would come the rest of her clothes, piece by piece. He would sniff and touch them and then her, checking for evidence. Lydia had learned to stand still and silent. No sense making a fuss, because that would only make it worse.

Another look at his watch. Twenty-seven minutes.

Roy jittered in his chair from excitement. He imagined how she would kneel in front of him on the carpet, the red rising up in the long snakes his belt left behind, while he confronted her with the truth. *You're doing it with the box boy in the back room, in some guy's van in the parking lot, out in the park for everyone to see, I know you, don't forget I know you. You're a whore who'll open your legs to anyone.* And then he would obliterate any trail, touch all the places they must have touched her, and finally fill her with his own seed. The way he did nearly every time she went to the grocery store, because, as both of them knew, it was almost impossible to walk the two miles to the store, shop, and walk back in the sixty minutes he allotted her.

Thirty-two minutes late.

In the three years they had been married, Roy had gotten Lydia just where he wanted her, trained her well, taught her how to think and act and talk just the way he wanted. He cared so much that sometimes he went a little too far, and then he would cry and say he was sorry. But deep in his heart, Roy knew Lydia liked it. And it wasn't his fault. She provoked him. And then she had to be taught all over again. He shifted to adjust his pants.

Thirty-six minutes.

Roy frowned. Even for Lydia, this was a record. Could she be stupid enough to try to take off? He considered the thought for a minute, then shook his head. Where could she go? He had given her sixty dollars for marketing, the way he did every week. And each and every week she had to account for every penny that she spent, so it was impossible that she had any money hidden away. And even if she did leave, where would she go? Lydia's parents were dead. In the past three years, Roy had weaned her away one by one from her old friends, gotten her to understand that she was the guilty one.

Thirty-nine minutes.

His excitement peaked and turned to anger.

Forty-seven minutes.

Fifty-two minutes.

How could she do this to him?

Sixty-three minutes.

Did she really think she could escape?

Three

On the twenty-minute ride to the hospital, there was silence in the truck's cab. Both Free and Casey were lost in their own thoughts. Fire trucks continued to race past them, toward the accident, but the road ahead was nearly empty and the dust seemed to have blown itself out. Despite the clear road, Free noticed that Casey still kept the truck down to about forty miles an hour.

Cars and ambulances jammed the parking lot of the hospital, a squat two-story concrete building. There was no place for Casey to park his rig, so after wishing her luck and asking twice to make sure she didn't need any money, he dropped Free off. Inside, the chaos was only slightly more organized than the pandemonium at the crash scene. Two dozen people in hospital garb scurried among more than one hundred people with various kinds of injuries, from broken fingers to people covered in so much blood that Free wondered if they were really still alive. She swallowed a sudden roll of nausea. While she waited at the front desk for someone to notice her, an older man shouldered open the door behind her. In his arms he carried a shoeless young woman in a business suit. She was arching her back and screaming that her ankles were broken.

It was half an hour before someone had time to talk to Free. Finally, a woman in blue scrubs put down the phone after begging for another Life-Flight helicopter, *"stat!"* She looked up at Free with distracted eyes.

"I'm looking for Jamie. I need to find Jamie. The ambulance brought him here maybe about an hour ago." The nurse looked at Free now, really looked. "He's wearing jeans and a polo shirt. He's got short hair that's dyed blond on the top and a tattoo of barbed wire around his wrist."

"Jamie." The nurse looked down at her desk and then back up toward Free.

"It's a Tommy Hilfiger shirt—big red, white and blue stripes."

"How old is he?"

This struck Free as a weird question. "I don't know. Twenty-two, maybe. I've got his bag, see." She offered it toward the woman. "He really wants it."

"And you are his . . . girlfriend?"

Free nodded, figuring it was too complicated to explain that she didn't know him at all. They were probably only letting immediate family back there, but she had promised Jamie. Her focus had narrowed down until she had only one mission: to return his bag.

"I'm afraid I have some bad news." The nurse's eyes were a really unusual color, Free found herself noticing. Green with yellow flecks.

"What?"

"Jamie didn't make it, honey. We tried to save him, but he had severe trauma." A cool hand rested briefly on Free's forearm. "Why don't you have a seat in the waiting area and I'll round up one of our volunteers to help you out. We'll need information about next of kin."

In shock, Free did as she was told, making her way to the only empty chair, tucked in the far corner of the crowded waiting room. Her feet were so far away it felt like walking on stilts, carefully balancing to keep from tipping over. Everyone she had tried to help today had died. Free had stopped by the side of the road to pick up Lydia, and she had died. And now Jamie, with his bleached blond hair and the stupid bag he had probably killed himself trying to get up for, he was dead, too. She had to get out of here. She couldn't stand to be here much longer, not in a place that smelled like blood and piss and smoke and echoed with shouts and screams.

Even the things she held were dead people's things. She put Lydia's purse on the floor between her feet. Lydia had said she was alone in the world, so there was no family to mourn her. But the nurse was right. Someone had to tell Jamie's family what had happened. Probably whatever information there was to find about him was in his wallet. Still, Free pulled the zipper on the bag and began to open it, although all she expected to see were balled-up socks and dirty underwear.

Instead, what she saw was gray-green. Money, old worn bills, stacks of them packed tightly in the bag. Almost reflexively, she zipped the bag closed, then looked around to see if anyone had noticed. But the other people had their minds on their own tragedies.

It was while she was sitting in a crowded hospital with someone else's money on her lap that Free first felt the baby move. And only then did she break down and begin to cry.

Four

From *The Oregonian*

14 KILLED IN OREGON'S DEADLIEST PILEUP; DUST STORM BLAMED
(*Clark City*)—*The day after a blinding dust storm triggered a 52-vehicle deadly pileup on Interstate 84, Oregon State Police are still reconstructing the blizzard of events.*

At 5:20 P.M. Saturday, a cloud of dust whipped up from dry, newly tilled wheat fields in Eastern Oregon crossed I-84 and swallowed up dozens of cars. The damage caused by the chain-reaction accident was compounded when a rig carrying gasoline exploded.

Six people were pronounced dead on the scene, included an injured man found in his car at 5:52 P.M., who died before frustrated state troopers were able to free him. Virtually every ambulance in the region was called into service to deliver 38 patients to hospitals in Clark City, Walla Walla and Pendleton, including two people who were pronounced dead on arrival. Six more later died of their injuries. Life-Flight took three badly burned victims to Legacy Emanuel Medical Center's Burn Unit.

Police identified the dead as Dorothy Campbell, 69, of Pendleton; Fred G. Carpenter, 76, of Redland, Wash.; DeWayne George, 52, of Tri-Cities, Wash.; Karen C. Marlowe, age unknown, of La Crosse, Wash.; Free Meeker, age 19, of Medford, Ore.; Gene Pavel, 37, of

Clark City; and John Phillips, 54, of Portland, Ore. At least one victim's body was too badly burned to identify late Saturday, police said. Police withheld the identities of others pending notification of family members.

Her hands shaking, Free put down the newspaper. That was it, then. She was officially dead.

She didn't feel like a dead person—but she didn't feel real, either. Wearing only a borrowed muumuu, she was sitting cross-legged on a sagging double bed in a room at the Stay-A-While Motor Inn, three blocks from the hospital.

The owner had been all clucks and sympathy when she saw the blood on Free's face and clothes. The basic outline of the story she already knew from listening to her CB radio. "Do you got any Band-Aids, honey? Or clean clothes? 'Cause Darlene can get you some," she had asked, her brown eyes sympathetic. Free had barely had the strength to shake her head. The woman, who turned out to be the Darlene in question, had loaned Free her own first-aid kit, polyester muumuu and white cardigan sweater.

During the night, Free had gotten only snatches of sleep. Each time she closed her eyes, she saw dead people, cars cartwheeling through the air, the orange bloom of fire. Over and over again, she had flinched awake, hearing the squeal of tearing metal and the terrible boom of impacts in her dreams.

Now it was 7:43 in the morning. The curtains in her room were closed, but they were so thin that the room was filled with a gauzy light. Spread out on the bed in front of Free were the contents of Lydia's purse and Jamie's bag.

Lydia's belongings took up only a small corner of the bed. Jamie's money covered the rest of the faded polyester coverlet— neat stacks of worn gray-green with a 100 printed in every corner. Each stack of one hundred bills was rubber-banded. Next to the stacks of money she had put other things from Jamie's bag. There was a compact gold-colored scale calibrated to weigh grams, a notebook, two small plastic bags filled with white powder, a large plastic bag filled with pot, and another small bag filled with brownish twisted shapes that Free identified as 'shrooms.

Leaning forward, Free counted the money again, tapping her finger on each rubber band. There were seventy-four stacks in all— for a total of $740,000. More money than Free could take in.

It was so much money the sweet, papery smell of it filled the room.

So much money that it could change her life. So much money that she would never have to worry again.

So much money that she could offer this baby in her belly a real life. A settled life. She could give this kid a house and a dog and a mother who never had to work. All the stuff Free had never had. Stability. Store-bought clothes. A car that ran reliably—and that had heat, a complete floor and no 'creative' paint job.

There was only one problem. It wasn't her money.

But whose money was it?

When she had first glimpsed the money, Free had wondered why someone would stuff a gym bag full of used bills. Real people, or squares, as her mother Diane still called them, would have put the money in the bank or the stock market. When she emptied out the bag on the bed and saw what was under the money, that had cleared up any confusion.

So Jamie had been a dealer. Diane and Bob had consumed more than their share of drugs, but the only one they had ever sold was home-grown pot, and mostly they just gave that away.

She picked up the notebook and began to leaf through it. It was filled with some kind of code, although she was sure that even if she knew how to read it, it would all be dates and dollars and grams. Where had this Jamie been going? Before he got caught up in the accident, his car had been headed west. Had he been driving to Portland or someplace farther away, like Seattle or San Fran-cisco? His car, Free remembered, had had Oregon plates, so he probably lived in the state. Who was he bringing the money to? Suddenly, Free remembered what Jamie had said about the bag while he struggled to get up. *Don will kill me if I don't give it to him.* At the time, she had thought Jamie was exaggerating. Now she guessed he might have been telling the truth. After all, someone was bound to get pretty territorial about $740,000.

How long would it be before this Don person came looking for the bag?

But if it weren't for Free's intervention, there probably wouldn't even be a bag to look for. She picked up the paper again, looked at the front-page photo of tangled trucks and cars burned down to charred skeletons. Wasn't it more than likely that this Don would assume that the money had literally gone up in a puff of smoke? If it hadn't been for Free, it would have. In a way, wasn't this like finding money nobody owned?

Free dropped her head into her hands and rubbed her fingers over the smooth contours. Too much had happened to her in the last few days. Her head didn't have enough room to hold it all. Figuring out she was pregnant—and then trying to figure out what to do about the baby. In the middle had come figuring out that her boyfriend was a two-timing asshole who had hooked up with the first hootchie that crooked a finger. And now this. An accident so bad that it made the front page of the paper. An accident that left a dozen people dead and her alive, sitting cross-legged on a bed surrounded by someone else's money. An accident that specifically left someone named Lydia Watkins dead, and another woman named Free Meeker alive. Only everyone thought that Free was dead and Lydia was still alive.

Everyone but Lydia, and she wasn't in a position to say any different.

Free looked down at the money again. She ran her fingers lightly over the stacks of bills, soft and slightly fuzzy. Too worn to be anything but real money. So much money. Enough money to solve everything.

Free turned her attention to the corner of the bed where she had spread out Lydia's things. Lydia hadn't had much, but what she had had was what Free thought of as "classy" and her parents would have described as "uptight." A flowered cloth bag full of makeup in matching marbled green containers that all read *Clinique* on the bottom. A pair of silver earrings shaped like crosses. An eel-skin wallet, more notable for what it didn't have than what it did. There was no checkbook, no Blockbuster card, no Whitchers card, no Visa or MasterCard or Discover card. Just a library card, a driver's license, a Social Security card, three crisp twenties and thirty-two crumpled ones. The last thing in the purse had been a little fabric-covered photograph album, fastened with a snap.

Free unfastened it and flipped through the photos. It began with a black-and-white picture of a dark-haired little girl in a dress and black patent Mary Janes. She was flanked by a woman wearing cat's-eye glasses and a man with a white shirt and a dark tie. Lydia with her parents, Free guessed. Next a photo of an older Lydia, recognizable now as the woman Free had picked up. In a brown fast-food uniform, she raised a knife with a grin, parodying a killer. Then Lydia, smiling with a group of women friends, their arms laced around one another's shoulders, all of them dressed in pastel dresses. Free felt a flash of envy at the sight of the tasseled graduation caps on their heads.

The last picture was of Lydia on her wedding day, her face almost lost in a veil made of layers of white lace. Free studied Lydia's husband—not tall but powerfully built, with dark eyes, slanted eyebrows and a heart-shaped face. He was beautiful in a totally masculine way. What had Lydia said about him? *He loved me so much that it was like we were still on our honeymoon.* Free's heart felt squeezed when she wondered who was left to mourn Lydia.

Normally, Free wasn't the type to pick up hitchhikers. Even Diane, Free's mother, said it wasn't safe anymore for a woman by herself to pick up a hitchhiker, even another woman. But Lydia had looked so out of place, so young and harmless as she stood beside the freeway on the outskirts of Pendleton, that Free had made an exception. For one thing, Lydia had been wearing a dress. A dress that looked as if cleaning it required a trip to the dry cleaner. Free herself didn't own a dress or an iron and had never been to a dry cleaner. She found herself pulling over for the other woman. How could Free leave her to the wolves who would surely scent her?

And Lydia, it turned out, needed all the help she could get. The words had poured out of her as soon as she got in the car. First a car accident had taken her parents, and then two weeks ago a machine at the disposable diaper factory where her husband had worked had literally eaten him up. The factory offered Lydia a tiny settlement. Instead of signing, Lydia had called this big-time Portland lawyer who advertised on TV all over Oregon about his ability to wring settlements from large companies. Lydia had been all set to drive into Portland, but that morning her car had blown a head gasket. Free, who was driving a 1972 Impala so old that mushrooms sometimes sprouted on the floor of the backseat, nodded sympathetically while Lydia rattled off her story.

Free hadn't planned on going to Portland, but after hearing Lydia's story she decided to take her there. She knew all about what it felt like to be abandoned, with no one to turn to. So what if she added a couple of hours to her trip? She figured the good karma was worth it. Besides, she was in no hurry to get back to Medford. The drive down from Portland would give her more time to figure out how to break the news about the baby. But they never made it as far as Portland. Thirty minutes after pulling over to pick up Lydia, Free had driven blindly into the dust storm.

Now that Free had looked inside Lydia's nearly empty wallet, it was clear that the other woman had badly needed whatever money the lawyer could get her. She wondered if Lydia had been forced to sell her engagement and wedding rings. The whole time the other woman had talked, the fingers of her right hand had absentmindedly circled the white mark on the ring finger of her left hand. It was strange to think that they were only a few years apart in age. The two of them had been as different as if they had been raised in separate countries. Some part of Free couldn't help envying Lydia her square parents, her graduation cap, even her poor dead husband who had looked at Lydia with such adoration on their wedding day.

Thinking about Lydia just made Free think about the accident, and she didn't want to go experience those memories again, so fresh she could still almost smell the smoke and blood. She decided to take another shower. A shower without shampoo or soap, since the Stay-A-While Motel cut down on overhead by not providing any toiletries and offering thin towels as rough as a cat's tongue.

From the mirror, still spotted with the white flecks of someone else's toothpaste, a stranger looked back at Free. Who was she, anyway? With her bald head, shadowed eyes and the cut on her forehead, she looked like a refugee. Leaning forward, she carefully peeled back the Band-Aid. The edges of the cut were holding together, set now in a bruise as black as midnight. Reaching down to grab the hem, she stripped off the muumuu. Naked, she looked like a battered wife, her body splotched with dozens of dark purple bruises. Her feet stung, and when she lifted one she saw the bottoms were dotted with dozens of small cuts from her barefoot escape up the hill. The shower head was below the top of her own head, but she stayed in for a long time anyway, as if the warm water could wash away the images of death and destruction. Free opened her mouth to the spray, swishing and spitting in lieu of her missing toothbrush.

Free took stock of herself. She was nineteen. She had a shaved head, a nose ring and a tattoo of Chinese characters around her biceps. They were supposed to mean something about happiness, but Free sometimes wondered if they really meant anything at all. In the last week, she had lost first her boyfriend and then her car. She had a career, if you could call it that, as a pet groomer at Petorium. And she was, as she had finally been forced to admit last week, pregnant.

After climbing out of the shower, she attempted to dry herself off. Not only was the towel rough, but it seemed to be made of some special fabric that actually repelled water rather than absorbed it. She still hadn't decided what to do, but she did know one thing. She didn't want to spend one more minute in this motel.

With no alternatives, Free pulled on the voluminous muumuu, abstractly patterned in turquoise and blue. From the floor, she picked up her jeans and T-shirt. They were stiff with dirt and blood and other stains she couldn't identify. She couldn't imagine ever getting them clean. Balling them up, she pushed them in the wastebasket, then washed her hands. The ring in her nose suddenly looked silly. She twisted it out and tossed it in the wastebasket, on top of her old clothes. Now she just looked sick, her brown eyes red-rimmed.

Free felt the baby move inside her again, a feeling like a trail of bubbles. The bottom had fallen out of her world. Somehow this baby seemed the only true thing she had. Free sat back down on the bed and stroked the money again, as soft as corduroy. Enough money to change everything. Maybe even to change who she was.

For nineteen years, she had been Free Meeker. Free's name had presented itself to her mother during a particularly stellar acid trip on the Fourth of July, the same night Free was conceived. And true to her name, Free had grown up free. Free of advertising, free of hang-ups, free to eat tofu and mung bean sprouts. Free of secrets and locked doors, free to run around naked as much as she pleased. Free of authoritarian hierarchies, bad trips, bad vibes, bad attitudes and aggressive dogs. Free to wear tie-dye dresses and toe-ring san-dals year-round, even in the rain. Free of rules, polyester, shampoo, the establishment, the government, shag carpeting and anything else that could be labeled square, mainstream or conservative.

Secretly, all Free had ever wanted to do was fit in. In grade school, the rest of the kids had lined up at lunch to get hot dogs on squishy buns, squirted packets of bright yellow mustard at each other. Between bites, Free hid the nubby brown bread of her alfalfa-sprout sandwich underneath the cafeteria table. From their first day of school, Free and her younger sister, Moon, had been allowed to decide whether they felt like attending on any given day. Free had had perfect attendance. Moon had usually opted out.

Deep inside herself, Free had longed to be something more, well, normal. When she was a kid she used to shoplift *Good House-keeping* magazine and clip out the pictures of mothers she could have had. Mothers who wore aprons over housedresses, instead of no bras under tie-dye. Mothers who whipped up meat loaf and mashed potatoes, instead of millet stew so thick you could stand a hand-whittled wooden spoon straight up in it.

And since Free's family moved around a lot, it was hard to make friends, leaving her feeling even more alone. The four of them had lived in a tepee, in a tree house, in a converted chicken coop, in an old VW bus plastered with Grateful Dead stickers, in a commune that fell apart in bitter jealousy after a few months. Over the years, Diane and Bob had made their living through one nonjob after another—making goat cheese, adjusting auras, crafting lumpy pots, selling beads with mystical powers.

Growing up, Free lied to the few friends she had about curfews and regulations and strictly enforced dinner hours. As if she had some. At her house there were no rules, so there was nothing to rebel against. Free hated it. It gave her an awful floating feeling, like going on a space walk, only her cord had come loose from the ship. In high school, her friends rebelled against conformity by stealing their parent's cigarettes, skipping class and getting stoned. Free had smoked her first joint seven weeks before her eleventh birthday. With her mother. Free craved conformity and rules. She wanted to wear a uniform, attend organized events and be the kind of person who had goals.

Diane and Bob, her parents, had rejected all that. Free and Moon never called them Mom and Dad. When Free was a kid, her parents had always been trying on different names—Summer, Rain, Apple, Sky, Diamond, Silver. For a while, they had given themselves Indian names, despite their pale skins. Diane had been She Who Runs, and Bob had finally settled on Thunder Cloud. Over time, they had gradually turned back into Diane and Bob again, giving in to the establishment in some small fashion. Still, they often accused Free of being "too uptight." They called her their "normie," with a hint of exasperation. They were appalled when they discovered that she was secretly shaving her legs, horrified when they caught her eating M&Ms. They believed that cops were pigs, the president was a crook, America was spelled with a K, and white sugar was poison.

The years hadn't changed them much. They still grew pot in the basement and organic vegetables in the garden, still danced around the kitchen listening to reggae while boiling lentils. They still sprawled in beanbag chairs, and divided the living room from the dining room with a rainbow-colored bead curtain. Bob still had a patchy beard, bad posture and a belief in conspiracies. Barefoot, Diane still marched right past the "No shoes, no shirts, no service" sign at the grocery store. And she certainly didn't wear a bra. Even now, in the summer she wore a crocheted halter that looked like two doilies. Bob and Diane continued in their countercultural ways, fond as ever of lava lamps, and, nearing fifty, the oldest attendees at rock concerts.

How would they feel if she were dead? Free amended the thought. The two of them already thought she was dead. The paper wouldn't have listed her name if her family hadn't been notified. As far as Bob and Diane were concerned, she had died yesterday. She pictured them at home, wrapped in each other's arms, weeping into each other's hair. Nothing she could do, including coming forward, could spare them from the grieving they had already done. In a few days, she bet that they would try to contact her spirit, see if she were doing okay, if she needed them to perform some kind of purification ceremony to free her in the afterlife. But the two of them had never really needed Free, or understood what she needed. In a way, it would probably be a relief to them that Free was dead, rather than having a live Free show up at home with the unexpected and probably unwelcome news that they were actually old enough to be grandparents.

Free looked back down at the money again, ran her fingers over its softness.

What if she took this money and ran?

What if Free Meeker became someone else—the woman she had always secretly wanted to be?

What if Free could really live up to the name her parents had given her?

Five

Don Cannon's private business line rang, startling him. It was connected to a special phone, one he had paid over two thousand
dollars for because of its state-of-the-art scrambling technology—
and the one he still preferred not to hold any substantive discus-
sions on.

"Yes?"

"Hey, dude." After nearly thirty years of friendship, Don didn't
need Barry Stevens to identify himself, scrambler or no scrambler.
"I've got some bad news. Our runner may have taken a runner."
Barry loved the fact that Don wanted any phone conversations
kept enigmatic, with no names attached. "People are calling me.
He never showed up in B or The D."

Using his own rudimentary code, Barry was referring to Bend
and The Dalles. These were the last two stops on a monthly circuit
that began in Portland, when Barry left a package of money for
whoever their current runner was—in this case, Jamie Labot. Then
Jamie would drive south to just over the California border. At a
rest area near Mt. Shasta, he would exchange the money for
drugs—mostly coke, a little pot, and more and more often, Ecstasy,
the top choice of kids both in and out of college. Then Jamie
would take the very long way back to Portland, dropping the drugs

off along the way. First he visited Medford, then Phoenix, Talent, Eagle Point, White City. Then Jamie would go over the mountain pass to Klamath Falls, and after that he would hit the little towns that dotted the dry eastern part of the state. Jamie's final stops would be in Bend and The Dalles. Except, according to Barry, this time Jamie had never made it that far.

Along the way Jamie accumulated money, much more than he had originally exchanged for the drugs. In a notebook, he recorded in code the name of each dealer, what they bought and how much they paid. Jamie then dropped the money off for Don— although he didn't know it was Don, and the drop site always changed. A few days later, Jamie would sign for a package from a messenger service. Inside the box he would find the same black Nike gym bag they always used for courier work, only this time with five thousand dollars inside. Pretty good for four days' work.

But now Jamie was missing.

"Could he have been hit?" It had happened before, when someone got a little too carried away by the entrepreneurial spirit and decided to take both the drugs and the money.

"Don't think so. All our contacts are where they are supposed to be, and no one seems to be flashing any extra money. The last place he was seen was P."

P as in Pendleton. That meant that Jamie had gone running with something approaching a million dollars. And that meant Don was going to have to arrange to get the money back and then to have Jamie killed. Which was too bad. Don had met Jamie a couple of times and liked him. In fact, Don was the one who had approved Barry's idea of hiring Jamie. The couple of times he had met him, the kid had kind of reminded Don of himself when he was that age. Don shrugged. Rules were rules, and Jamie should have known that.

He realized he had been quiet for a long time, leaving Barry waiting patiently at the end of the line. "Can you take over the rest of the route this once? There should be enough in the safe to cover what's left."

"No problemo."

"Thanks." Don hung up without saying good-bye. He sighed and turned to look at the orange maples next to the windows and beyond them, to the city that lay cupped between the hills. Each house on these terraced slopes was situated to take full advantage of the view. The neighbor on his left was an architect who had designed a house made mostly of Plexiglas, the one on his right a lawyer with a sprawling three-story house that looked as if it had been modeled after Tara from *Gone with the Wind*. Don's house sat smack in the middle, a beautiful Craftsman bungalow with pillars made of river stones bracketing the porch.

There were always a handful of large orders Don handled himself, and he was going to have to arrange for Barry to take a cut of one or more of these to meet the immediate demand in Bend and The Dalles. Then he was going to have to figure out how to replace the missing drugs.

But that wasn't the real problem. The real problem was going to be getting the money back before the next link in the chain realized it was gone. This kind of problem, even if it wasn't his fault, could kill him.

He was going to have to take care of this mess, and soon. There had already been rumors that Enrique was making noises Don was too old, too American. The top guys now were ten, maybe even twenty years younger than he was. And these new guys were ruthless. Last year, when a drug deal in Mexico had gone bad, Enrique had arranged for a whole family to be lined up against the garage wall and mowed down, from the two-year-old to the eighty-nine-year-old great-grandmother. Enrique had said it was about teaching a lesson, about making sure that he left behind so much fear that no one would ever dare to fuck with him again. Don thought it was sloppiness. That kind of killing attracted the attention of even the most corrupt cops.

Then again, Don certainly had no personal desire to be found with a neat little stitch line of bullets across his chest. He swiveled his chair back around to look at his desk calendar. Today was October 15. He figured he had until the end of October to come up with the money. One way or another.

Six

Sunday, OCTOBER 15, 10:05 A.M.

Holding tightly to Jamie's bag, which was filled once again with the $740,000, Free ventured forth from the motel for breakfast. Before she left, she spent a long time deciding what to do with the drugs. If she left them in the room, the cleaning lady might find them. And the Stay-A-While's locks looked like they wouldn't thwart a bobby pin—let alone someone with a heavy boot. Although chances were slim that someone would break in during her absence, Free now knew from personal experience that the worst could and did happen. But if she took the drugs with her, she would be putting herself in danger if someone caught her with them. No one would believe her if she said they weren't hers. And there were enough of them to add up to years in jail. Finally, she had decided to get rid of them by flushing them in batches down the toilet.

As Free walked down the main street, which doubled as the highway, drafts from passing trucks blew the too-large borrowed muumuu from one side to the other. Even though she was wearing the damp panties she had washed out in the sink and squeezed dry, Free felt naked as the wind pressed the dress against her and then tugged it away. Every step made the cuts on her feet sting and her bruised legs ache.

It felt dangerous to be carrying the money, as if any minute someone might snatch the bag away. Free also realized that even the act of taking the money with her, and the fact that she was worried about it, meant that she had crossed a line and was beginning to think of it as belonging to her.

There weren't very many other candidates. Jamie was dead. And this guy Don he had talked about probably thought the money was nothing more than a pile of ashes.

Even if she wanted to give the money back, how would she go about doing it? She couldn't exactly run an ad in *The Oregonian*: "Found. $740,000 in used hundred-dollar bills. To claim, please describe dead man who once owned it."

Free tightened her grip on the straps of the bag. If she went to the police now, she would be back where she had been the day before—nineteen, alone and with a baby in her belly. And that money would just end up moldering in some government evidence locker. Or—and it seemed quite possible—some cop might just keep it all for himself. Who wouldn't be tempted when faced with a stack of used, untraceable hundred-dollar bills?

But what if she kept it and this Don guy came looking for it? Then again, how would they ever trace the money from Jamie to a woman he had never known and who didn't even officially exist anymore? They could no more trace the money forward from Jamie's possession than she could trace it backward to where it really belonged.

The town of Clark City was small, barely qualifying for the word. In addition to the Stay-A-While Motor Inn, there were two hotels (one a generic Best Western, the other a more rundown mom-and-pop affair), two gas stations, a grocery store, a hardware/feed store and five restaurants. Free didn't think she could take the cheerful plastic decor and plastic food of McDonald's. The Dairy Queen and the In-N-Out (a tiny A-frame shack) were both closed. One of the remaining restaurants was really a tavern, a weather-beaten, windowless structure that probably served just enough food to keep its liquor license. Free opted for The Roost, which had a fading, flapping banner that read BREAKFAST SERVED ALL DAY.

Once inside, she had to fight back a moment of panic. The place was crawling with cops in a variety of uniforms. Taking a deep breath, Free reasoned with herself. Of course there were a lot of cops here. Fourteen people were dead, and dozens more had been injured. Blame must be assigned. Still, she couldn't help feeling nervous, as if they might sense she was carrying nearly a million dollars of drug money. She was glad she had flushed the drugs away. She had a sudden childhood memory of yelling out "I smell bacon!" from the back seat of their Volkswagen bus as Bob drove past a police car hidden in an alley.

A new thought occurred to her. What if this Don person were here, trying to figure out where his money had gone to? Her gaze swept over the restaurant again, but she didn't see anyone who looked like a dealer, who in Free's experience always used as well as dealt. No, all the guys in the restaurant seemed clean-cut and uniformed. Free realized she was still rooted to the ground next to the gumball machine in the entryway. Everyone did seem to have noticed her, something that had happened to her all of her life as she moved from place to place, showed up at each new school dressed in thrift-store outfits, was picked up by her dad with his long hair and love beads. Maybe she should leave. Or maybe she should walk up to one of these cops right now and hand over the gym bag. Even as she told herself she was seriously considering the idea, she found her feet walking past the full tables. Taking a seat at the counter, Free put the bag on the floor and planted her Birkenstocks squarely on top.

When the harried waitress finally stopped to take her order, Free asked for French toast, coffee and an orange juice, then called the woman back to add a glass of milk. She had to remember that she was eating for two now.

As she ate, Free tried to weigh her options. An hour ago, she had decided to take the money and start a new life. But now as she tried to picture this new life, to see exactly what she would do, where she would go, who she would be—Free failed. The only thing she knew was that she couldn't go back to Medford, back to her parents and her job at the Petorium and Billy pleading with her to take him back.

The sensible thing, Free supposed, would be to fly to a different city in a faraway state, someplace where this Don guy would never find her. The idea scared her. The only time she had been on a plane was at the Jackson County Fair, when her parents paid a man to take her and Moon up above the fairgrounds for a five-minute ride that cost a penny a pound. Free didn't remember how old she had been, just that the two of them together hadn't cost more than a dollar.

The only big city Free had been to before was Portland. Maybe it wasn't such a bad choice, at least not to start. It was a big enough city to get lost in, but not so big she couldn't find her way around.

Free popped the last bit of French toast in her mouth. It was time to leave both the restaurant and this town, before anyone came sniffing around. The only problem was she no longer had wheels.

The tab came to $4.70. "Keep the change," Free said, pressing a twenty dollar bill into the hand of the waitress. Free was halfway to the door when she heard the woman gasp when she realized it wasn't a five. Maybe I can get used to this, Free thought.

As Free walked back to the motel, she passed a ramshackle apartment complex, tiny one-story apartments strung together like beads. An old blue Chevette was parked on the street in front, with a sign propped on the dash. FOR SALE BY OWNER. ASK AT APT. 6A. $500 OBO.

She circled around the car, feeling a momentary pang for her lost Impala, the low rumble of its motor, the amazingly intact green upholstery. Even the slightly musty smell of the interior was associated in her mind with freedom. Having a car meant she could go where she wanted—and take whoever she wanted along with her.

Five hundred bucks wasn't much to pay to have that freedom

back. She picked her way to Apartment 6A through the dozens of broken toys that littered the shared yard, like colorful debris washed up by the tide. On the mat lay a red plastic fire engine missing its front wheel.

A scrawny woman with burnt-out eyes answered the door. Behind her, five children who all looked to be under the age of six were sitting in front of the TV watching Scooby-Doo. The woman didn't say anything, just looked Free up and down.

"I'm interested in buying your car."

"You want to take it for a drive?" Free nodded. "I'll come with." Not even turning her head, she let out a yell that made Free jump. "Kids—I'm going out for a minute! Don't let me catch you fighting when I get back!"

The woman shuffled over to the car in dirty pink plastic sandals. She pulled a key chain with a clear red heart from the pocket of her cutoffs.

"Here ya go." The woman handed over the keys and pulled open the passenger door, accompanied by screeching metal. Free got in the driver's seat. Maybe it had been the sound of metal on metal, but her palms were starting to sweat. She groped behind her, but the car didn't seem to have any seatbelts. Feeling off balance, Free fumbled the key into the ignition, but didn't turn it.

The skin on her face felt tight, and her scalp prickled. The air was heavy. It didn't seem to contain enough oxygen. Breathing through her mouth, Free finally managed to turn the key. Her hands were trembling and she felt like she was choking. Her chest and belly hurt. Was she going to pass out? Was something wrong with the baby? Was she having a heart attack? A miscarriage?

"Aren't you going to drive it?" The woman's nasal voice pulled Free back a little bit. But then she had a sudden flash of Lydia, the last woman who had sat beside her in a car.

The woman repeated the question, and the word "drive" caused Free to feel even worse. She was passing out, she was sure of it. She barely had the strength to turn off the key. "I'm sorry, I just can't do this."

Unexpectedly, the woman patted her on the shoulder. "That's all right. It needs a new head gasket. I'm not supposed to say that, but it does."

Free threw a "thank you" over her shoulder as she opened the door. She left the keys dangling in the ignition.

Seven

Five minutes after freaking out in the Chevette, Free was beginning to feel better. Her breathing had loosened and her stomach didn't hurt nearly as bad. Maybe she just wasn't ready yet to get back behind the wheel. After all, just yesterday she had been in a huge car accident, seen dead people for the first time. Eventually, her memories would fade. But she didn't want to wait around, in case this Don guy came looking for his lost bag, or someone asked why she had the exact same name as one of the accident victims. But how was she going to get out of this town? Driving was out, and she certainly wasn't going to hitchhike. When Free checked out of the motel, Darlene was still there, sitting in the living area that was set up just behind the counter, like some sort of weird display. As one of a half-dozen cats twined about her ankles, Free asked about Greyhound.

"You can buy your ticket at the hardware store and catch it right out front." Surrounded by the plump flesh of her face, Darlene's eyes looked like raisins stuck in dough. Today she was dressed in a muumuu twin to the one Free was wearing, only in purple instead of blue. "Unless they've changed the schedule, it comes by at one-fifteen." She patted Free's hand. "Darlene is so sorry about your not having a car anymore."

The touch almost made Free start to cry. She felt so alone. "I need to give you back your dress. Is there any place around here I could buy something to wear?"

"No, hon, the last clothing store in town closed about seven years back. Now most people in town just do mail order. Or drive into Bend. Darlene ordered this dress in seven different colors off the Internet. She can live without one of them for a while." She scribbled something on a piece of paper. "When you get orientated again, just mail it back to this address." Instead of sliding the paper toward her, Darlene surprised Free by flipping back a section of the counter, walking through to the other side and pulling Free into a hug.

Enveloped in the older woman's softness and the smell of baby powder, Free didn't know she was crying until she felt the wetness on her face. Darlene pulled back a bit, but didn't let go, her hands still resting on Free's shoulders.

"Don't be surprised if it takes you a while to get to the point where you're not thinking about it all the time. I was in a car accident on my graduation day." This was the first time Free had heard Darlene use the word *I* instead of referring to herself in the third person. "Two of the other girls in the car were killed." Her gaze was unwavering. "I think I dreamed about that accident every night for a year."

Free closed her eyes. "I don't think I could take any more nights like last night."

"Oh, each night does get a little better. It's just a slow process."

According to the schedule posted in the window of the hardware store, Free had forty-seven minutes before the bus came. She roamed the aisles, selecting a combination lock, a spiral-bound notebook, a pen, and, giving into temptation, *Ladies' Home Journal* and *Redbook*. Sitting on the bench in front of the store, she threaded the lock through the gym bag's two zipper pulls. Of course, any thief could still simply run off with the bag and slit it open later, but Free no longer had to worry about the zipper working itself open, exposing her secret.

The bus was nearly empty, so Free put Jamie's bag, Lydia's purse and the sack from the hardware store next to her, on the seat by the window. The first few minutes after she boarded, she was afraid she would freak out again about being inside a vehicle, but the size of the bus, the squeal of its air brakes and the reek of disinfectant made it seem completely different from a car. For the first hour of the trip, Free flipped through the magazines. It was hard to believe that she had enough money now that she could live in any of the houses pictured, buy the appliances, create the crafts, wear the clothes, cook the casseroles. The money opened up so many possibilities that it seemed like too many. Instead of feeling excited, Free felt empty and anxious.

Then the baby kicked her, right underneath her heart, and the odd sensation brought her back down to earth. This baby in her belly was real, Free reminded herself. Putting down the magazine, she picked up the notebook and pen. She wrote "Things I Could Be," but didn't get any further. Now that she had enough money to be anything she wanted, what did she want to be?

She had spent too much time around surly cats and dogs to want to be a vet. Could she be a lawyer, a chef, an artist, an architect? Free could picture the clothes each one might wear, but when she tried to think past the outfit to what each one actually did moment to moment, her imagination ran out of steam.

Figuring out what she was going to do with the rest of her life seemed too overwhelming. Instead Free turned to a new page and started on a list of possible names for the baby.

Sienna
Nora
Claire
Keegan
Caleb
Charles

Each name brought with it the image of a child. Nora, for example, would surely have a head of black curls, like her own had been before she had chosen to shave them, and a wide-legged, defiant stance that Free had never had. Sienna would have blonde hair, like Billy, and his blue eyes, too.

How long had it been since she had spoken to Billy? Just six days, Free realized, the answer such a surprise that she had to count on her fingers again before she believed it. Six days ago, she had had a car, a job, a boyfriend, and a settled if boring life. Six days ago, baby names had been the furthest thing from Free's mind.

Last Monday morning, Free had just stepped out of the shower when what she saw in the steam-shrouded mirror made her stop reaching for the towel. She rubbed the edge of her hand over the mirror, then turned to the side. Her belly jutted out in a way that couldn't just be chalked up to her recent weight gain. Her breasts looked bigger, too. She almost looked like she was pregnant. But Free knew that was impossible.

When she was sixteen, Free had had to have pelvic surgery courtesy of some sexually transmitted disease she had never known she'd had until she was doubled over in pain and the damage was already done. One tube had had to be removed. The surgeon left the other one, although he said it was nearly as useless as if it were tied in knots. "You'll never get pregnant," he had informed her bluntly on her follow-up visit, not even looking up from Free's chart when she had started to cry. "You're lucky you didn't come down with something worse. We sell condoms out at the front counter for fifty cents a piece. You'd better stock up."

He had talked to Free like she was a slut, but the thing was that she wasn't. She certainly was a lot less wild than her own parents expected her to be. Since she was twelve, they had always been sure to let Free's boyfriends know they were welcome to spend the night. The first time that happened, she had flushed to the tips of her ears. She'd only slept with a half dozen guys, far less than her mother or even her younger sister. But after the doctor's warning, she had become vigilant. She and Billy had both gotten checked out for AIDS as well as every other sexually transmitted disease before she stopped insisting on condoms.

After Free finally stopped staring at her belly and got dressed, she drove to the Petorium. She was scheduled to work the day shift, but when she came in she asked her boss if she could have the morning off to go the health clinic. It was a slow day, and there was another groomer on duty, so he let her go. He didn't asked why she wanted to go, and Free didn't volunteer. She was afraid to say the word even to herself. Cancer. That was what it had to be. Some kind of female cancer caused by stuff backing up, things not working right, hormones with nothing to work on. Her periods had always been wildly irregular, thanks to that missing tube, but for the past couple of months there had been only some light spotting on and off, and lately, nothing at all.

After checking in at the Jackson County Health Clinic, Free took her number and settled in to wait. The job at Petorium paid a dollar over minimum wage with no benefits, so she only went to the doctor when she had to, and then to the county clinic, which charged a sliding scale.

While she waited on the orange plastic seat someone had still managed to stain, she prodded her stomach with three fingers. It felt hard. Too hard. Like a growth. Why had she ignored it for so long? Was it too late already? She remembered that show she had watched with Billy one time, *Ripley's Believe It Or Not,* and the woman with the tumor bigger than a basketball.

Free had never been one of those girls who fretted over her shape. Her body was something to get her from point A to point B, not something to be dieted into submission. Normally, she dressed in elastic-waist shorts and graphic T-shirts she borrowed from Bob's closet. At work, the uniform was black draw-string pants and a loose white polo shirt. She guessed she had noticed her waistbands were getting a little tight this past month, but she had chalked it up to all the snacking she had done a few months ago when her stomach had felt funny a lot of the time. That is, until she looked in the mirror this morning. Her arms and legs had still looked the same size. Only her belly was bigger.

The only reason Billy hadn't noticed Free's changing shape was because lately he had been shut down, preoccupied with his own problems. She wasn't even spending the night there much lately, because he paid no attention to her except to bitch about his parents.

Free's mind went back to her belly again. Maybe it wasn't cancer. Maybe it was a cyst or something. Then she thought of her grandmother, a thought she had been trying without success to push away since she got out of the shower. Diane's mom had died two years before of uterine cancer. At the end, she had been skinny and yellow, thrashing from side to side in the hospital bed they set up in the living room. Didn't that kind of thing tend to run in families?

When the clinic nurse eventually asked Free to pee in a cup, she was clueless. Everyone knew you could tell a lot about a person's health by analyzing their urine.

Including, it turned out, whether or not that someone was pregnant.

Free argued with the doctor. Standing there wearing a thin white gown that tied at the back, she told him he must be wrong. What about that other doctor at this very same clinic, the one who had told Free three years before that she could never get pregnant?

But the second doctor insisted that the first doctor was wrong. Way wrong. As in approximately twenty-two weeks pregnant wrong, an educated guess the doctor made after measuring her belly. And no one in southern Oregon, the doctor informed Free, did abortions on any woman more than sixteen weeks along.

In a panic, Free went to Billy's apartment, which was really in his parents' basement. She knew Billy would be there because Billy was always there. Billy raised ferrets, and both he and his parents pretended this was like a real job. It was through a ferret that Free had met Billy seven months before, when he smuggled one into the store that ended up getting loose before she managed to trap it in the grooming area.

Free knocked on the basement door to the apartment (which was really one big room interspersed with support beams and a water heater). When no one answered, she let herself in, figuring Billy was probably napping. Instead, she found him putting it to the Taco Bell counter girl on his new Sleep Country USA mattress. The mattress that Free had helped pay for, since she had been halfway living there already. They were going at it doggy-style, which somehow struck Free as funny, given the fact that she had met Billy through the Petorium. It was so funny that she didn't even realize she was throwing her new bottle of pregnancy vitamins at them until it smashed against the wall next to the woman's head.

So Free figured it probably didn't much matter to Billy that she was dead. She had never even told him about the baby. She hadn't spoken to him since that morning six days before, not uttered a single word while she packed up her stuff and left. A crying, naked Billy had followed her everywhere on his knees. Neither of them spared a glance for the counter girl while she put back on her uniform and left with a flounce. When Free went home, obviously upset, she found Bob and Diane too stoned to ask her what was wrong. Needing to get away, she had picked up the phone and called Moon, asking if she could come visit.

Now Free yawned. What had happened six days ago seemed as distant as if it had happened to another person, in another century. She yawned again, her eyes closing. In ten minutes she was asleep, her body curled protectively around her bags and the bulge of her baby.

Eight

Where could Lydia have gone? Roy was going crazy just thinking about it. The first thing he had done was to drive to the super-market. He asked the three checkers and the guy behind the meat counter and the kid who counted pop cans if they had seen Lydia come in that day, but they all said they hadn't. Only none of them would meet his eyes. Were they afraid of him, were they disre-specting him—or did they know something he didn't? But then the manager told Roy he had to leave.

Then he went to the neighbors who lived on either side. They hadn't seen Lydia, or if they had, they wouldn't admit to it. The woman who lived across the street just shut the door in his face without saying a word. Roy knew right then that she was the one who had called the cops on him before. She was the one who had messed in his business. What happened between family was pri-vate, didn't she know that?

Roy spent the rest of the evening and most of the night driving up and down the streets of Pendleton, looking for Lydia. Any sec-ond he expected to see her wide dark eyes caught in the glare of his headlights, just like when you jacked deer out of season, pin-ning them in a beam of bright light. But he saw nothing.

By two in the morning, Roy was back in his own neighborhood, peeping in his neighbors' windows to see if Lydia was there, maybe hiding in someone's back bedroom. But all the houses were dark and still, although he had to run when a dog started to bark where the stupid biddy lived. That one time she had gotten so upset about, that one time in the car she had seen, he had only put his hand over Lydia's mouth to shut her up for a goddamn second because she was screaming at him so loud he couldn't think. And maybe some of Lydia's hair had gotten pulled out, but that was only because Roy had had to grab her and stop her from jumping out of the car when it was moving.

Finally he had gone to sleep, after checking three times to make sure the phone was working okay. But when he woke up Lydia was still gone, and there was still a dial tone, and the message light on the answering machine still wasn't blinking. Lydia had been gone for nineteen hours. Roy felt pissed off and worried, all at the same time. Lydia was naïve. She didn't know what was out there. They'd had a little fight yesterday, and maybe she thought she could make things better by running away and putting a scare into him, but she was wrong.

He couldn't think of where she had gone to. Her parents were dead, and he made sure she never talked to her old friends. And she didn't have any money. So where could she go? How could she just disappear into thin air? Softly, he thumped his head on the door frame, the way he used to when he was a kid, but it didn't help clear his mind. What Roy needed was some crystal. Lydia was always on him about it, but what was the difference between crystal and some yuppie drinking a triple mocha special? You used coke at a party to be social, you smoked some weed to be mellow, maybe you had a belt or two when you were angry, but when you wanted to concentrate, you used crystal. And that's what he needed to do. Concentrate. Figure out what to do next.

If only things could be the way they used to. Roy remembered what Lydia had been like when he first met her. Big brown eyes, shy, ducking her head when she caught him looking at her, hiding behind her hair. So nervous that the first time he took her out, she trembled all the way through the movie in the seat next to him. When he went to kiss her, her teeth chattered. Roy had found all that innocence exciting. She was like a little girl in an eighteen-year-old's body.

He met her just a few months after his grandmom had died. He had bought this place out on the edge of town, but it needed a woman's touch. And Lydia was looking to get away from her parents, who fought all the time. Drunks, both of them, with the house scarred from their fighting, holes in the wall from their fists, doors that had been kicked down so many times they didn't close tight, not a dish in the cupboard that matched.

Three months after they met, they were married. Then slowly Roy found Lydia was not to be trusted. She lied about little things and big, and when he caught her she just pulled into herself. When she broke the little china ballet dancer that had belonged to Roy's mom, she hid the pieces. He asked her and asked her to keep the house clean, and he would come home and find dishes in the sink, crumbs on the counter. He hated dirt. He couldn't stand disorder. And he had told her that. The first time he hit her, he expected her to cry, but she did nothing. Nothing! It drove him crazy.

Then he began to wonder if she was tricking him. Cheating on him. He set more and more rules, but even still, he figured she could find ways to wiggle out of them. And maybe she was. He followed her whenever he could, just to be sure. He had seen her with his own eyes, seen her smile at strangers, seen her laugh with other men.

Roy had hated then how he had let Lydia know one or two of his secrets. He had always been careful to keep his shirt on around her, but then one time she saw him after a shower and touched the knot on his collarbone. He had told her what had happened and his eyes had even gotten a little wet. For all he knew, maybe Lydia had been laughing at him, or telling his story to strangers while she rolled her eyes. About how his grandmom had shoved him down the cellar steps for a chore not done to her liking. When Pop-pop came home from work hours later, he fixed up a splint for Roy's arm, but Roy's collarbone never healed up right. Roy had been down there in the blackness for an eternity, cradling his arm to his chest, barely able to breathe because of the pain and his face swollen from crying and the dank smell of mold.

He had been too scared to move. In the dark, the spiders had worked their webs all around him. He was four. He knew better than to call out.

Nine

Sunday, OCTOBER 15, 4:30 P.M.

Free jerked awake as the Greyhound bus pulled into the outskirts of Portland. Reflexively, she checked to make sure Jamie's bag was still located on the seat beside her. It was. At the sight of the cluster of tall buildings marking Portland's downtown, the hairs along Free's arms rose. She was really doing this. She was both frightened and excited, and not sure which emotion was stronger.

She ignored the pain from the cuts on her feet as she walked out of the terminal building. A line of homeless people—men and women, young and old, black and white—stood on the street corner opposite, waiting, she guessed, for the doors of a soup kitchen to open. For the most part, they stood without moving or talking, faces expressionless. Their body language said that they had waited in line for hours and expected to wait for hours more. The exception was a jittery mumbling man dressed in a plaid flannel shirt and a blue and white cheerleader's skirt.

In the many times she had dreamed about living in a large city, Free certainly hadn't pictured all these street people. In Medford, bums were mostly drunk old white men with six days of sparse white growth on their chins—not this variegated mix of people of all ages and colors, all of them looking as if they were in trouble or wanted to cause trouble. What Free wanted was to be in the section of the city where people had real jobs, not addictions. Glancing left and right, she decided to walk toward the cluster of tall buildings.

After a block or two, she knew she had chosen the right direction. There were fewer people on the sidewalk now, and they mostly looked like they worked at full-time, well-paying jobs. A man in a suit held the door of a restaurant open for a woman wearing a long dark skirt decorated with sequins. Another man walking toward Free she initially pegged for a crazy, despite his expensive-looking suit, until she realized he wasn't talking to himself but to the tiny bud of a microphone, part of a miniaturized headset he wore over one ear.

Now what? Free had never been good at being spontaneous. She made lists all the time, on paper or in her head if she didn't have anything to write with. She liked instructions, maps, assignments and knowing what was expected of her. That had been the good part about her job at Petorium—the white coat, the checklists, the instructional videos about dematting fur or performing CPR on dogs.

It was only when two well-dressed women made a point of detouring around her that Free realized what she must look like. With her shaved head, Birkenstocks and her four-sizes-too-big borrowed cardigan worn over an iridescent polyester muumuu that kept slipping off one shoulder, she didn't look too much different from some of the homeless people she had been taking pains to avoid earlier. Evening was beginning to fall. Tonight she would check into a hotel and think about finding a place to live. Tomorrow would be time enough to think about what to do next. But first, her stomach reminded her, she needed to eat. She hadn't had anything since breakfast. So far, all the restaurants she had passed had had white tablecloths—not the kind of places Free would feel comfortable.

A block later, she found a deli. Out of habit, Free nearly ordered the vegetarian sandwich special (sprouts, avocado and Swiss cheese on stone-ground whole wheat). Then she realized that she had always hated alfalfa sprouts. What she really wanted, Free decided, was the roast beef on white, a bag of Lay's Kansas City Barbecue chips and (with a guilty nudge from her conscience as she felt the bump in her belly move) a salad and a glass of milk. She took the number the clerk handed her and went to find a table.

It was the kind of restaurant decorated mostly with big signs reading PLEASE BUS YOUR OWN TABLE. As instructed, the last patron had left Free's table clean, but on the chair was a folded copy of a tabloid newspaper called *Willamette Week*. After putting Jamie's bag down under the table and resting her foot on it, Free picked the newspaper up and began to page through it. It was filled with listings of movies, books, plays, gallery openings and musical acts coming to town. Free had never gone to an art gallery. With the exception of the one time in junior high when they were all bused over to a dress rehearsal of *Midsummer Night's Dream* at Ashland's Shakespearean Festival, she had never seen a play. But Free could be whoever she wanted to now. Maybe she could be the kind of woman who ate at restaurants with white tablecloths, who went to the opera, who wore skirts shimmering with sequins.

The newspaper's back pages were devoted to personal ads. In the Women Seeking Men section, women described their sense of humor and intelligence and seemed to have few requirements of a potential mate. The Men Seeking Women seemed to be seeking to fulfill their fantasies. White men sought "Asian beauties." Half-a-dozen men were looking for women willing to be "submissive." There was more than one man over the age of fifty who required any potential mate to be under the age of thirty-five. And a lot of the ads specified "child-free" and "slim." Free was perilously close to fitting in neither of these last two categories.

There were also sections for Men Seeking Men, Women Seeking Women, and Other. Even these weren't eye-opening to Free. Her parents had tried communal living when she was six. Free had shared a bedroom with three other children, and when she had a nightmare, she never knew which room to seek Diane or Bob in.

Her parents almost split up over Diane's relationship with a seventeen-year-old runaway who called himself Horse. Bob and Diane had arguments that raged for hours, while Free sat outside on the porch, playing with her stuffed dog with the torn ear, and her baby sister howled, unheeded, in the bedroom. Her mother claimed to be rejecting the establishment and its hang-ups. Her dad just cried.

And eventually, Free was never exactly sure how or why, her parents decided to leave the commune and move out. A few months later, on the dawn of the spring equinox, they exchanged vows in a service of their own making. Diane braided flowers in her hair and Bob wore an antique black silk vest, cracked with age. They had even jumped the broom. They had drawn the line at having an actual minister or even a justice of the peace. That would have been buying into a power trip.

Outside the windows of the deli, the sky was growing dark. Free's eyelids were heavy with exhaustion. She supposed the baby and the food in her belly were taking what little energy she had available.

After busing her own table, Free approached the cashier and asked if she knew of any nearby hotels. The cashier glanced upward, thinking. Free looked at the young woman's green hair and the two rings piercing her eyebrow. Maybe her transformation to middle class was already taking place, because she thought the girl looked a little odd. Finally, the cashier pointed down the street. "Try the Leonardo. It's two blocks down. I hear it's pretty quiet." Then she looked back at Free, focusing on the bruise that had now spread far beyond the edges of the bandage. "I know it's really none of my business, but my old boyfriend used to hit me. You need to get out of it while you still can."

Free couldn't think of what to answer. Finally she settled on, "It's really not that simple."

The other woman surprised Free with a deep laugh. "Don't I know it."

Ten

Sunday, OCTOBER 15, 5:47 P.M.

On her way to the hotel, Free passed a small outpost of Fred Meyer. Freddy's usually sold groceries, clothes and small appliances, but this branch was more like a drugstore. She bought a toothbrush, a tube of Crest, a new box of Band-Aids and two Payday bars (figuring the peanuts counted as needed protein). The only clothes she could find were in a small display of discounted men's sweatshirts and pants, so Free picked out one of each in black. She would have given anything for a new pair of panties, but she would just have to wait until tomorrow when the department stores opened.

As she walked past the book and magazine section on her way to the checkout counter, she spotted a map of Portland and added it to her basket. The magazines, with their tempting glossy colors, called to her. What the hell? She had thousands of dollars, didn't she? Hundreds of thousands. Giving into temptation, she picked up some more magazines suitable to her new life—*Good Housekeeping*, *Women's Day*, *Family Circle* and, after a second's hesitation, *Parents*.

As she was straightening up from taking the *Parents* magazine, Free glimpsed something out of the corner of her eye that stopped her cold. On the bottom of a rack of newspapers was a stack of

The Medford Mail Tribune. The headline on the front page read
TUESDAY FUNERAL FOR MEDFORD CRASH VICTIM. Underneath the
headline was a picture of Free. She recognized the photo. It was
taken from her junior yearbook, the last full year she went to
school. Was this how everyone was going to remember her, as the
girl with a buzz cut, hunched shoulders and downcast eyes? She
had had a buzz cut for years, after one particularly bad day in
seventh grade when she decided there was no use fighting the
labels the other kids gave her.

The clerk was busy talking to another employee. When she
put her purchases on the conveyor belt, Free kept the magazines
and the newspaper in a stack, with the newspaper on the bottom.
She certainly didn't need anyone noticing that she wasn't actually
dead. As the clerk rung up her purchases, Free's head hummed and
her chest felt tight, but he only glanced down long enough to find
the bar code on each item.

When she checked into the hotel, Free faced a dilemma. What
name should she put on the form? Seeing the newspaper had
brought home to her that it probably wasn't a good idea to continue to be herself anymore. Not only was Free Meeker officially
dead, but she didn't want to leave a trail for anyone who might
come looking for her. The clerk drummed her long red fingernails
on the counter. On impulse, Free wrote down Lydia Watkins, followed by a made-up address in Pendleton.

Her hotel room proved to be small but very clean. Free put
her bags on the floor and then sat on the edge of the bed and read
about her own death.

The Medford Mail Tribune paraphrased her mom ("Diane
Meeker, 44, said her daughter was a kind and generous young
woman"), quoted her boss at the Petorium ("Free had a special way
with animals") and her sister, Moon ("I'm glad we got to hang
together before she died"). No quotes from her dad or from Billy,
either. No mention of the baby, but then again, Free hadn't told
anyone about the baby yet. Anyone reading the article would think

she had been little more than a failure, a high school dropout with a dead-end job.

For the first time, Free wondered who had identified Lydia's burned body as Free's. Unlike all the true crime shows on TV, the identification couldn't have been made based on dental X rays. Diane and Bob had never bothered to take Free or Moon to the dentist, and they had been lucky enough to escape with reasonably straight teeth and no known cavities. It must have been Moon who had had to do it, Free realized. Knowing that a body had been found in Free's car, and then being confronted with a charred corpse—it was easy to see how Moon had made a mistake.

Free read over the article again. Her family seemed to have already come to terms with her being gone. Bob and Diane had always been the most important people in each other's universes, anyway. Sure, they had loved Free and Moon, but their passion had always been reserved for each other. And Free had never been that close to her sister, even before Moon had gotten so wrapped up in playing Mrs. Charles Morton.

In a way, it was Moon's fault that she had gotten in all this mess. If Moon hadn't gotten married to Charles, Free never would have gone to visit her in Pendleton. And if Free hadn't gone to Pendleton, she wouldn't have been indirectly responsible for Lydia's death and ended up with $740,000. Three months before, Free's sister had been working at Club Carnival when she met her husband-to-be, who was in town for a visit. He was seventy-two and in a wheelchair, but he could still wolf whistle. And he still liked the "ladies," as he invariably referred to any female over the age of about ten. He had stopped by the club to order a chicken-fried steak and a lap dance at 7:30 in the morning. Moon provided him with both. He so admired her talents that he hired her to jump out of a cake at his grandson's bachelor party the next week. And it was at the party that he popped the question.

Two weeks later, they drove down to Vegas (well, really it was Moon who drove the old man's Cadillac) and got themselves married by an Elvis impersonator. After becoming Charles's sixth and current wife, Moon moved with him back to Pendleton. When Free had called Moon after discovering Billy with the Taco Bell counter girl, the only thing she had told her sister was that she needed a chance to get out of town and get her head together. Tucked carefully away was the thought that visiting Moon would make her feel better about her own mistakes. Free had been surprised to find her sister happy, prattling about going back to school to get her GED while her husband looked on fondly. Free had been ashamed that Moon's happiness had made her feel even worse.

Really, would anyone be hurt if she stayed dead? Billy could have the Taco Bell counter girl. Diane and Bob already had each other. Even Moon had Charles. Free had no one but this baby. That and the cash fate had dropped in her lap.

Free had thought she would fall asleep as soon as she crawled between the motel bed's stiff sheets, but instead her thoughts refused to stop racing. If only her brain had come with an off switch. She had to decide not only what she would be, but who she would be. Free Meeker was officially dead. And to avoid being connected with the missing money, it would be best if she stayed dead.

Lydia, on the other hand, was really dead, even if no one knew that but Free. Would anyone really be hurt if Free kept quiet? Whether Free told anyone or not, Lydia was dead, and nothing would change that. From her chatter, Free knew that Lydia didn't have any family left. And she must not have had any close friends, either, if a square girl like her had had to rely on hitchhiking to get to Portland.

Free couldn't use her old name any more.

And Lydia no longer needed hers.

With a sigh, Free sat up, turned on the light. What should she do? Picking up Lydia's purse, she found the other woman's driver's license and stared at the thumbnail-sized picture, as if Lydia's eyes or expression could tell her what to do next. In a way, the other woman looked the way Free might have if she had been brought up by square parents. Their differences were minor. Lydia was twenty-two to Free's nineteen. Lydia was five foot seven, Free five foot eight. At one hundred thirty-five, Lydia had been about ten pounds thinner. Both had snub noses, brown eyes, and brown hair, although Lydia had worn hers in a shoulder-length bob with the ends turned under.

What if Free became Lydia?

Free's thoughts returned to the idea again, turning it over, examining it. Was it ghoulish of her to be thinking about stealing Lydia's life for her own? After all, if Free had been a better driver, maybe Lydia would have still been alive. Although she didn't really believe that. It seemed a miracle that she was even alive herself.

She put Lydia's driver's license back and then picked up her notebook. At the top of a fresh piece of paper, she wrote down the word "Need," underlined it twice, and then started a list under it.

Name (Lydia's?)
Story about past
New clothes
Place to stay
Place to keep $

The nice thing about adopting Lydia's story more or less wholesale would be that it answered the first two needs on her list. New clothes she could buy tomorrow. That left a place to stay and a place to keep the money. Part of her didn't want to let the money out of her sight, but she couldn't keep lugging the Nike bag around everywhere she went. Free supposed she could put the money in a safe-deposit box, but she didn't want it that far from her. And what if procuring a box entailed filling out all kinds of paperwork? She already knew that she couldn't put the money in a regular checking account. Her parents had hung with enough drug dealers that Free had learned the IRS required paperwork on any trans-action involving $10,000 or more in cash. That meant the idea of depositing the money was out by about a factor of seventy-four.

Maybe once she found someplace to live it would offer a hiding place for the money. She had enough cash to buy a house of her own, but again that idea wouldn't fly past the IRS. *Willamette Week*, Free remembered, had had apartment ads in the back. She picked the paper off the floor and began to thumb through it, consulting her map of Portland to figure out the approximate location of each address. Then she realized her plan had a major flaw. Renting an apartment would require more than just first, last and a deposit, which she could easily afford. It would also require paperwork. But what could she put down on any form that asked for personal references or job history? Sure, she had someone else's Social Security card and a license with someone else's picture on it and a shit-load of money, but those were more likely to make any landlord suspicious rather than reassured.

Then an ad at the top of the next section, "Shared Housing," caught her eyes. "Professional woman seeks same. Share large, beautiful old home with fireplace, garden. Close in SW, walk to downtown. No pets/smoking. Large room with bonus room. $600 month plus deposit."

Professional woman seeks same. That sounded good. Free imagined a manager, a lawyer, a dietitian, an advertising executive. The kind of person she had always wished Bob and Diane were. The kind of thing that maybe, just maybe, Free could now be herself.

And maybe someone renting a room would be less likely to require the filling out of complicated forms, credit checks and four different types of ID. Free imagined that the most important part of the whole equation would be that she have enough money to pay her share of the rent and the utilities. That, Free thought, eyeing Jamie's bag, wouldn't be an issue.

There were a bunch of other ads for shared housing, but they sounded more like ads the old Free would have answered, with requirements that any potential roommate be vegan, nonsmoking and willing to help till the organic garden. While the baby swished inside her, Free's attention kept returning to the ad at the top of the page. Finally she tore it out, set it on top of the Nike bag, turned off the light, and fell into a fitful sleep.

Eleven

Carly woke up when she felt his weight settle at the foot of the bed.

"Jamie, baby," she murmured sleepily, without opening her eyes. "Where've you been?" She sat up, then leaned forward to pull him into her arms. In the dark, her eyes suddenly went wide.

Before she could scream, a stranger's hand clamped over her mouth. A man's hand. Wearing a glove. With a twist, he pulled her back against his chest. Carly kept quiet, figuring she was already in so much trouble it wouldn't do to make him mad. Not right now. Not when the gun in her nightstand drawer was just three feet away.

She felt him lean over to turn on the bedside lamp. That was when she saw that he had his own gun, only this one had something gray screwed onto the barrel.

"If you scream, I'll kill you right now. Do you understand?" His voice was a harsh whisper against her ear.

Carly nodded and he took his hand away. She scrambled higher on the bed, until her back was against the headboard and her left hand rested on the nightstand, a scant foot from the lamp. It would only take her a second or two to turn off the switch, roll to the left, and come up with the gun in her hand.

She thought about pulling up the sheet to cover herself better than the ivory camisole and matching satin tap pants from Victoria's Secret were, but decided against it. Her breasts, Carly had found, made a useful ally. Maybe they would buy her the second of distraction she would need to shoot him between the eyes. While he looked her over, she did the same for him.

He was a big man, at least six-three. For a rapist, he was dressed unaccountably neatly. Dark dress pants, black shoes with heavy rubber soles, a dove-gray polo shirt pulled taut across his chest and well-muscled arms. His head was shaved as bald as a bullet, and his eyes were so black that Carly couldn't see the pupils. There was something strange about his face, but she didn't have time to think about that now.

"Where is Jamie?" No longer a whisper, his voice was quiet, with a flick of menace.

Carly made a rapid recalculation. This wasn't about her, then. When she had a second, she would think about what this might mean for Jamie, but right now Carly had to worry about Carly.

"I don't know." It was an honest answer, and she made sure she delivered it honestly.

"When were you expecting to see him?"

"Yesterday. But he didn't come." It was an effort not to keep her gaze focused on the round eye of the gun, but she managed.

"Has he been in contact with you since then? Has he called you, E-mailed you, sent you a postcard?"

She shook her head.

"And do you know what Jamie was doing?"

She couldn't see any point in lying. "Carrying something."

"Carrying what?"

Her gaze dropped to her lap. "Money. Or drugs. I think one way it's drugs and the other way it's money."

"And what does he get in exchange for doing that, Carly?" Her name in his mouth was meant to tell her everything—that he knew exactly who she was and that he could find her again if he wanted to. She thought about the gun again and then discarded the idea. This guy didn't miss a trick. Besides, she didn't think he wanted to kill her, or even that he wanted to rape her. If she was right—and if she was lucky—all he wanted was information.

"He gets five thousand a trip."

"And was he ever tempted to keep that money, that money that belonged to someone else?"

Unexpectedly, Carly's heart foundered at the past tense being applied to Jamie. Even if Jamie wasn't dead yet, she wouldn't place any bets on how long he was going to stay alive. "No. I don't think he even daydreams about it. He thinks it's too stupid to risk it." The man with the gun nodded for her to go on, so she did. "He's just a college kid. But he likes thinking he knows things other people don't, that he's part of things other people aren't. He has one of those cell phones, you know, with a headset, and the part that clips on his belt buzzes him whenever his stock prices change. He likes thinking he's a player."

He heard the way the tone of her voice changed. "And what do you think he is?"

She bit her lip and looked up at him through her lashes. "I think maybe he's just getting played."

He smiled at her, as if he liked her bravado. His teeth must have set him back some, they were so white and even. Carly knew the look. She had a mouth like that herself.

"Jamie likes his little walks on the wild side, but mostly he just does it to pay for school. Lewis and Clark is expensive. And he's going to go to law school next year."

"And are you one?"

"One what?"

"Are you a walk on the wild side?"

"Of course." She shrugged her shoulders. One of her straps slid down. She made no attempt to pull it back up.

"Where would he go if he did decide to take the money and run? Does he ever talk about a particular country? Does he speak any languages, like Spanish?"

Carly thought for a moment, then shrugged. "He never talks

about other countries that I can think of. And I know he doesn't speak Spanish, because once he ordered chicken off the menu in a Mexican restaurant and called it polo. Like your shirt."

He smiled for a second time, but the smile was absentminded. Carly thought he was making a decision, and despite the appreciative smile he had given her earlier, she was no longer so certain what it would be. She tried again to imagine throwing herself sideways, turning off the light, yanking open the drawer and grabbing the gun. She knew she would be dead before her fingers even touched the light switch.

When he moved, she couldn't help flinching, but he was only getting a business card from the pocket of his shirt. It was cream colored, with nothing on it but a number. "Call if he shows up. Leave your number and I'll get back to you."

Carly nodded. The man leaned forward, and she froze again, but he was only turning out the light. In the sudden darkness, she heard his sure footsteps walking toward the door. His face had only been a foot from hers before he turned out the light, and now she realized what had struck her as strange. The man's eyebrows had been tattooed on.

twelve

Free had slept with the Nike bag on the pillow next to her, and she woke up with her left arm curled around it. During the night, her entire arm had gone numb, and now she massaged it in an effort to get the blood flowing. Bruises were still flowering on her legs. After taking a long shower, she stuffed Lydia's purse, Doreen's muumuu and the things from Fred Meyer into Jamie's bag and then locked it up again. She had begun to think of herself as different, as if she had already become Lydia, but the mirror put the lie to that. Her head and feet, her buzz cut and Birkenstocks, looked like they still belonged to some hippie chick. In the middle, the combination of a man's sweatshirt and pants and the beginning bulge of pregnancy made Free look like the kind of suburban matron who shopped at Walmart.

Professional woman seeks same. Free rubbed her hand over her smooth head. If she really were Lydia Watkins, the woman running the ad would surely rent to her. But not to Free, not to Free with her bald head and cheap sweat suit. Taking out the nose ring hadn't made much of a difference. If she were going to start on a new life, the life that Lydia might have lived, then she needed to look more like Lydia had.

She ate breakfast at a nearby McDonald's, savoring every bite of the Egg McMuffin and the crisp oval of hash browns, still hot from the fryer. Back on the street, Free eyed her reflection in the large window of a beauty salon, then focused on what was behind it. Next to a pyramid of sculpting gel jars was a display made out of a foot-square piece of black velvet. Piercing the velvet were thirty plastic flesh-colored index fingers. Crooked downward, each nail displayed a different color of nail polish. The effect was macabre, like looking at the souvenirs of a serial killer. Free was about to walk on when she noticed the second to last item on a sign listing services offered by the salon—Erica Young wigs.

Thirty minutes and one hundred and forty-nine dollars later, Free emerged from the salon wearing what the saleslady had called the Maui model. Made from human hair about the same shade as Lydia's had been, the wig came pretty close to Lydia's style, too. Now Free had a dark brown bob. The bangs hid the cut on her forehead, and the ends turned under in a line even with her chin. Each time Free turned her head, strands brushed against her neck. The unexpected touch made her flinch. Even though her new hair didn't quite go with her sweat suit, Free noticed immediately that it did cut down on the number of stares she got.

She had one more stop to make before she would be a reasonable facsimile of "professional woman seeks same." It was definitely time to go shopping. Although she was in a part of the city that offered a dozen clothing stores, many of them were small boutiques where she was sure to be the center of attention. That was the last thing she wanted. She kept scanning the people on the sidewalk, alert for the mysterious Don, who would probably do anything to get his money back. The sooner she looked like someone else, the better. Then no one would be able to connect her to the girl who had picked up Jamie's money.

Up ahead, Free spotted a Whitchers. The chain had an outpost in Medford, and from the time or two she had ventured in (seldom with any money to spend—Diane had been proud that she "mooched" most of their clothes), Free had found it far less intimidating and much more jumbled than most clothing stores. It catered to everyone from the just plain cheap to the bargain-loving crowd to the people who could afford something—anything—prominently displaying a designer's logo.

Once she walked through the doors, she automatically headed for the stuff she normally wore—short dresses, embroidered jeans, crop tops. Then she remembered. She wasn't nineteen-year-old Free. She was twenty-two-year-old Lydia now. A widow. A woman who probably had a job at an office. A woman who wore serious, grown-up clothes.

After consulting the directory, Free went to the fourth floor. Here she found what were described as career clothes. It was all stuff that one day at Petorium would have left snagged and permanently stained. There wasn't a single serviceable drip-dry multicolor polyester item in sight. Instead there were matching skirts and jackets made of the finest wool gabardine. Silk blouses that slipped through Free's fingers when she caressed the cloth. Cashmere twin sets as soft as clouds. It was only when she pressed a silk shirtdress up against herself, trying to gauge what size she should take to the dressing room, that Free remembered that with all her money, she still couldn't have any of these clothes.

She was pregnant. Which meant that none of these outfits would fit for more than a month or two, at the most. And most of them probably wouldn't fit right now.

Reluctantly, Free went up a floor to the maternity clothes. The clothes here were a cruel contrast to those on the fourth floor. Everything seemed to be either pink, decorated with ribbons and ruffles, patterned with tiny flower prints or all three. She didn't want to look like a kindergartner who'd accidentally gotten herself knocked up. The first salesclerk she saw took one look at her cheap sweat suit and heavy bag and gave her a wide berth. The second, a woman who looked nearly seventy and barely came to Free's shoulder, bustled over with a smile on her face.

"May I help you find something?" Osteoporosis had pushed the woman's shoulders into a permanent curve, making her head jut forward like a turtle's.

"Do you have anything more—dressy? I'm looking for something, um, like a professional woman would wear."

If the salesclerk thought this an odd request coming from a woman wearing poly-cotton sweats and Birkenstocks, she didn't let on. "To work? Like a skirted suit?"

When Free nodded, the woman darted unhesitatingly from rack to rack. She came back with a black suit with French cuffs, a cream-colored twin set, a pair of black pants, and a burgundy colored dress with a sweetheart neckline. "What would you like to try on?"

"All of it!" Free's spirits were rising. She'd never owned a jacket with lapels or a dress that had to be worn with nylons.

As the clerk hung Free's clothes in a dressing room, she told Free that she would wait to see if Free needed different sizes. Part of Free wondered if the older woman was really afraid that she was going to steal something. Maybe she was listening for the telltale sound of someone trying to pry apart the plastic antitheft device that dangled from each garment.

After pulling on the twin set and black pants, Free hesitantly stepped out of the dressing room to look in the three-way mirror. The clerk tilted her head to one side, looking even more like a bird.

"Are you wearing a maternity bra?"

Free shook her head, knowing it was pretty clear she wasn't wearing any bra at all. Overnight, it seemed, she had developed breasts like a milkmaid's. "Do you sell any?" She had never known there were such things, but she had seen more than enough of Diane's boobs to know that a little support might not be a bad thing.

In answer, the woman came back with several white bras. Free studied the hang tag of one before trying it on. It promised to grow right along with her—the pregnant woman's version of a training bra. The idea of more growth was a little bit scary. Her breasts already seemed huge.

By the time Free and her helper—Helen—were through, she

had selected two bras, seven pairs of maternity underwear, a nightgown, three pairs of maternity stockings and nine different outfits—including all the clothes Helen had originally chosen for her. The older woman even hunted down items from other departments, coming back with shoes, socks, stockings and even a strand of pearls and matching earrings. And after asking if she might make a suggestion, Helen went down four floors and came back with a tube of red lipstick. The bright slash of color lit up Free's whole face.

Free realized she couldn't carry around armfuls of bags all day, so Helen even went up to the luggage department and came back with a black Samonsite suitcase on wheels. She and Free had taken to bursting into giggles for no reason.

"Can I wear one of the outfits out of the store?"

"Certainly. Do you want to keep your old clothes?"

The sweat suit had cost twenty-four dollars, and she had worn it only one day. Feeling more than a little bit daring, Free shook her head. She took the black pants and the twin set back into the dressing room with her, along with the maternity underwear, knee-high stockings and the black flats. While she dressed, Free added the total up in her head. It was pretty clear she would have to dip into Jamie's bag to pay for everything.

"Look at that, Joe." The younger of the two security guards nudged his partner.

They had both long since gotten over the thrill of seeing nude strangers, especially since very few of them bore any resemblance to a Penthouse Pet. And the store always made sure to assign two of them to the dark room the size of a walk-in closet and lined with video monitors. Unstated was the reasoning that having company meant there was less chance of a security officer treating the room like his own private peep show and taking matters into his own hands, so to speak.

They were there to watch for theft, and they saw that a lot, but they also saw interesting things all the time that didn't fall under their purview. Men dressed as women, women dressed as men, men who wore women's panties under their staid suits, women who hid their stick-thin bodies with voluptuously padded undergarments. Once or twice they had witnessed a daring couple sneak a tryst in an isolated dressing room. The tapes for those rare events got passed around the various shifts, sometimes even sold.

By the time Joe turned, there wasn't much to see but a girl with brown hair and a nice body, even if she was a little bit pregnant. Insisting he had seen something, the first guard rewound the tape a bit and played it back. And there it was—underneath some other stuff inside a zippered gym bag, there was a flash of what looked like stacks of money.

They rewound it and watched it again. Then Joe shrugged his shoulders and hit the rewind button, so that the tape would be used again. They were there to catch people stealing, that was all. If some woman wanted to carry a lot of cash in a gym bag, well, that was her business. He just hoped she had the good sense to keep a tight hold of the bag.

Thirteen

Monday, OCTOBER 16, 1:14 P.M.

From the pay phone in Whitcher's lobby, Free called the daytime number listed in *Willamette Week*. She closed her eyes for a moment while the phone rang. A wave of exhaustion washed over her. Less than forty-eight hours ago, she had been surrounded by the dead and dying.

"Alexis Ashburg." A deep voice for a woman.

"Yes, I'm calling about your ad. Is the house to share still available?" Somehow she felt that the different clothes made her sound different. More mature, more responsible. *Professional woman seeks same.*

"Yes, it is." Her voice reminded Free of honey. Or money. Or both. If Free hadn't been acting, she would have been nervous. "You don't have any cats, do you?"

"No." The ad had clearly stated no pets.

"I've had two women now who've told me they didn't consider a cat to fall under the category of pets." The woman cut her laugh short. "Would you like to come by this evening?"

"I could come by right now if you wanted." Free refrained from saying she had no place else to go.

"I have an afternoon meeting, but I could meet you after work. Would five-thirty work for you?"

"Sure. I'll need directions, though. I just moved here from Pendleton." She didn't want to say she didn't have a car.

After killing as much time as she could in the tenth-floor cafeteria, Free went back out onto the streets pulling her suitcase behind her. She noticed both that different people looked at her and that people looked at her differently. Well-dressed businessmen smiled and nodded at her, while street kids asked her for spare change. Both of these experiences were novel. Her new clothes and hair felt like camouflage. Even though she looked around a few times to see if anyone was following her, she began to relax. No one looking at her would ever guess that she was really Free Meeker.

At 5:30, Free was bumping her new suitcase, now filled with all her purchases, as well as Jamie's bag and Lydia's purse, up six flagstone steps. The house was two stories, with a high, pitched roof. Painted gray, it had decorative white shutters framing every window. Free couldn't help contrasting it with the house she had lived in with her parents for the past three years. Bob and Diane had built much of it themselves, and it had showed. She put out her hand to ring the bell, then hesitated. *Professional woman seeks same.* This woman would probably think it strange if Free trundled in her suitcase. A professional woman would have a place to keep her stuff. Tall arbor vitae grew on either side of the door, pressed up close to the outside wall. After a moment's hesitation, Free wedged the suitcase behind one, then stepped back to make sure it couldn't be seen. She stepped forward and rang the bell.

The woman who answered the door was strikingly beautiful. Even though she was only an inch shorter than Free, Free was sure she was no more than a size two. Kinked black curls framed her triangular face and fell loose around her shoulders. Her large gray eyes were tip-tilted, and she wore a short black skirt topped with a loose red silk shirt that drew the eye like a candle's flame. Standing in front of this vision, Free was sincerely glad she was no longer wearing an oversize iridescent polyester muumuu.

"Come in, come in. As I said on the phone, I'm Alexis Ashburg, but all my friends call me Lexi."

Which didn't exactly settle the question of what Free should call her. "I'm Lydia. Lydia Watkins." Even though Free had rehearsed the words, she had to force them from her mouth. She felt like a hermit crab, scuttling into an empty shell after its original owner had died. She followed the other woman inside. "You have a beautiful home."

Smiling slightly, the other woman nodded without speaking. It was beautiful, with a feeling of light and space. The oak floors were polished to a subtle gleam. Ornate glass lighting fixtures shaped like flowers hung from the ten-foot high ceilings. Mahogany trim framed all the windows and doors. At the same time, the house was strangely unfurnished. The book-lined living room held only a well-worn Morris chair and a leather ottoman. Beyond it, the dining room was empty except for two folding chairs set on either side of a card table.

"Would you like to see the room?"

Free nodded in agreement. She followed Lexi up the stairs and into the first door on the right. She was relieved to find a completely furnished bedroom with a maple queen-size sleigh bed and a matching dresser and nightstand. There was an old-fashioned blue and white quilt on the bed, and white curtains at the window.

"This used to be the guest bedroom." Lexi opened a door that led off the bedroom. "This is a private bath." It was as clean and tidy as if it were in a *Good Housekeeping* pictorial, with yellow-and-white tile and thick towels the color of egg yolk folded precisely over the towel rack next to the shower stall. They walked back through the bedroom and into the hall, where Lexi opened the door next to the bedroom. "This is the bonus room. It's currently unfurnished." Even though the pale gray carpet had been freshly vacuumed, it still showed indentations where furniture— Free guessed a desk, a chair and bookcases—had recently been. "It would make a nice office." Or a nursery, Free thought.

They went back downstairs and Lexi showed Free the kitchen,

which was mercifully without bare spots. Free guessed that whoever had taken the furniture hadn't been much of a cook. Tucked underneath the cabinets was a row of expensive appliances, including an espresso maker and a cobalt blue KitchenAid mixer. The six-burner stove and refrigerator were both faced in stainless steel. Overhead hung a row of copper pans.

"There's a little laundry room back here, right off the garage," Lexi said. She led Free through it and then out the back door and into a small garden, planted in a colorful riot of wild flowers. Free recognized hot pokers and bachelor buttons, Queen Anne's lace, poppies and foxglove, as well as a dozen other flowers she couldn't name.

Lexi reached inside an empty red flowerpot. When her hand reappeared, it was holding a pack of Merit Lights and a silver lighter. The line between her brows eased as she sucked the cigarette to a glow.

Free was surprised to hear herself speak. "I thought your ad said no smoking."

"It does. It does." Lexi turned her head and carefully blew a stream of smoke behind her. "I only smoke outside. I hadn't smoked for seven years. Then my husband left me for somebody else. And the next day I was surprised to discover myself at the 7-11 at three in the morning, buying a package of Merits." She took a long drag on the cigarette. "Bastard."

"I'm sorry," Free said. "I know what that's like. I caught my boyfriend with the Taco Bell counter girl." Then she remembered she was now officially a widow. "Once," she added. "That was a long time ago. Before I was married."

"Hah!" A bitter laugh spurted from the other woman. "At least you caught him with a woman. Two months ago, I decided to leave work a couple of hours early. I work in public relations, and the banquet I had organized the night before had gone very well. Everyone was happy." The corners of Lexi's mouth turned down when she said the word "happy." "The client was happy. The firm was happy. I was happy. And I thought Gene was happy. So I decided to surprise him. I stopped by Elephants Delicatessen. I got a bottle of wine, some of that great rustica bread, a triple crème cheese from France, a little box of Niçoise olives. It was a picnic in a paper bag. When I let myself in, he was talking on the phone in the kitchen and didn't hear me. But I heard him." Lexi's words were for herself now, speeding up, changing to present tense. "And he's complaining about me, calling me a bitch to someone he's calling honey. But the worst part is that when he hangs up the phone, he says, 'I love you, too, Brad.' Brad! It's another guy. Somebody he worked with. My husband left me for another guy." Lexi stubbed out her cigarette and lit another, keeping her hand half over her mouth even when she wasn't inhaling. "Now I feel like people are staring at me all the time, wondering what's wrong with me that I made my husband turn to men. Or what's wrong with me that he thought I wouldn't notice he preferred boys to girls." Her nostrils flared and her cheeks sucked in as she took another drag on her new cigarette.

Free had thought Lexi had forgotten about her presence, but now the other woman eyed her shrewdly through the veil of smoke. "You're expecting, aren't you?"

The old-fashioned word struck Free as exactly right. "Yes, I am expecting. My husband, umm, he was killed in an accident a couple of months ago." Free was surprised by the prim way she heard herself speaking. It was like hearing Lydia again. She listened to her own words the way she might have watched a magician pull forth a string of scarves from an empty top hat.

"I'm so sorry. Did he know about the baby before he died?"

Free thought of Billy, the tears streaming down his face as he followed her on his knees. "No." She looked away, the spell of pretending to be Lydia temporarily broken.

"What do you do? Or have you found a job here in Portland yet?"

Free thought quickly. She didn't want to come up with the wrong profession for herself, not when she hadn't decided what she wanted to be yet. Then she realized that sticking with a slightly modified version of Lydia's story offered a simple explanation—and one that would reassure Lexi that she could afford to pay her share of the rent.

"Right now, I don't have to work. There was a settlement from the insurance company. I decided to move to Portland to get away from all the memories. I know I should have planned it all out and everything, but it was an impulsive decision. I just suddenly realized I had to get away."

"I know what that's like," Lexi said. "Only I'm stuck here. Gene is refusing to help me pay the mortgage, even though both our names are on it. I came home from work one day and he'd taken anything he thought was his and a lot of stuff that was mine from the beginning. I mean, he even took the Duncan Pfyffe dining room set I inherited from my grandmother. He's trying to force me to sell this place, and give him half the money, but I won't. I love this house. But the only way I can afford to keep it is to get a roommate." Free could tell she had reached a decision. "There's room in the garage for two cars. Did you park on the street?"

"I, um, don't have a car right now."

"Don't have a car?" Lexi echoed. She turned her head away to blow a stream of smoke sideways, but Free could tell the other woman was surprised and a bit perturbed. Then Lexi supplied her own answer. "Oh," she said, her voice as soft as a sigh, "that accident that killed your husband. It was a car accident, wasn't it? Were you with him?"

Free found herself nodding. "I was driving, but it wasn't my fault." Tears sprang to her eyes as she remembered how awful the real car accident had been. "Now I can't bring myself to drive." There was a lot of truth contained in her lie, but still she wanted to change the subject. "Have you talked to a divorce lawyer about making your ex-husband give you alimony, or at least give you your stuff back?" Free ventured. This was uncharted territory for her. Aside from her sister, no one in Free's circle of family and friends was married. And Moon's husband had been torn between adopting and marrying Moon, trying to figure out what would be the best way to prevent any of his real children from inheriting.

"Yes. And about the most he's done so far is charge me quite a lot of money." Lexi stubbed out her cigarette, then looked up at Free. "Well, Lydia, what do you think? I'm asking first, last and a five-hundred-dollar deposit. Half of the utilities runs about one hundred and twenty-five dollars every month. Are you interested?"

When Free went to bed that night she slipped between strange sheets and lay surrounded by unfamiliar things. But in a way, she had never felt more at home. She rolled onto her back and put her hands on her abdomen, feeling the baby stir. She had noticed that it liked to move when she was still. Tonight it felt as if whatever was in there was busy grabbing on to everything it could find, pulling and tugging.

This week she would definitely have to find a doctor. A real doctor, for once. She was tired of the drill at the county clinic, where they had tested her vaginally, anally and orally at every visit for the presence of syphilis, chlamydia, herpes, HPV and AIDS. They never listened when she insisted she was in a mutually monogamous relationship.

She ran her hands lightly across her belly. Maybe she was too imbalanced and insecure to be anyone's mother. Free sighed. It was too late to worry about that. Instead, she made the baby a series of promises. She promised this kid that there would always be enough food to eat. Warm clothes to wear. That she would never leave hash brownies where he or she could get into them. That this kid would never be exposed to wood heat except in the form of a festive Christmas fireplace. And that there would always be indoor plumbing.

When she finally went to sleep, Free dreamed she really was Lydia Watkins.

Fourteen

Tuesday, OCTOBER 17, 3:03 P.M.

Roy wound up and let go. Lydia's bottle of Eternity made a popping noise as it shattered against the wall. Then the only sound in the room was his own harsh breathing. Trembling with rage and exhaustion, Roy looked around the bedroom for something else of Lydia's to destroy.

There was nothing left untouched. He had been awake and raging all night, and now all of her things were strewn on the floor, stamped on, smashed, cut, torn, crushed. The pages from her books lay everywhere, like drifts of leaves. He had pulled her necklaces until they burst into beads, ground her tubes and pots of makeup until they smeared into paste on the bathroom floor. After finding them discarded in the back of a bathroom drawer, he took the hammer to her wedding and engagement rings. He had smashed the glass on the framed photo of her parents that had hung above the couch, then ripped the photo into a hundred pieces. Now Roy saw a bright bead of blood on the end of his index finger and realized that he had cut it on a piece of glass. He sucked on it, the hot, salty taste of blood mingling with the sour tang the whiskey had left on his tongue.

Finding the brochure hidden in Lydia's panty drawer had been what did it. He had been touching all the slick and shiny things,

83

thinking of how much he needed her, when his fingers brushed against something stiff. Paper. From the back of the drawer, he had pulled out a purple leaflet.

"Love doesn't have to hurt," it said on the front in curlicue writing. Roy could feel the red climbing up the back of his neck. Where had Lydia gotten this? Had she been talking out of turn, nattering on to people about things that were none of their business?

He opened the brochure and began to read. "Are you in a close personal relationship that has become frightening? Is your partner controlling, abusive or violent? The danger is real. If you have a controlling partner, don't ignore or try to excuse abusive behavior. It is not the result of stress, anger, drugs or alcohol. It is learned behavior that a person uses to intimidate and manipulate. It is destructive and dangerous. Every year, thousands of people are seriously hurt or killed by their spouses or partners. But we can help. We can offer you a safe house where you—and your children—can be secure."

The stupid bitch had even put checkmarks after nearly every item on a long list:

Does your partner:
— hurt you by pushing, hitting, slapping, kicking, or choking you?
— threaten to hurt or kill you?
— call you names and humiliate you?
— blame you for the abuse they committed?
— limit where you can go and what you can do?
— control your money?
— tell you that you're crazy?
— force you to have sex against your will?
— apologize and tell you it will never happen again (even though it has already?)

Until he found the brochure, Roy had been thinking about taking Lydia back. Then a crank-fueled rage had come over him when he realized that she must have told a bunch of strangers what was none of their business. What had happened between them had nothing to do with outsiders.

He picked up the brochure again, ready to throw it in the burn pile, but for the first time he noticed something on the back. No address, but a phone number. A phone number that started with 503—the area code for Portland, three hours away. So that's where Lydia had taken herself off to. Was she really dumb enough to think he wouldn't get her back? A long time ago, before she knew better, Lydia had always been pestering him about going to Portland. She had even wanted to go there on their honeymoon, instead of the old cabin near the Zig-Zag River he had inherited from Pop-pop. He had set her straight about that pretty quick.

Roy picked up the phone. The phone and the TV and the stereo were all in one piece, little islands in the sea of broken things. He thought of them as solely belonging to him, because Lydia was never allowed to touch them. He dialed the number from the back of the brochure.

"Gabriel House."

"Let me speak to Lydia Watkins."

"I'm sorry, sir, but we have no one here by that name."

"Yes, you do, you stupid bitch. Let me speak to my wife."

"She is not here. But we do have Caller ID, and we do make tape recordings of all calls, and we do bring harassment charges when necessary."

The woman's words were a blur of noise. Lydia was there, Roy could feel it. And in his mind's eye, his wife was dressed in a short skirt and some dyke with a crew cut had her arm around her, and Lydia was laughing. Laughing at him. "You tell Lydia that I will come get her if she doesn't get her butt home now. You hear me? You tell Lydia I will find her and put one bullet in her eye and one straight in her heart if she's not here by tomorrow."

The only answer was a dial tone. He called 411 and said he needed the address for a Gabriel House in Portland. Even though Roy had expected it, he still felt a surge of anger when the recorded voice told him, "I'm sorry, but that information is unavailable."

Staggering toward the doorway, he kicked a mound of her clothes out of the way. He had cut them up, scissoring out the crotch and the places where her breasts had rubbed. Just wait until she came back. He'd make her earn new clothes, piece by piece.

Roy ran his hand roughly down the front of his pants, then took another hit from the nearly empty bottle of Jack. If he left the clothes here, though, she would just sew them up. Lydia was clever, in a sly sort of way. She could always think of ways to fix things, make it as if they had never happened. If he tossed her dinner on the floor, he might get up in the middle of the night to find her picking off the top bits and eating them. If he hit her, she covered up the bruises so she looked as if he hadn't left a mark on her.

Well, she wasn't going to have these clothes to make over, to make nice, to piece together until the eye couldn't even see the scars. Leaning down, Roy gathered up an armful of dresses and pants and blouses and then took them outside, bumping the screen door open with his hip. He stuffed them into the burn barrel, then went back for her underwear.

What if Lydia didn't come back? Because she might not, Roy knew that. He probably was going to have to find her. He would find her, and then he was going to have to teach her a lesson. Teach her that she couldn't talk about private things to outsiders. But first he had to think about how to find her when she had gone to ground at a place that specialized in hiding wives from husbands, children from fathers.

Roy ran his thumb over the wheel of his lighter until it flicked into flame. Her bras and panties twisted as they melted and burned. He pitched the empty bottle of Jack on top and stepped back as it exploded. How could she have humiliated him like this?

From the laurel bushes came a questioning sound, almost a moan. Roy jumped, then saw two eyes glowing back in there. Without thinking about it, he crossed himself. The reflex had been beaten into him by his grandmom, starting when he was three, after his mother decided to drop him off for good.

Squinting, he made out the form of a black cat, thin as a shadow, hidden way back in the branches. He swore to himself. For weeks, he had suspected that Lydia was feeding a stray out in the backyard. Once he'd even found an empty tuna can out in the middle of the grass, licked clean. She had claimed it must have fallen out of the garbage, and had stuck to that claim even after he whacked her a few times.

He had never liked cats. From his grandmom he knew that they were sneaky, dirty, Satan's familiars, and that they sucked the breath right out of newborn babies. Now here came this black cat slinking around as soon as Lydia had taken off, taunting him with its slanted yellow eyes.

Slowly, a smile curled Roy's lips. He would track down Lydia, wherever she had gone, and then he would show her what she would get for lying to him. He couldn't wait to see Lydia's face when she saw this stupid cat after he was done with it. He bet she wouldn't be able to hide behind her dead eyes then.

"Here kitty, kitty," he called. The cat didn't budge. That was okay. Roy went into the kitchen and opened a can of tuna. He went back out in the yard, settled down on his haunches and set the can of tuna a foot in front of him. He could be patient when he wanted to be.

Thursday, OCTOBER 19, 7:15 A.M.

From *The Oregonian*

POLICE SEEK IDENTITY OF MAN KILLED IN OREGON'S DEADLIEST PILE-
UP *(Clark City)—Oregon State Police are seeking the public's help to
identify a young man, one of the 14 victims of a 52-vehicle deadly
pileup on Interstate 84 on Oct. 14. The police have released a photo
of the dead man's face. He was a white male in his early twenties, 5
foot 11, 180 lbs., with blue eyes. He had dark brown hair cut short
and bleached blond on the top. There was a tattoo shaped like barbed
wire around his wrist, and he was wearing a Tommy Hilfiger long-
sleeved polo shirt and denim jeans. His first name may have been Jamie.*

*Police would also like to hear from a woman who witnesses at Holy
Redeemer Hospital believe was traveling with the dead man. She is
described as a white woman in her late teens or early 20s, 5 feet 8
inches tall, weighing 130 to 140 pounds. She had a shaven head and
was last seen wearing a tie-dye T-shirt, jeans and sandals. There was
a silver ring in her nose.*

Don carefully refolded the Metro section and slipped it back into
the newspaper, aligning everything until it was as neat as if it had
just come off the press. Margherita often chided Don for the way

he cleaned up after himself, saying he left her with no work to do. But it wasn't in Don's nature to be untidy. And he couldn't abide loose ends. While he tamped the pages back into place, he thought about his now no-longer missing courier. *The Oregonian* article—as well as the accompanying photo, recognizably of Jamie, even though his face was oddly puffy and his eyes were closed—had solved one mystery while posing a dozen others.

The leather soles of Don's French loafers ticked hollowly as he walked across the dining room floor, custom-crafted out of pale bamboo. He went down the hall and into his office, then sat down in the black leather chair. The room was warm—a necessity since without hair on his head, or any place else on his body, Don was often chilled. Turning away from his desk, he looked down at the city without seeing it, caught up in the puzzle of what had transpired Friday.

One piece of the puzzle had just been snapped into place. Jamie was dead—not kicking back in Costa Rica or Thailand, his only luggage a Nike bag filled with nearly a million dollars. It seemed more than likely that Jamie had just been doing his job when he got caught up in a severe bit of bad luck. Don had heard about the accident, but had figured Jamie was in Bend by the time it happened. He must have been running a half a day or more behind. Maybe he had planned on cutting down on sleep to make up for lost time, before the accident took all worries from him.

And maybe this other girlfriend, this one the paper mentioned, the one Carly seemed to know nothing about, had slowed him down. At that idea, Don had to shake his head. Olive-skinned Carly, with her black eyes that snapped like firecrackers—why wouldn't she be enough for a man? He shrugged. Maybe you could just chalk it up to being twenty-two, a time when everyone thought he was unconquerable and then went on to make a dumb mistake or two.

Even Don. He had once been a Jamie, a human mule who was supposed to never question its load. But unlike this dead boy, Don had dreamed of working his way up, not out. And he had, fighting fiercely for possession of each rung. There were a few things he had been forced to do back in the old days, things he still regretted.

Don was a professional. That was how he thought of himself. He treated everyone with courtesy unless or until they tried to cross him. He was polite, well-mannered and never raised his voice. He didn't chatter and he never let down his guard. You were wise not to make any friends in this business.

Unfortunately, sometimes being a professional meant performing an unpleasant task and then moving on. A professional did not dwell on what couldn't be helped. He seldom thought about them, the people he had killed. Don did not allow these dead people to enter his thoughts, and he tried to keep them out of his dreams.

In the days since the money had gone missing, though, a parade of the dead had marched through his dreams, and he was helpless to stop them. It started with Skip. The night that Barry had called Don, he had dreamed about Skip, who had been underground for twenty years now. In Don's dream, Skip had followed him around, wanting to talk, wanting to be friends, even though there was a red-rimmed hole like a third eye right in the middle of his forehead. A hole that Don had put there. He awoke in his wide bed, panting for breath, his own eyes wide in the dark. But in his mind's eye, he saw the dead walking.

When Don had shot Skip, the circuit-rider who had the job before him, he had been just twenty-two, the same age Jamie had been. He knew now that that first death had been manipulated. They had set it up. It took care of so many problems. It got rid of Skip, who had been skimming off the top, a little bit more each time, and replaced Skip with Don, someone who had a reputation for being reliable, honest and without a drug habit of his own— three rare things in the world of the syndicate. And the fact that they knew the truth about who had killed Skip was an unspoken threat in case Don was ever tempted to rejoin the world of civilians.

They hadn't told Don to go out and kill Skip. They just gave

Don the order that he was to take over, and a gun that he stuck in the back of his waistband. Skip had been on a meth binge for eighty-two hours straight and had the resultant hair-trigger temper. Red-eyed with rage, Skip drew a gun, but Don had had a good night's sleep and was half Skip's age. Skip finally dropped to the floor with one bullet in his chest, another in his arm and a third in his head. Afterward, Don was frightened all over again by the sound of his own grunting as he hopped around, pointing the gun at the empty corners of the room, the grip slippery in his sweaty hands. When he realized what he had done, Don walked out to his car on rubber legs and threw up in the passenger seat. He'd had to give that car to Barry to sell, because even though he cleaned it, to Don it would always stink of vomit and fear and blood.

The second death had been a young Hispanic guy outside of Chiloquin. He had jumped Don when he bent down to unlock the car door. Don had seen a flash of movement reflected in the window, and had turned and shot the guy as easy as you would point a finger. The bullet caught him in the throat, and he was dead before he even hit the ground. Don had never seen him before. He didn't even touch him, just hightailed it out of there. For a few weeks, he had scanned even the smallest articles in the paper, looking for a notice about the man's death, but there was nothing. Maybe the death of what was more than likely an illegal immigrant was deemed too unimportant to mention. Or maybe his buddies had dragged him off and buried him someplace out in the high desert.

There were just two deaths Don would have regretted, if he had allowed himself to have regrets. Ten years ago, he had arranged to sell three kilos of coke on a dirt road outside of Forest Grove. It was a big enough deal that Don decided to handle it himself. But Les, the local dealer, paged Don, saying that his baby was sick and there was no one to watch it, and asking Don to meet him at his house, which was off the highway in an unincorporated area. Normally, Don would have said no, but he had known Les for more than a decade.

The house was a hovel on the verge of falling down, listing enough that there wasn't a single true angle left. Don walked up splintered boards on the front porch and knocked on the door, which didn't quite fit inside the frame. Les answered the door with a grin pasted on his face and sweat on his forehead, so it wasn't even that much of a surprise when he went to get the money and came back with a gun instead. Don shot him in the heart before the other man had even summoned up the guts to pull the trigger.

Somewhere in the back, a baby started crying. Blood frothed from Les's lips. Don kicked the gun away from his hand. He turned away, not wanting to watch the man die. Exhaustion fell over him like a heavy quilt. He knew he should look for the money, even knowing it was more than likely gone or had never existed in the first place.

Suddenly, a woman jumped out from a closet with a hatchet in her hand. She was screaming like a banshee and her eyes were on fire with craziness and grief. Don shot her once, in the chest, but she just kept coming at him, so he put the second bullet in her face. The baby was crying louder. Rachel was about four months pregnant then, just starting to feel their own baby kick inside her. Don didn't think he could bear to look at this baby, but its room would be one of the places he would have to search. He would have to take the mattress out of the crib and inspect it, even look in the folds of the baby's diaper. He was afraid, suddenly, that he might kill it when he laid his hands on it. Don yanked a dishtowel from the refrigerator handle and wiped down everything he had touched, then turned on his heel and left.

He couldn't stop thinking about the baby. He stopped at a pay phone and called the hospital in Hillsboro, thinking it was less likely that they put an automatic trace on calls. He told the woman who answered that he had heard shots at his neighbor's house, and now he could hear their baby crying and crying, only no one was doing anything about it. He gave her the address, but when she started to ask questions, he hung up, then wiped the phone down. In another town, twenty miles away, Don threw the dishtowel away.

At the time, Don had tried to chalk it up to just business, something he had been forced to do. He had been given no other choice. When he came home, he had stayed away from Rachel, feeling his hands were too dirty to touch her or to cradle her belly, filled with innocent life. A distance had grown between them, and she had raged at him, but he had not told her the truth of it. Maybe things would have been different if he could have broken down, if he could have confessed to her and found absolution. But he hadn't been able to take that chance, to see her face reflect horror and disgust and maybe even fear.

Don was considered an old-timer in this business, with old-fashioned quibbles and morals and self-made rules. Now the business was run by new people, kids really, boys barely older than Jamie but with a ruthlessness Jamie had never possessed. Kids who had no respect for history or hard work, and no regrets when blood was shed. And these kids were eyeing Don, circling, wondering how long he was going to be around, wondering when they could take over his particular rung of the ladder. Not if, but when.

And if word got out that nearly one million dollars of the syndicate's money had gone missing on Don's watch, well, that would be all the chance some people would need to take him down.

He had maybe a week at the most before hard questions would be asked. The important thing was to find out where the money had gone. Then he could get it back—and if he couldn't, he would have to look into how to replace it. Had the money burned up, as many of the cars had? Had a cop or a fireman stumbled over the bag as he worked the accident scene, unzipped it, and decided then and there to never report its contents? Or maybe it had even been turned in, all official. Don guessed it was possible. Maybe the police weren't saying anything, because they wanted to see if the owner of what was clearly dope money would come forward and implicate himself.

Or, in what seemed the most likely scenario, had this woman, this unknown girlfriend of Jamie's, this young woman with a shaved head and a silver ring in her nose, taken the money? Was she the loose end that would unravel the entire knot of questions?

Don allowed himself a small smile. If she was, he could think of one good thing about the whole situation. She certainly wouldn't be too hard to find.

Sixteen

Thursday, OCTOBER 19, 7:32 A.M.

After just three days of living her life as Lydia Watkins, Free had fallen into something of a routine. Each morning she awoke to the muffled sounds of Lexi moving around the house. The click of the front door closing at 7:30 was the signal for Free to get out of bed. Until then she lay warm and snug under the quilt. It was so different than what she was used to. No lingering smell of marijuana, no sounds of an early morning sun chant, no sight of an unexpected stranger who had crashed in a sleeping bag in the corner, as when she had lived with her parents. No ferrets scampering over her head, as they had when she spent the night with Billy. Instead Free now had a life that was all hers.

Well, hers and, Free guessed, Jamie's and Lydia's and Lexi's. She owed part of her new life to each of them.

Free still wasn't sure what she and Lexi would end up being to each other. Roommates? Friends? Something in between? The other woman, with her slender legs and perfectly made-up face, fascinated, attracted and intimidated Free in equal measures. Lexi's feelings seemed to mirror Free's. She could be generous and helpful—as she had been when she made Free dinner the night she moved in—or seem distant and judgmental.

That had been the case the next night, when the two women

fixed meals for themselves side by side in Lexi's gourmet kitchen. Lexi had made Greek pasta with black olives, feta cheese, garlic and fresh tomatoes. Earlier in the day, Free had walked to the neighborhood grocery and bought whatever she desired.

"Is that what you're having for dinner?" Lexi's expression was dubious as she watched Free slide a can of Campbell's cream of mushroom soup, still retaining the shape of the can, into a dish containing cooked noodles and tuna. It was a naughty treat Diane sometimes served if Bob was at an out-of-town demonstration and thus unavailable to deliver his lecture on how tuna fishing led to dolphin by capture.

"Yes," Free said, topping the whole thing with a crunched up bag of potato chips. She had never really learned how to cook. Diane's cooking was haphazard at best, as she endeavored to pre-pare whatever was dictated by that month's diet—dried beans as tough as pebbles, "chocolate" shakes made with carob and tofu, certified organic potatoes full of bruises and boreholes. Mostly their meals were marked by whatever they didn't eat, having decided it was poisoning their bodies or the earth. At various times, Diane and Bob had refused to consume wheat, dairy, white sugar, choc-olate, gluten, meat, eggs, fish, commercially grown fruits or vege-tables, chicken, vinegar, rice of any color, processed junk foods or coffee. The day Free had left, they had decided to stop eating corn or products containing corn, fearing genetic engineering.

Lexi was teaching Free how to cook. Both women took plea-sure in their roles. Lexi lost something of her fast-paced edge while she was teaching, and Free liked the feeling that she was becoming someone different, someone who knew how to cook, how to tell when pasta was al dente and how to taste and adjust seasonings and flavors.

One evening as they worked companionably side by side, Lexi asked Free who she was planning on seeing for obstetrical care. Free's hesitation was answer enough. The next day, Lexi came home and announced that she had talked her very own OB-GYN into making room on her schedule at 11:30 A.M. Friday. Free had thanked Lexi, while mentally cautioning herself to remember to tell each woman the same stories about her past.

Outside of the kitchen, though, Free kept mostly to her room when Lexi was home. She leafed through magazines, clipping out recipes to try and articles about child rearing. In the mornings, she waited until Lexi left the house before she got out of bed. Not only did she want to respect Lexi's privacy, but she also enjoyed going wigless. The wig was hot and made her feel confined, a prisoner under her bangs.

This morning, Free went to the bathroom as soon as she heard Lexi's car pull out of the driveway. It seemed like she always had to go to the bathroom now. Then she went downstairs, poured a glass of orange juice and sliced a banana over a bowl of Wheaties. She sat down at Lexi's makeshift table. If she had been at home, breakfast would probably have been a cup of chicory and a bowl of gravel-like kasha topped with almond milk. The Wheaties represented a compromise between Free's desires and fears. If she hadn't been worried about what it might do to the baby, she probably would have started the day with Count Chocula, one of the forbidden foods Free had longed for growing up.

She picked up the paper, turning first to Ann Landers and Dear Abby. Everyone else's issues, which mostly revolved around annoying coworkers and ex-wives, seemed tame in comparison to her own. *Dear Abby, I have assumed a dead woman's name and made off with a drug dealer's cash. If you were me, what would you do next?*

If only Free could hide the money as well as she had hidden herself. All her dreams seemed to be nightmares now, either of the accident or of vainly trying to hide the money while it spilled out from a cupboard or a drawer or even her own pockets. Her fantasy of finding a good hiding place in Lexi's house had proved just that. The house was well maintained, without a single loose floorboard or brick. And there was simply too much money to tape it to the bottom of a drawer or even stuff it under the mattress. At the same time, she couldn't carry the gym bag everywhere. But where could she hide it? Free smiled at the thought of Ann and Abby putting their combined one hundred and fifty years or whatever it was of experience into helping her hide seven hundred thousand dollars in small used bills. Maybe they could even throw in some etiquette advice—dos and don'ts when assuming a new identity.

Free was still smiling when she turned to the back of the Metro section and saw the photo of Jamie. She slumped back in her chair, her heart beating a million miles a minute, the baby leaping underneath as if it felt her distress. It was a minute before she could bring herself to look at the photo again.

Free had recognized Jamie right away, and now wondered how she had. Dead, he looked completely different than he had alive. A shell, a husk, as empty as Lydia had been after the last collision snapped her neck. Finally, Free's heart slowed down and she was able to regard his picture calmly. The caption said the police were seeking his identity. She had more clues than the paper or the police did, but she still didn't know his last name or who his next of kin was. What could she tell them? That he had been driving a brown Honda with Oregon plates and a sock monkey dangling from the rearview mirror? That wasn't the kind of information they were seeking. They wanted to know who his family was. And it was more than likely that someone else leafing through the paper today was going to be even more shocked than she was, when they saw the picture of their dead son or lover or best friend.

Then Free read the article that accompanied the photograph. Panic overtook her. Why had that one overworked nurse, in the middle of the chaos, remembered Free? By blabbing to the paper, the woman was telling whoever cared to listen that there was still a loose end. She remembered Jamie writhing on the ground, determined to get the bag, his panic greater than his pain. *Don'll kill me if I don't give it to him.* Would this Don start pulling at the thread to see what unraveled?

Trying to control her thoughts, Free took a deep breath. She had made sure to snip every connection between herself and her past. She had a new name that no one who had ever known Free would know, she lived in a place where the phone and the utilities and the mortgage were in another woman's name, she had even let her family and her old boyfriend continue to think she was dead.

She could only think of one small catch, so small that it couldn't possibly matter. Yesterday, she had mailed the muumuu back to Denise. She hadn't put a note inside or her name on the outside. "You have to have a return address. It's the law," the clerk at the post office had insisted, and after a moment's hesitation Free had scribbled down Lexi's address. The address only, no name.

Seventeen

Thursday, OCTOBER 19, 8:10 A.M.

"Road trip?" Barry echoed Don's invitation. "Just like old times, huh?" They were standing in the alley behind the Burnside branch of Java Jiant, leaving only the sullen redheaded girl inside to deal with the morning rush all by herself. Barry held his palm out and said, "Give me five, my man!"

Don's hand met only air as it descended. Barry laughed while he jerked his hand back. The ritual was as old as their friendship.

Barry could always make Don smile, and there wasn't much Don could say that about anymore. Basically, Barry was still the same person he had been in fifth grade, when he had moved into the apartment across the hall. He still had shoulder-length blond curly hair, only now it was held back by a ponytail and the front had retreated into an M-shape high on his forehead. He still had a child's love of physical humor. (His favorite movie was *There's Something About Mary*.) And he was still the closest thing Don had to a best friend.

Despite the fact the two were the same age and lived in the same apartment complex, it had taken Don and Barry a long time to become friends back when they were kids. They both had a lot to hide, but slowly they figured out each other's situation. Don had no dad, just a mom who worked two jobs and drank in between shifts. Barry had a succession of "dads," and a mom who believed that bad love was better than no love, even if she was telling Barry that through a split lip and a mouth full of cracked teeth.

To the outside eye, they had been as different as two boys could be. Don dressed neatly in the clothes he washed and ironed (and originally shoplifted) himself. He got good grades thanks to his natural intelligence (supplemented, when necessary, by cheating). He always had plans to go someplace far away from Southeast Portland.

Barry wore whatever clothes he found on the floor, and barely managed to pass each grade as they grew older. He had no plans past the next hour. He had a sweet spirit, though, and an easygoing attitude. And he could work hard when he wanted to.

The most striking thing about Don was his lack of body hair. Around the age of thirteen he had noticed a bald spot on the back of his head about the size of a quarter. Over the next six months, it just kept growing, and his hair got thinner and thinner and finally vanished altogether. The hair on his arms slowly disappeared, as did the hairs on his legs. Even his pubes. Even the hairs in his nose. In the end, he was as slick as a seal. The school nurse diagnosed alopecia areata. In a medical dictionary in the library, Don found out that he wasn't contagious and nothing worse was going to happen to him. Still, he beat up the first kid who dared tease him about it. And he spent as little time in the locker room as he could.

Even before he turned into the hairless wonder, as he sometimes thought of himself, Don had already begun to feel a certain distance from other people. Part of him was always separate from whatever was going on, looking on and making comments. The alopecia only exaggerated this feeling. He watched as people stared at him, sometimes openly, sometimes trying to be subtle. He could and did wear a hat most of the time, but without eyebrows, his face looked perpetually displeased. He tried using an eyebrow pencil of his mother's, but the results just looked strikingly weird. When he was thirty, he heard about a tattoo artist who had a sideline, tattooing eyebrows on people with alopecia. He endured the pain without a murmur. Up close, he still caught people eyeing his brows, but from a few feet away it wasn't noticeable.

Before he lost his hair, Don had been friends with Barry and a few other kids. Afterward, only Barry saw past his face as smooth as an egg. That had been true for a long time, until he met Rachel. Ultimately, though, even she had left him.

Although Don was seven weeks younger, Barry had always looked up to him as if he were a big brother. And as they got older, Don did get big—bigger than the other boys his age, both in height and in the way he filled out with slabs of muscle. Twice he even made it clear to Barry's latest "dad" that neither Barry nor his mother were to turn up with any more bruises. The first guy was scared by this strange bald kid who was supposedly fourteen, but looked and acted like he was forty, and who had such a calm, methodical way of talking that every word was freighted with quiet menace.

The second guy wasn't as smart. Not one week after Don had delivered his message, Barry showed up at school sporting a new black eye. That had been the last anyone saw of that particular "dad." Barry never even asked Don what had happened to the guy. He didn't want to know. He was just happy that he was finally being left alone.

Don had planned on going to college and then becoming a lawyer, making lots of money in a genteel way. But his plans took a left turn when he was sixteen and was caught cheating by a teacher on a math test. The teacher offered to forget about everything—just as long as Don consented to a blowjob. A hot anger welled up in Don, breaking through the calculated approach he took to most things. Plastic surgery was able to restore most of the teacher's face, but in the meantime Don was arrested, expelled and sentenced to sixteen months at MacClaren, Oregon's detention facility for juvenile offenders. Knowing it was hopeless, Don let the teacher's version of events stand, barely speaking during sentencing except to say "Yes, sir" and "No, sir."

After his release, Don started rebuilding his life. He had gotten his GED at MacClaren, but he knew that his old dreams were just that. No college would want him now. But he still intended to get rich, to get away from his mother's drunken rantings and the frequent shootings and knifings in their part of town. So he looked around for other ways to make money. The best way, he figured, was to offer a service to people who were more than happy to pay for it.

And in Don's neighborhood, that meant drugs. First he worked on the corner, but then he moved up, taking the job Jamie would have twenty years later. Once a month, Don drove the circuit, starting with a couple of kilos of cocaine and a few other drugs and ending up with stacks of money. It paid well, because anyone who took the fall with that amount of coke was going to end up doing hard time. Don didn't let anyone else's drugs go up his nose or anyone else's money stick in his pocket. When he wasn't running drugs, Don offered his services running errands, mostly following other people's girlfriends to make sure they were staying faithful and coworkers to make sure they weren't skimming. And he took the money he made and looked for an investment, something that provided a service that others needed. Something legit.

In the early 1980s, Don opened a copy center near the Portland State campus. He started small, with two copiers in a room not much bigger than a walk-in closet, but he kept it open twenty-four hours a day. Soon he had a lot of money coming in, but it seemed to go right back out again. The machines were always breaking down, or he would spend money to train someone who quit two weeks later. On paper it looked like Don should be making quite a bit of money, but it never quite worked out that way.

On paper. The thought gave Don an idea, and he took that idea to his bosses. He knew that one of the big problems with selling drugs was it was a cash-intensive business, generating vast amounts of payments in the form of bills in small denominations. But you couldn't just go and deposit the money in the bank, or buy a new car with cash, not without triggering an investigation.

The government was very interested in asking questions about people who had a lot of unexplained cash.

Don's copy business offered a way to change that money into something that looked, at least from the outside, legit. Fake invoices. Loan repayments on money he had never borrowed. And on paper, at least, Don always had a lot of customers who paid in cash.

Over time, Don added more businesses that were also good places to hide cash. He caught the West Coast wave for coffee early, opening a Java Jiant next to the university. Outside the store, he put a campy statue that looked something like the Jolly Green Giant dipped in brown paint. He wholesaled coffee beans, too, to two dozen restaurants in town. The coffee business offered a carefully calculated side benefit. Everyone knew that coffee beans were grown south of the border. So if Don had occasional dealings with dark-skinned businessmen with soft Spanish accents, well, that was to be expected.

Three years ago, Don had opened up a couple of high-end steak restaurants, one downtown for the businessmen, one in Beaverton for the folks who didn't want to venture out of the 'burbs for their celebrations. A steak sitting on a plate, naked except for a piece of parsley, cost thirty-nine dollars. And that was for one of the less expensive cuts. You wanted the creamed spinach, you wanted a baked potato, you wanted a glass of red, you wanted the flan for desert—pretty soon you were talking $100 a person. Easy. And with the way the economy had been going for the past ten years, people were willing to pay that. Even now, with the stock market down, there were still plenty of people with cash and the desire to spend it.

And as his various businesses grew and prospered (both on paper and in reality, although there was a difference) Don built a tangle of legal and illegal enterprises that intersected in ways only he knew. To create even more confusion, he added a complex web of transfers, both domestic and international, that made tracing the original source of funds virtually impossible. The money got changed around eight ways to Sunday, and came out smelling as sweet and innocent as a chocolate-chip cookie.

The whole time, Barry was like a little fish swimming in Don's wake. Back when Don was working his way up, he used to bring Barry along on the circuit where drugs were exchanged for money and money for drugs. After being jumped one too many times, Don had wanted someone who could watch his back. It had been strictly against the rules—just like Jamie's bringing this girl with a shaved head along for the ride had been strictly against the rules.

Then Barry started helping Don out with little favors. At first, he just got Don whatever was needed. License plates to replace some on a stolen car. Hookers who could serve as human party favors, but who weren't all used up and clapped out. Given a liter bottle of diet Coke, Barry could watch someone's front door, happily, for hours. Don joked that Barry had a bladder the size of a five-gallon bucket. He was protective of his old friend, though. He tried not to let Barry know so much that he would be a danger to himself or others. And although the syndicate knew about Barry's errand running by now, Don kept him away from the dirtier work. Barry had never had to wash blood from his hands, because Don knew that would destroy his old friend.

About five years back, Don had been between managers at the original Java Jiant. In desperation, he turned to Barry. To the surprise of both men, Barry actually turned out to be pretty good at it. He got along well with the teenagers who worked the counters, and he could tell the difference between Arabica and Robusta beans with just a single whiff.

"How many days will we be gone?" Barry asked now. He jittered from foot to foot, one of the occupational hazards of drinking espresso concoctions all day. The rain had come in the night before, and now it drizzled steadily. The two men ignored it like the native Portlanders they were.

"I don't think any more than two. Can you get us a car?" Don was sure there were no listening devices in Barry's office, but he was always careful. That was why they were outside. You didn't survive and prosper for twenty years without being careful. He would never even ask how Barry had gotten the car, whether it was stolen, purchased or borrowed, or some combination of all three.

"No problemo. What kind?"

"Something boring, I'm afraid. Four-door dark-colored sedan, say about ten years old? I want something no one will look at twice." The first step, Don had decided, was to check out Jamie's car, or what was left of it. If it was a burnt-out heap, then maybe the money had turned to ashes inside of it. If it wasn't, then the next step would be to find this girl with the buzz cut and the nose ring.

"You just took all the fun out of it." Barry tried to pout but couldn't hide his grin. When was the last time they had done anything together? Don couldn't remember.

Eighteen

Thursday, OCTOBER 19, 11:20 P.M.

Roy had been high on meth for fifty-two hours and counting. He hadn't eaten much since Lydia left, but with meth, you didn't need to eat. He had gone to work yesterday, and had actually done a pretty good job. There was a reason they called it go-fast. His hands had been a blur as he worked the line, pulling off defective diapers as they rolled past. Dri-N-Fresh Diapers was the only place within a fifty-mile radius where a person could make more than eight dollars an hour. They took just about anybody with a pulse and the fortitude to stay off drugs long enough to have a clean urine sample for the new-hire drug screen. Man, it had been hard to stay clean for a week. He had drunk so much water he had been pissing every fifteen minutes.

He liked crank because it gave him focus. Maybe too much focus. Things looked brighter and he had a lot of physical energy and jumpiness. Roy saw things so clear. When he wasn't pulling defective diapers from the line, he picked at his skin, working on little scabs and blemishes until they bled again and scabbed over, only bigger. He barely noticed that everyone was staying clear of him—the blacks, the Mexicans, the few Indians, even the other whites. At work, people stayed in their own groups. The whites got the clean work—they were mostly mechanics or supervisors, or, like Roy, had easy jobs, where it wasn't so clear whether you were working hard or not. The Indians got the in-between jobs. The niggers and the tacos and the inmates in their green uniforms on work release got the shit jobs. The jobs that demanded your hands move so fast that you got carpal tunnel, or where you had to reach into machines that had been known to chew off a finger or even an arm.

Yesterday, Roy had bounced up and down on his feet the whole nine hours. Inside the Dri-N-Fresh factory, which was basically a giant metal shed, there was no clock, no window, nothing to show the world outside. Sometimes Roy even jumped up and down for no reason. Just because he had to. And at the end of the day, his feet didn't even hurt. He could have worked another shift, easy, but they weren't asking anyone to do overtime that night. Instead he went home and didn't go to bed. He started one project and then another—cleaning his guns, picking up the house a little, heating up a can of chili he then forgot to eat.

Today his thoughts were all over the place. The work burned his muscles and dulled his mind. When the line had to be shut down for a few minutes, Roy went into the restroom. In the handicapped stall he did a huge line, which burned like hell. Five minutes later it hit. He was back on the line and all of a sudden he had a grin on his face. But the good feeling quickly faded. The endless series of white puffs rolling past just irritated him. He was supposed to look for places where the tape was defective, where the leg gathers had failed, but he found himself looking at everything too closely, seeing the smallest of flaws, yanking off diaper after diaper.

At break time, the spics stood around talking in groups. Roy never knew what they were saying. They took Americans' jobs and did them for less. Some of them had houses in Mexico, while he was living in a prefab on a brick foundation way out in the woods. Here he was, born in this country, and he had to listen to Spanish. The world was going to hell. "This is America and I want to start hearing some English, now!" he screamed. One of the women told him where to stick his head and listen for the echo. "Then you'll hear some English." He wanted to pick up a box cutter and slice her open, but managed to walk away on stiff legs.

When Duane, the supervisor, came by in the afternoon, and went through the pile of rejects, he complained that most of them were actually okay. Then he started in on Roy. Duane didn't like his work ethic. He went too slow. He cut out to the bathroom too much. Roy could hardly make out Duane's voice over the hammer of compressors, the screech of pulleys, the grind of the belts. It got so loud that sometimes the only way to get somebody's attention was to lob a diaper at them.

"Got a bladder infection?" Duane asked thirty minutes later, standing in Roy's spot when he returned to the belt after snorting another line. "That's it. You can't go to the toilet unless it's break time."

Roy had a hard time focusing on what Duane was saying. His vision was totally locked up and he felt like he was going to explode. He knew he was going to start cussing out Duane if he said another word. When Duane reached down and tossed a diaper from Roy's reject bin back onoto the line, that was it.

Roy started cussing at Duane, hitting him around the head, calling him a motherfucker. Time slowed down and had gaps in it. It was like he was watching a series of snapshots, not a movie. Then Roy had Duane down on the ground, had Duane's ears in his hands, and was pounding his head on the cement floor.

Two minutes later, two security guards hustled Roy out to his car, getting in a few belts along the way. Even though Roy was a white guy, that hadn't stopped Dri-N-Fresh from firing his ass. That's why there were security guards, to stop the only kind of mixing there was in the plant—fighting.

Once in his car, Roy started banging his head against the steering wheel. It felt right, somehow, so he didn't stop for a while. It was all Lydia's fucking fault that he had gotten fired. If he hadn't been so worried and frustrated, wondering how to find her, this wouldn't have happened.

Later on, when he was at home, Roy felt a little better. His job hadn't been fit for a donkey. It was okay, really, that he had quit. Down at the bar this afternoon, he had heard about a guy who might be hiring for a roofing crew. And with Lydia gone for now, maybe he could start making meth again, start making more money without her whining about how the house smelled, about how he was going to set the place on fire, about how she didn't like him when he was using. Lydia didn't understand that he had just wanted to get ahead a little bit.

And then Roy had another idea. An idea so good it made him smile. He knew this guy, Warren, this guy whose wife worked for the DMV. And he'd heard that for a little consideration, Shari could sometimes get numbers. Girls' phone numbers. Addresses for them if all you had was their license plate number and you thought they looked pretty. For the right amount of money, she could even tap into the state's database and get you a Social Security number for someone who had died and didn't need it anymore.

He had met Warren up at the old canyon. People liked to go shooting up there. Guys would shoot rock formations or into the walls. Animals, if they saw them. Didn't matter what season it was or who had a fucking permit. This place had been there for thousands of years, long before there were permits. You could get drunk, build a bonfire, dress out a deer, buy whatever you wanted. Drugs, guns, home-brewed whiskey that would take off the back of your head, use of somebody's girlfriend or maybe even daughter. And, Roy hoped, the information he needed. After all, even if Lydia was at a shelter, eventually she would have to interact with the system in some way.

That night, Roy called Warren. "Want to go shooting up at the canyon sometime?"

Nineteen

After breakfast, Free went back upstairs and took a shower. Under the warm spray, she rotated her shoulders, letting the water massage the back of her neck. Afterward, she picked out one of her new outfits to wear. Free had grown up wearing clothes that came from thrift stores and other people's kids' castoffs. The whole idea of having to cut off tags was novel to her, and she had walked around all day yesterday with a tag dangling from her neck. In the evening, Lexi snipped it off.

Today Free chose the burgundy dress with the sweetheart neckline. After she pulled it down over head, her breasts threatened to spill out the top. With some jiggling, Free was able to stuff them back down into another of her Whitchers purchases, a bra with a frightening back fastener three hooks deep. If Billy could see her now, he certainly wouldn't find her sexy. Certainly not in this bra. And not in these huge-o maternity underwear that Free had discovered she could, if desired, successfully pull up and over her oversize breasts.

By nine-thirty she was out the door. Although it was supposed to be in the low seventies later, the air was crisp as she walked the mile into downtown. Her first stop was the library. She had discovered it her first day in Portland while looking for a place to kill time until Lexi got off work and could show her the house. Courtesy of the all the libraries in the towns she had lived in, Free had grown up on a steady diet of books about kids with normal, boring problems, like lost dogs or who to take to the prom. They never dealt with issues like your mom smoking pot with the boy you liked.

This morning she spent an hour reading from *The Big Book of Careers*, mentally trying professions on for size. On a piece of scratch paper she listed possible professions. She could be a lawyer. Run her own catering business. (Lexi's cooking lessons had inspired this particular fantasy). A biochemist. An arbitrator. Even a writer. There was a whole world out there she had never even guessed at.

The book managed to make every occupation sound fascinating, even those jobs Free knew would be terrible. Taxi drivers got to meet new people while learning more about their own city. Waitresses got the chance to sample different types of cuisine for free. There was even a section on pet grooming, but it focused on the high-end jobs—the groomers who worked the show circuit.

Working at Petorium certainly hadn't been anything you could call a career. The book made no mention of the kinds of things Free had considered drawbacks while working at Petorium—teeth and claws, tapeworm and ringworm and flea bites. And groomers couldn't wear gloves, because they needed to feel each animal to check for lumps. Cats, with their smaller, sharper teeth and claws, were more dangerous than dogs. Plus they could be temperamental. One groomer could handle almost any dog, but it always took two to handle a cat.

After a couple of hours, Free put the book back on the shelf. She wished she had a library card so she could check it out, but for that she would need a driver's license that showed her current address. Well, Lydia's name and Free's current address. Free was still working up the courage to go to the DMV. Would the clerk notice that the woman standing in front of her wasn't Lydia Watkins at all? Would she ask for some secret password—Lydia's mother's maiden name, for example—that Free would not be able to produce? Sooner or later, though, Free knew she was going to have to get at least one piece of ID that reflected her new reality.

After lunch, Free found a store called Baby Togs, which sold all the hundreds of things she guessed you needed as soon as you brought the baby home from the hospital. She got a cart and began to fill it. Syrup of ipecac in case the kid ate something it shouldn't. Cabinet latches to make sure she never needed the syrup of ipecac in the first place. Plastic covers to fit over electric outlets, bottles of baby shampoo and baby lotion, a tube of diaper rash cream. Even though she had weeks until the baby was due, Free felt the urge to prepare.

She was moving to the section that held the advice books when she saw a pile of something called a Boppy. A Boppy was a C-shaped pillow covered in brightly printed fabric. According to the packaging, it was supposed to go around your waist when you were nursing. And as the months went by, it could prop up a baby just learning to sit. But Free didn't want it for any of these reasons. Instead she pinched and prodded the Boppy through its plastic covering. The pillow was very firm. It gave her an idea, one that made her forget about putting anything more in her cart. She picked out a turquoise and yellow one and put it in her basket, then wheeled it straight to the counter. When the total came to nearly one hundred and fifty dollars, she didn't even blink. On her way home, she stopped at Fred Meyer and bought a needle, a spool of turquoise thread, and a seam ripper.

Before Lexi came home from work, Free removed most of the pillow's stuffing and replaced it with twenty-dollar bills. She used just enough of the old stuffing to fill out the curved shape, then stitched it closed with nearly invisible stitches. When she was finished, she had something that looked exactly like a brand-new Boppy—only this one was filled with $92,700.

As she fixed dinner with Lexi that night, Free felt more relaxed than she had since she first found the money. Her success with the Boppy had inspired her. As she followed Lexi's instructions and rolled out fresh pasta dough so thin you could see the counter through it, she tried to calculate just how much money could be used to replace the insides of a largish stuffed animal. Perhaps as much as fifty thousand dollars. Still, a herd of two dozen stuffed animals might inspire comment. Then she had another brainstorm. All the cribs in Baby Togs had had fat bumper pads hanging from the sides. What if she bought a crib, mattress and bumper pads and had them delivered to Lexi's house? The bumper pads might hide as much as another couple of hundred thousand dollars. Maybe even more.

"It's good to hear you humming," Lexi said. "I think it's the first time I've heard you sound happy. God knows one of us in this house deserves to be."

Free came back to reality. "I didn't know I was."

Lexi smiled at her. "It was that old Beatles song. The one where the guy sings about giving him money, because that's what he wants."

twenty

Even though he was alone in the house, Don closed the door before picking up his private line, the one he used only for business.

"Our 'paperwork' hasn't shown up yet. It was due this morning." A man's voice. Quiet. Educated. A stranger's voice, but one that Don had been expecting for three days. Paperwork was code for the deposits in the offshore accounts, the last step in Don's money fan dance.

He supposed he could throw himself on the syndicate's mercy, but he knew there would be no mercy if he said the money was gone and he didn't know where.

Instead, Don said, "Have you seen wholesale coffee prices lately? The commodities market has gone crazy since the big storm in Honduras. It's been a lot harder to move things around. Half the country's infrastructure was wiped out. I'm getting everything together, it's just taking me longer than usual." Even to his own ears, he sounded excessively wordy.

"When can we expect it?" It was clear from the man's voice that he wasn't listening to Don's excuses. Don was just a link in a chain. And when it came right down to it, a link that could easily be replaced. If the money was gone, these people didn't care

119

how it happened. They just wanted the money back. Like all good financial executives, these people had their eyes focused solely on the bottom line.

"I should be able to get everything together in about six weeks."

"Six weeks is too long. We'll give you ten days."

"Ten days?" How could he possibly figure out where the money had gone, get it back, and then do all the paperwork required to turn three-quarters of a million in worn bills into two dozen untraceable overseas deposits? Even if he had the money in his hands right now, it would take him nearly a week to process it. "That's not enough time."

"I'm afraid that's all the time we're prepared to offer you."

"And if I can't?" Don had never said anything like this before, and couldn't quite believe he was saying it now.

"Then there will be consequences." With a soft click, the connection was severed.

"There's just no way, Don," Marianne said. Even without being able to see her face, he could hear her exasperation. He had called her to try to work out a backup plan in case this trip to Clark City didn't yield results. So far, though, he was getting nowhere. "I'm sorry, but there's just no way we can squeeze that kind of cash out of your holdings in such a short timeframe. If you gave me six months, a year, then maybe. But it's a bull market. I don't have to tell you that."

"What about selling this place?" Don asked. He had been going to Marianne for financial advice for ten years. In this line of work, you didn't have a retirement plan unless you created one yourself. And Marianne was careful never to ask exactly where his money came from. "This house is easily worth a million. Maybe a million and a half."

"And those kinds of deals aren't done overnight."

Don was running out of options. "How about a line of credit?"

"For what business purpose?" Marianne's voice was skeptical, and she didn't wait for him to think up an answer. "The economy overall is going south. People are getting cold feet about laying a lot of money on the line. No one's going to lend you that much money unless you have a solid business plan. And even then it would take months before you had the money in your hands. But you're telling me you want it in ten days. It's impossible."

The doorbell rang. Don looked at his watch and realized it was Barry. "Excuse me, but I have to go. I'll call you soon though, okay?"

"Sure. But I'm afraid I still won't have any better answers for you," Marianne said before hanging up.

Twenty-one

Friday, OCTOBER 20, 12:07 P.M.

The Oregon Obstetrics Group, a practice shared by five physicians, had an office on the seventh floor of a downtown office building. The space was decorated in aqua and salmon and had plenty of fresh copies of *Talk* and *Mirabella*. The whole setup was much more pleasant than the Jackson County Clinic, where you were given a number that was announced over an intercom whenever they were ready for you.

Free got a raised eyebrow when she told the receptionist she had no insurance and planned on paying in cash. The woman acted as if she had never seen money before, carefully examining the hundred dollar bill that Free handed her before putting it in a drawer full of checks.

Even though this place was more upscale, it did share one feature with a county clinic—a long wait. Free's appointment had been for 11:30, but now it was past noon. Since she had passed a good portion of her childhood in health food co-op checkout lines, Free was used to waiting. She leafed through a copy of *Vogue* so heavy that it threatened to slide right off her lap. It was hard to believe that anyone ever dressed like the women pictured in it. Maybe it was as much a fantasy for women as *Playboy* layouts were for men.

123

Finally the nurse ushered her back to the examination room. She handed Free a gown and told her to put it on. Even the gown was infinitely better than the cheap thin polyester ones the county used—this was luxurious pale blue brushed cotton.

After knocking on the door, the OB-GYN walked in with her right hand extended. She was a tall, slender woman in her mid-forties. "I'm Dr. Peggy Davenport. Call me Peggy, unless you would feel more comfortable calling me Dr. Davenport." Her mane of ginger-colored hair, threaded with strands of silver, was pulled back into a thick braid that brushed her hips.

"Peggy is fine," Free said, taking in the ears with multiple piercings, the makeup-free fair skin, and the brown Birkenstocks Peggy wore with her green scrubs. Free was willing to bet that Peggy had once been a lay midwife, someone who had "sold out" as Bob and Diane would say, gone back to school and mainstream. She started to smile at Peggy, really smile, but stopped when the other woman's friendly but impersonal expression didn't change. Free realized that she did not feel the same sense of kinship. Peggy might have been looking at Free, but she was seeing Lydia. Lately, Free herself hadn't been too sure who she was.

"So Lexi said on the phone that you just moved here from Pendleton and you're house sharing with her?" When Free nodded, she said, "Before you leave, ask the receptionist for the form to get your prenatal records transferred."

Free didn't have to fake a blush. "I'm afraid there really aren't any. I only found out a little while ago that I was pregnant."

A frown flickered across the doctor's lips. "Do you know the date of conception?"

"No. I was told years ago that I could never"—Free was going to say *have a baby*, but then realized it wasn't the way Lydia would talk—"never conceive. I had pelvic inflammatory disease when I was a teenager. Maybe Lexi didn't tell you, but my husband is, ah, deceased."

"Oh, I'm so sorry." Peggy's voice became as gentle as a caress. "From an illness?"

"He died in an accident a few months ago. I was in shock for such a long time that it took me a while to realize I was pregnant."

"Well, scoot back and put your feet up in the stirrups and let's have a look. Then I'll send you on down to ultrasound. The tech can take some key measurements that should allow us to give you a fairly accurate due date. Of course, even though the average pregnancy is forty weeks long, it's perfectly normal to give birth anywhere from thirty-seven to forty-two weeks."

It took Peggy less than five minutes to perform pelvic and breast exams, her hands made efficient by long practice. "So far, everything looks like it should. I'm going to listen for fetal heart tones now." She took out a black wand attached to a long black cord. "This magnifies the sounds so that you can hear them, too."

She slipped the buds of the stethoscope in her ears. The cool instrument roamed over Free's belly. Silence. Peggy's eyes were focused on the middle distance, her expression absorbed and serious. The wand stopped near Free's hipbone. "Here we go."

Clomp, clomp, clomp, clomp. The sounds so rapid they ran together. A burst of static, then more clomping, each sound coming on the heels of the next.

Peggy listened intently, looking at her watch, and then looked up. "One-hundred sixty-eight beats per minute."

Free felt a spurt of anxiety. "Isn't that too high?"

"Not for a baby at this stage it isn't. It's right in the mid-range."

"What about those staticky sounds? What causes that?"

"Hmm—oh, fetal movement." Peggy must have noticed the expression of Free's face, because she added, "What's the matter?"

Billy had once rented the movie *Alien*. It had been three nights before Free had been able to sleep without nightmares. Now Free could identify with the character who had arched back over the dinner table, an expression of terror on his face, as the alien burst from his abdomen. "I just feel—weird. I mean, I've got some little thing inside me that is moving around on its own and has its own

heartbeat." She found this knowledge more frightening than reassuring.

Peggy smiled and patted Free's hand. "Maybe there's a reason
human pregnancies last nine months. It gives us time to get used
to the idea." Her smile receded as she looked down at Free's arm.
Free followed her gaze, to the greenish, fading bruise on her forearm. Peggy ran a finger gently across it, and then in quick succession she lightly touched another bruise on Free's thigh, and a third
on her shin.

"I've noticed that you have a number of bruises. And you have
a cut in your hairline, as well." Her voice was carefully neutral.
"Can you tell me how you got those? Is someone in your life hurting you?"

"No." Free started in surprise. It was getting harder to lie to
this woman who presented herself to the world without artifice.
She decided to stick as close to the truth as she could, and hope
that Peggy wouldn't compare notes with Lexi. "I was moving to
Portland when my car was totaled in that big pileup near Pendleton."

"That big one caused by the dust storm?"

Free nodded. "Even though I was wearing a seatbelt, I really
got slammed around."

Peggy gave Free's hand a comforting pat, although there was
still a faint line between her brows. Free could tell the other
woman was still worried that something wasn't adding up, that
someone might really be beating her. "I'm really sorry that the past
few months have been so traumatic for you. Is having this baby
something you want to do? There may still be a few options open
to you."

The phrasing was nonjudgmental, but Free's hands went immediately to her belly, cradling it. "I don't want to have an abor-
tion."

"There's also adoption. And most adoptions are open these
days, meaning you could be part of this child's life—"

"No." There were times when Free felt ambivalent about this

pregnancy, so she was surprised at how fiercely protective she suddenly felt toward her unborn baby. "I can raise this child."

"All right then. Let me send you downstairs for an ultrasound."

A few minutes later, Free was again lying on a table and again having someone running something over her belly, only this time it was Lewis, a compact black man in his mid-fifties. With his eyes on the screen behind him, Lewis ran a wand over the mound of her abdomen, occasionally adjusting one of the dials on the console in front of him. Free watched, too, but the ghostly images on the monitor meant nothing to her.

"Oh, you don't often see that," Lewis said.

"What?" Free lifted her head, but still couldn't identify a thing.

"Look, it's sucking its thumb." Lewis pointed at the black-and-white monitor.

"I can't see anything," Free said. There were vague white shapes against the blackness, but it was like those people who saw Jesus in a tortilla—everything seemed open to interpretation.

"Look here, here's the head." A white round blob. "The spine." A railroad track. "And there, see, it just kicked." A squiggle.

And finally Free did see, began to make sense of the pale images on the screen. Lewis talked to himself while he inventoried all the vital organs, naming off the kidneys, liver, heart and brain. The dim shapes slowly began to make sense to her. She watched the baby swim and flail, and was amazed at how little of this movement she, the container, felt.

"Does it look like it's all right?" Free asked, gripped by the sudden worry that some vital part might be missing or deformed.

He tipped her a wink. "That's really for your doctor to tell you, okay? Not Lewis." His unhesitating grin made his reassurance plain. "The one thing I can tell you, if you want, is what sex the baby is."

"What do most people decide to do?"

"It's about fifty-fifty. Some women think if they don't know, it gives them a little extra reason to push right at the time it's the hardest. Other folks feel like it gives them a jump start on bonding with the baby." He smiled. "The one advantage to knowing is you don't end up with a bunch of yellow and green baby clothes."

Free thought of the ugly gender-neutral clothes she had seen at Baby Togs and had to agree. Still, she guessed she was still her parents' daughter, because knowing the baby's sex in advance seemed unnatural. "I think I'll let it be a surprise."

It wasn't obvious that Peggy's office belonged to an ex-hippie— there were no bead curtains or lava lamps—but there was one clue that let Free know her guess had been right. It was a wedding photo, although the couple wasn't dressed in traditional wedding garb and it had been taken in a park. The woman, a much younger version of Peggy, wore what looked like a vintage white cotton slip. Her hair was loose around her hips, and she wore a crown of bright yellow dandelions. On the green grass, her feet were bare. Beside her was a thin man, his face nearly hidden behind a wild beard and hair past his shoulders. He wore plaid bellbottoms, and in his buttonhole was another dandelion instead of a boutonniere.

Peggy caught Free looking at the photo. "Young love, circa 1973. Every time he sees it, my husband always threatens to steal that photo so no one will see him in those bellbottoms."

Free counted back. "Twenty-seven years. That's a long time." She and Billy hadn't even lasted for a year.

"Yes." Peggy's gaze went to the photo, and then back to Free. "I'm so sorry about what happened to your husband." She hesitated, then said in a rush of words, "I know this sounds like a cliche, Lydia, but you're young. You may find there's someone else in your future."

"I don't want anybody," Free said, meaning it. She'd had boyfriends of one kind and another since sixth grade, when she discovered that normal boys would invite her to their normal houses in exchange for her willingness to kiss them after school with her mouth open. She had been willing to trade her tongue for a chance to watch TV, eat Ritz crackers and walk around houses with curtains in the windows and beauty products lined up on the bathroom counter. She was sick of guys, with their games and their lies and their needs. And now Free had the two things a man might have been able to give her: a baby and financial security. She didn't need a man. She didn't need anyone.

Peggy turned all business, looking down at her notes. "I'm estimating your due date as February nineteenth." She went on to warn Free about watching for the warning signs of premature labor—the obvious things like cramps or bleeding, and less obvious ones like a persistent ache, low in the back. "If you are experiencing any of these symptoms, go to Good Samaritan immediately and have me paged. The fetus won't be viable until twenty-four or twenty-five weeks, and you are currently right on the edge— about twenty three weeks. There are a lot of things now we can do to delay a baby from coming too soon—if we start in time."

Free left Peggy's office armed with a sheaf of pamphlets, a list of recommended books, and an appointment to attend a half-day birthing class in a week. The receptionist had told Free she could bring whoever she wanted for her birthing partner. It sounded as if she imagined Free had an unlimited number of friends, relatives and lovers to choose from. Free was too embarrassed to tell the woman she would be attending by herself. When the elevator doors opened, a man and his very pregnant wife were waiting, holding hands. At the sight of their clasped hands and happy faces, Free's determination that she didn't need a man suddenly faltered. She wished someone else had been with her today to watch and listen and marvel as the baby moved.

twenty-two

FRIDAY, OCTOBER 20, 1:10 P.M.

Eastern Oregon was dry and nearly flat, with scattered clumps of low vegetation instead of forests of fir, pine and spruce. When Don had taken his first courier job, at the age of twenty-two, it had also been the first time he had been east of the Cascade Mountains. In the beginning, all that empty space, all that solitude, had bugged him. Miles of nothing, broken up only occasionally by clusters of manufactured homes with a gas station or two, maybe a general store and a restaurant that nearly always advertised "homemade pies." Sometimes you couldn't even pick up a radio station. Taking Barry along with him had offered Don not only a measure of safety, but also someone to talk to.

Don looked over at Barry now. He had cranked up the cheap stereo on the tan Ford Tempo (a car they had immediately christened "The Lumper") and was now tapping both hands on top of the steering wheel, singing along with Foreigner's "Double Vision." Maybe that was why Don still spent time with Barry, because when he was with him, Don could pretend he was still fifteen. He could go back to some less complicated time when life had seemed full of possibilities instead of a careful tightrope walk that never ended.

Nine days. Nine days to produce the money. Don had already done as much as he could without actually having the money in his possession. The paper trail was all ready—but it was useless without the cash to back it up.

While Barry drove, Don spent an hour with a calculator, a Mont Blanc pen and a notepad, considering if there was some way he could scare up enough to replace the missing money with his own. Maybe if he sold the house for half its worth? Could he find someone who would hand over the money in nine days? On paper, his businesses were probably each worth as much as what was missing—but it might take him months to find an interested buyer. And anyone who went over his books with a fine-toothed comb might begin to realize that there was no way Don was making the amount of money his balance sheets showed.

Sure, Don had lots of other stuff—cars, stereos, an in-home theater system, leather furniture, designer clothes, custom golf clubs—but nothing that could be easily turned into cash money. Certainly not what it was worth. And he couldn't exactly hold a garage sale.

In the end, it was clear there was no way he could get his hands on that much money, that fast. Which left just one alternative, the original one. Find out who had taken his money—and take it back from them.

But who did have his money? He had already ruled out Jamie's parents. They had given birth to their son, but knew nothing about him. He had called them yesterday in Seattle, after *The Oregonian* said they had identified the body as that of their missing son, Jamie. Jamie's mother was a waitress in a coffee shop, his father a janitor who worked nights. They had no other children.

Giving a made-up name, Don told them that he was seeking his own daughter, and that she matched the description of the girl thought to have been with Jamie during the accident. They were shattered, bewildered—and clueless. Why had Jamie been caught up in a car accident five hours away from Portland? What had he been doing out in the middle of nowhere? And why had there been a girl in his car? As far as they knew, Jamie wasn't dating anyone. And they knew nothing about a bag. They had reclaimed only his body and the clothes that had been cut off it.

Don had also put a tap on Carly's phone, but the expense hadn't been worth it. If she knew anything about Jamie's death or where the missing money had gone to, Carly was smart enough not to talk about it. For two days, Don had had Barry get someone to fill in for him at the Java Jiant, and then follow Carly around. The only places she had gone to were the grocery store and her job. At My Fair Ladys (the misspelling grated on Don), guys paid one hundred dollars to watch Carly "model" lingerie while they sat in chairs draped with towels (changed after every customer) and were encouraged to get "comfortable" while she took off her own clothes. The second day, Barry even went in to see exactly what Carly did, terming it "research." He reported that he thought Carly's tits were real, but that she was a bit full through the ass. Then he had the balls to ask Don to be reimbursed. It was such a Barry thing to do that Don had just laughed and peeled off two fifties from his wallet.

So if Jamie's friends and family didn't know anything about the missing money, that meant that Don had to start out at the scene of the accident and figure out if and where the money had gone after that. More and more, this girl with the nose ring looked like his best chance, his only chance. He had decided to start at the beginning, which he figured was Jamie's car. Yesterday, Don had called the Clark City police station and asked where the cars from the wreck were being stored. He had been prepared with a story about how he was a relative who just wanted to see where his cousin had died, but the clerk hadn't questioned him. She just said all the vehicles were at the local tow yard. He had thanked her for the information and then hung up the pay phone that was located nowhere near his home or any of his businesses. He didn't know whether they routinely logged incoming phone calls, but Don liked to be careful.

———

Now Don gave Barry the last of the directions he had printed off the Internet. Five minutes later, they parked to one side of a sprawling compound. Behind a chain-link fence topped with razor wire, hundreds of cars were slowly rusting. Don had Barry stay in the car. It was easier to keep a story straight if just one of them was telling it. He went over and knocked on the door of the shack that stood next to the gate.

The man who opened the door was dressed in black polyester pants and a white polyester short-sleeved shirt with the word *Dave* embroidered over his left breast pocket. His square face sported white bushy eyebrows that looked like two strips of fake fur. Even though the temperature couldn't have been above thirty, he wasn't wearing a coat. "What can I do ya for?"

"I hear you folks are storing the cars that were involved in that big pileup on Eighty-four."

"Yep, we got 'em all. You with an insurance company?"

Don had considered and rejected this approach, ultimately deciding he didn't know enough about the business to lie convincingly. "I'm a family member. We just want to see where—where it happened." He looked away, as if overcome with emotion. He had dressed down for this occasion, wearing a black Trail Blazers sweatshirt and Levi's. He wore a ball cap on his head, both to cover his bald head and to shade his face.

Dave didn't seem interested in his reasons. "Kinda car is it?"

"1989 Honda Accord. Brown."

"Plate number?"

"Oregon plate SVT 983."

After consulting a pile of papers blotched with greasy fingerprints, Dave reached down for the ring of keys that was hooked to his belt loop on a retractable lead. He picked one out and used it to open the padlock.

The gate swung open. Stepping over puddles of rusty-colored water skimmed with ice, Don followed as Dave picked his way among the dozens of disabled vehicles. Some looked like they might be driveable, but the vast majority were crumpled, ruptured or crushed too badly to ever drive again. Others were slowly being parted out, with missing tires or hoods that gaped to reveal absent engines.

Dave finally came to a stop in front of a large section of freshly churned mud that had been marked off with sagging lines of yellow caution tape. The space held about four dozen cars, SUVs and light pickups, and a dozen truck cabs and trailers. Some of the cars appeared relatively undamaged, but the rest bore impact marks at all angles, making it clear each car had been struck numerous times. About a third of the vehicles had been bured down to nothing but the frame. Most of the rest were scorched, with blistered paint and tires melted flat.

Dave waved his hand. "I think the Honda's in the back there someplace. You want I leave you alone for a few minutes?"

"I would appreciate that," Don said, his eyes on the ground, as if he were overcome with sadness. He figured the less time Dave spent looking at his face, the better. The problem with having alopecia was that people seemed to remember you better, even if they didn't consciously know that they were noting your total lack of hair.

After the other man left, Don found himself distracted by the terrible tales the cars told. Doors were ripped off and bumpers torn away. On one minivan, crumpled to almost half of its original length, he could even read the word Kenilworth, stamped into the metal of the trunk in reverse. What might have once been a station wagon was now so flattened that it wasn't any more than three feet high. The driver's side had been sliced into and peeled back by the Jaws of Life, although in this case there couldn't have been any life left to find.

When Don finally tore his gaze away from the station wagon cut open like a tin can, he spotted Jamie's Honda. It was badly damaged. The windshield had been reduced to a few broken bits around the edges. A sock monkey dangled from the rearview mirror. Since there were only a few pieces of glass on the inside, he figured Jamie must have flown through the windshield. Slowly he circled the car. Blue paint had been tattooed on the driver's side door, but the door had kept its shape, so the two cars must have only grazed each other as they moved in the same direction.

Don continued his circuit of the car. In addition to the missing windshield, the front of the car was damaged across the full width, heavier on the passenger's side. The hood had assumed a noticeable V-shape. On the passenger side, another impact had punched a hole in the rear corner. On the backseat of the car, something caught the light. Leaning forward, Don shielded his eyes to look inside. It took him a minute to identify it as part of a turn signal assembly from another car. He moved up to check the front seating area. There was nothing on the seat itself, but on the floor he saw a pair of binoculars and an oversize paperback book. He squinted. *Gambol's Field Guide to Birds of the Western States.*

From this angle, he saw something else. A black-and-red bag tucked far under the dash, out of sight. He looked around. The yard seemed empty—no sign of Dave or any customers. Both doors refused to yield, so he had to lean far in, avoiding the broken glass, and grope unseeing for the bag. When he finally snagged it, Don eased open the passenger side door, then set the bag on the hood. Even before he opened it, he knew whatever it held inside wasn't what he was looking for. The weight was wrong, for one thing. And the bag itself wasn't the Nike bag they used. This one said Converse on the side in three-inch-wide letters.

The bag held two pairs of silk boxers, a pair of Hilfiger jeans, a balled up pair of socks, and the latest issues of *Maxim* and *Vanity Fair.* In addition, there was a whole bunch of personal grooming aids that Don didn't need anymore—a razor, lime-scented shaving lotion, and no less than three different hair products. Don bundled all the stuff back in the bag and put it back where he had found it. Presumably they would eventually ship it all back to his parents, and he knew they would be torn between keeping it and throwing it all away. Don knew what it was like to be left with only scraps of a person. After Rachel had gone, he had thrown her things in the trash, white hot with anger and despair. But for two years afterward he found pieces of her that he had missed—an earring lost in a corner, panties that had somehow fallen behind the headboard, a tube of red lipstick that had rolled to the back of a drawer. Each time, he had been pierced to the heart, the pain as fresh as ever.

Don drew a deep breath. He was here on a mission. If he spent too much more time here, old Dave might come wandering back out to see what was up.

In the end, the most interesting thing was not what the Honda held, but the fact that it was here at all, and more or less in one battered piece. Except for some faint scorching on the passenger side, there was no sign of fire. The things inside the car had been untouched by the flames. If the money had been left in this car, it certainly hadn't burned up. It was possible that the money had flown out of the windshield at the same time Jamie did. And if so, then the fire that had only licked the Honda, which was made of metal, might have entirely consumed a bag full of what was essentially paper.

Don walked back through the gate and over to the shack's half-open door, where Dave was listening to Mozart on the radio, his hands cutting through the air as he conducted an imaginary symphony. He flinched when he realized Don had appeared behind him.

"I just wanted to thank you for letting me look."

"I hope you found closure." The word sounded funny coming out of Dave's old-timey mouth.

Don nodded, although he was leaving with just as many questions as he had brought with him. When he walked back to the Lumper, he found that Barry had tilted the driver's seat all the way back and was sound asleep. The long, tangled blond curls had a lot of gray in them now, and, without his spirit to animate it, Barry's sleeping face fell into lines of age. It was kind of a shock to see him looking like an old man.

Twenty-three

FRIDAY, OCTOBER 20, 1:25 P.M.

As Free walked home from her first doctor's appointment, she thought that downtown Portland seemed easier to traverse on foot than it would be by car. It was a maze of one-way streets punctuated by "Turn Only" lanes, "No Turns" signs, and stretches where "Buses Only" were allowed. Just thinking about trying to navigate Portland from behind the wheel made Free feel a little faint.

That truck is really driving too close to that car, Free thought as she looked up the street at the oncoming traffic and waited for the light to change. The two vehicles were a block away, and so close there was no visible space between them. The car was a baby blue Firebird, splotched with gray primer spots and red rust. It was even older, Free judged, than her departed 1972 Impala. Right behind it was a brand-new oversize red Dodge pickup, riding the Firebird's bumper. Free could tell that the pickup's driver wanted the Firebird to close the gap between the Firebird and the car ahead of it. Stubbornly refusing to tailgate, the Firebird's driver kept twenty feet back. Free thought he even let the space ahead of him open up a little farther. The two vehicles were only about a half block from her now.

The pickup suddenly jerked sideways into an opening in the

139

middle lane and then speeded up, pulling even with the Firebird. Then it began to cut back into the right-hand lane, in front of the Firebird. Free could see the pickup driver, a guy about her own age with a blond crew cut, grin.

Free was never sure what happened next—if the Firebird speeded up, or if the pickup driver misjudged the angle or speed. All she knew was that there was a grinding crash as the two vehicles, for a brief moment, endeavored to occupy the same space. A space directly in front of Free. With no place to go, she pressed herself against the cement wall of the building behind her. In one slow-motion second, the back end of the pickup tore off the Firebird's front fender on the driver's side, and then, for good measure, the front bumper. Something small and silver flew past Free's head. The brakes on both cars squealed and smoked.

Free saw the blond man driving the pickup swivel his head back for a stunned second—and then he took off so fast his tires spun for a moment on the rain-slicked pavement. The pickup's back bumper was no longer a smooth stretch of silver, but bent and crumpled on the right side. The driver quickly wove around the other cars ahead of him before taking the corner on two wheels and disappearing from sight.

The impact had slewed the rear end of the Firebird around, so that the car now blocked both the right and middle lanes. The driver, a guy in his fifties with long hair and a Harley-Davidson T-shirt pulled taut over his potbelly, stumbled out of his car. A small brown car had to swerve to avoid running him down. It careened across the street and crashed into a parked car. Third Avenue was now effectively closed off.

Horns began to blare. Shouting, people leaned out their car windows. The Firebird's driver began circling his car, his face blank with shock. With both hands, he picked up the fender and pushed it against the battered body of his car as if the part might simply snap back into place.

Free still had her back pressed against the wall behind her. She could feel her heartbeat pulsing in her temples. Even though her eyes were wide open, she didn't focus on the scene in front of her. Her mind's eye saw a kaleidoscope of images. An old woman lying on top of a hood, the steering wheel still clutched in her hands. Lydia, silenced in mid-scream. A young woman with her legs cut off. And finally Free saw Jamie, blood trickling from his ears. Her scalp prickled, and her insides felt hollow.

Putting one hand over her heart and another on her belly, Free took a deep breath and tried to force herself to focus on the here and now. A dark-haired man had run up and was now directing traffic. With the fluent gestures of a man working an airport runway, he began to guide cars, one by one, through a narrow gap between the Firebird and the brown car. Free looked back up the street. There was a cop car back there, caught up in a traffic jam, and even changing to a different-sounding siren could not make the cars part before it.

A uniformed cop left the stranded police car and took over for the man directing traffic. They exchanged a few words, and the dark-haired man pointed in her direction. Free was having trouble paying attention. It was like she had double vision, seeing both what was in front of her and what had happened only a few days before. She strained to focus. As the dark-haired man began to walk over to her, she looked down at his feet. Something red was puddled on the ground.

The world narrowed to a dark tunnel and then blinked off altogether.

The next thing Free was aware of was a finger. A thick finger, tasting of soap, probing her mouth. Gagging, she opened her eyes. At first, all she could see was an ear. Dimly, Free became aware that someone must be checking to see if she was breathing. The man who owned both the ear and the finger sat back on his heels and looked at her. He was about thirty, she guessed, with close-cropped brown hair. His greenish eyes were set in a face that still looked tan. It took her a minute to recognize him as the man who had been directing traffic. She turned her head. She was lying faceup on the dirty sidewalk next to a mailbox.

Everything came back to her in a rush—the accident, the memories of dead people, the way the world had suddenly receded from her. Free moaned. She wanted to spit, to rid herself of the soapy taste of his hand, but still felt too dizzy to risk turning her head.

"I think you may have had a seizure," the man said. His voice was low with a little bit of a rasp. "I was trying to keep you from biting your own tongue."

Which was worse—talking or shaking her head? Free chose speech as the lesser of two evils.

"No, I didn't have a seizure. I think I passed out. I watched what happened and then all of a sudden I just felt dizzy." A wave of tightness rippled through her abdomen. "Oh, God, did I hit anything when I fell?"

He hesitated. "I'm not sure. You may have hit the mailbox."

Her hands found the zipper on her jacket. She pulled it down and touched the mound of the baby. It seemed still under her hands. Had she hurt it?

"How far along are you?" Free realized that he must be a doctor, asking such unruffled questions about seizures and pregnancies.

"Twenty-three weeks." The number was still fresh in her mind. She remembered Peggy's warning that if the baby were born now it would die. "Could I have hit the mailbox with my stomach?"

As he answered, she tried to anchor herself on the calm green gaze. "I'm not sure. It's possible you hit it with your belly or maybe a bit higher up, on your ribs." He ran his hand across her chest, and then more lightly over her breasts and belly, and she didn't protest. "Do you feel any tenderness here? Or here?"

"No. I don't know. I don't think so." Then the muscles of her abdomen contracted again, harder, and she cradled her belly in her hands. "Oh, no!"

"What's the matter?"

"I think I just had a contraction."

He nodded. "Well then, we've got to get you to the hospital. But there's no way I'll be able to get an ambulance down here, not with all the backup. Wait a minute."

The doctor bounded to his feet and hurried toward a yellow taxi that was slowly inching by the accident scene. With one hand raised in a halt gesture, he ran in front of the taxi. Even though the driver stopped, he honked his horn while leaning out his window and complaining. Free watched all of this from the strange canted angle afforded by lying on the sidewalk.

"I'm not on duty, man!" she heard the driver protest.

"This is a medical emergency. We have a woman here who may be in labor. You will either take me and this young lady to Good Samaritan Hospital or I will take your cab and do the driving for you." His voice brooked no back talk.

"You heard the man!" the cop chimed in.

Then the dark-haired doctor was back, bending over Free, his arms outspread, ready to scoop her up.

"I can walk," Free said. She half-sat up, causing her head to spin.

"Of course you can. But why take that chance?" With a muffled grunt, he lifted her in his arms. He deposited her in the cab, then swung in beside her. She caught a glimpse of the driver, who was wearing a white turban, before her rescuer pulled her back down into a prone position. "Here, put your head in my lap and brace your feet on the window. Do you feel like you have to push? Because under no circumstances should you push."

Pushing—wasn't that what you did when you were about to give birth? She'd seen enough movies with doctors exhorting women to push. But those took place in sterile hospitals with fully grown babies, not in cabs that smelled like cigarette smoke and to women who were only twenty-three weeks along.

"I don't think I need to push." She tried to pay attention to what her body was telling her, what messages the baby inside of her was sending.

"Good." She felt him shift under her, then a cell phone appeared in her line of sight. "Do you want me to call your husband?"

"I'm not married," Free said. Couldn't he just leave her alone? Something awful was happening to her, and she wanted to concentrate on it.

"Your, um, partner?"

"There's no one, all right? There's no one at all you can call. Would you just leave me alone!"

The cell phone was put away. "Hey, I'm only trying to help here."

Free was no longer paying attention to him. Under her hands, she felt her abdomen tighten again. "Oh no, I think I'm having another contraction."

He touched her chin, tilting her head back until she met his gaze. "What's your name?"

"What?" The question briefly distracted her from her panic. "Um, F—Lydia."

He didn't seem to notice her hesitation. "I'm Craig. Now the way we're going to get through this, Lydia, is by keeping calm. I want you to focus on my face and take a deep breath. As deep as you can." She did as ordered. "Again. That's good. We're almost at the hospital. You're going to make it. But even though it's not going to happen, if we had to, we could do this thing in here. I've delivered three babies outside the hospital."

"But it's too little! It can't live if it gets born now." Tears leaked from Free's eyes as she remembered Peggy's words. She felt the unfamiliar sensation of mascara rolling down her cheeks.

"We're just turning onto Twenty-third Avenue. Almost there," he said, leaning down closer. Not only did his finger taste like soap, but he smelled of it. Ivory soap. "I'll make sure they get you triaged right away."

Craig's hand started to smooth her hair, then she felt him pull back. Even though her eyes were closed, Free knew he was trying to guess why she was wearing a wig. She didn't care what he thought. All her thoughts were concentrated on the baby, willing it to stay inside.

Twenty-four

The interior of Clark City's Holy Redeemer Community Hospital was hushed, the corridors empty. The only people Don could see were an old woman in a pink jacket, arranging magazines on a table in the empty lobby, and a young woman in blue scrubs sitting behind the emergency room counter. She was typing on a computer. Behind her, a swinging door led to the emergency room.

Don gave her an easy smile. "Excuse me, doc, could I talk to you?"

She returned his smile and tucked a strand of hair behind one ear. "I'm a nurse."

"Oops, sorry, my mistake. Anyway, I wanted to ask if you were on duty the evening of the dust storm accident?"

She took her hand down from her ear, her manner noticeably cooler. "If you're with the media, you'll need to talk to someone in administration."

Don raised his eyebrows, miming disbelief. "I'm not a reporter. I'm a relative. I'm looking for my half-sister. She's missing." He had thought of saying that he was a friend or relative of Jamie's, but decided he couldn't pull it off, not after the real friends and relatives had presumably just been in contact. "You know that article that was in the paper, that one about the unidentified man who died here? Well, the description of the girl who was with him, the one the cops wanted to talk to—it sounded a lot like my sister."

"But we don't have her. We only had one unidentified patient—and that turned out to be Jamie Labot. His parents called the day after that story ran in *The Oregonian*."

Don nodded. "I saw that's who he was. See, since the accident, my sister hasn't come home and she hasn't called, and my mother's frantic to find her. Some of her friends say that she knew this Jamie guy and might have been traveling with him. And then somebody told us about the article in *The Oregonian*—and the description sounded just like her. I was hoping I could talk to someone who might have seen her that night."

"I was on that night." She glanced at the empty space behind her, and when she turned back the expression on her face was far away.

"You were? That's great. Did you happen to see my sister?"

"Do you have a picture of her I could see?"

Don shook his head, making eye contact with her the whole time, his expression only of disappointment. "The last picture anyone could come up with was before she got her braces off and cut off all her hair. Even our own mother wouldn't be able to tell it was the same girl."

The nurse offered his feeble joke a polite smile. "Is your sister a runaway?"

"More of a free spirit," Don hazarded a guess, based on the newspaper's description. Late teens or early twenties was a bit old to be a runaway. But anyone who shaved her head and stuck a silver ring in her nose was probably not a cog in a corporate machine. "Since she moved out from living with my mom, she's been crashing with various friends. But no one has seen her since the accident. My mom's worried she might have been badly injured, maybe even wandered off someplace and laid down in a ditch, or be unconscious in some hospital with no ID." Don added, "Although I guess you've said you don't have any unidentified patients."

"What's your sister's name?"

"She told you her name?" That really would be a bit of luck. It would be a lot easier to find this girlfriend of Jamie's if Don knew her name. Even if she had taken off, even if she had changed her name and gone to ground in a different city, if he knew who she had been originally, then he could find her. In Don's experience, people who ran off didn't really become different people. They just became the same person in a different place.

Just as quickly as the nurse had inflated Don's hopes, she burst them with her next words. "She never told me her name, and we never admitted her, so it wouldn't be in the medical records." She gave Don a look as if he were as dumb as a box of rocks, then repeated her question. "So what's your sister's name?"

"Oh," Don said, realizing he should have thought of the answer to this question in advance, "it's Rachel." His wife's was out of his mouth before he could call it back. Where had that come from? He didn't know. It had been years since he had said her name out loud. Sometimes Don believed that if he just perfected the illusion that Rachel had never existed, then it would be as if she had never gone. By forgetting about her existence, he would not have to acknowledge her absence.

"And does Rachel have brown eyes and a silver ring in her nose? Is she around nineteen or twenty?" She waited for his nod. "Is she tall, with a buzz cut? Does that sound like your sister?" When Don nodded again, she said, "Can't be too many girls like that wandering around." Her mood seemed more skeptical now, as if she sensed something about his story was bullshit.

"Drive over to Portland and look in Pioneer Courthouse Square and you'll see a thousand girls like her. That's why I wanted to see if I could find anyone who talked to her that day—to make sure it was really Rachel." Don had to find a way to working the topic around to the missing gym bag, but he knew the woman expected him to ask questions about his "sister." "So did you see her that night?"

"I even talked to her. I'm the one who had to tell her Jamie was dead."

Don leaned forward. "You did? You really saw her? Was she hurt? That's what our mom was really afraid of."

The nurse looked away. "Your sister did have a nasty cut on her forehead, over her left eyebrow, near her hairline." She ran her index finger, the nail clipped close, over her own smooth skin. "I asked her to sit down and wait in the waiting area until we had time to deal with her. Even though she did have that cut and she looked like she was in shock, that type of injury wasn't a priority right then." She answered a protest Don hadn't made. "I'm sorry, but we had people dying back here, and basically she was young and healthy. Sometimes you have to make decisions about your resources. It's called triage. They do it in war zones, and that's what we were. We had people in gurneys out in the hall, and even then they were still bringing them in. We didn't have enough blood. We ran out of bandages. Your sister was in shock, but it wasn't life threatening. Six people died here that night. Maybe I should have paid more attention to her, but there frankly wasn't time. We're just not equipped to handle something like this. But we had to, didn't we? People were dying whether we liked it or not." Her eyes were fixed on something past Don. "And then when I finally went to find her after things had quieted down, she had just disappeared."

"Did you see her go? Did she leave with any one?"

"She could have left with a drum major at the head of a marching band, and I wouldn't have noticed. I'm sorry if that sounds sarcastic, but we were racing against time back here. And we were losing. It's one thing to lose an eighty-year-old man to pneumonia. It's another to lose kids like this Jamie Labot."

"No, no, I understand. You did the best you could. So you said she had a cut on her head." Don tried to sound properly upset. "How deep was it?"

"Not too bad. If it was, we would have treated it right away, don't worry about that. It had bled a lot, because there was blood all down the side of her face and on her clothes, but facial cuts are real bleeders. And by the time your sister got here, it wasn't bleeding anymore." Something compelled her to be honest. "At least not much."

"But you do think she was with this guy, this Jamie Labot?"

"Yes, she came up and asked for him and then her eyes got real wide when I had to tell her he was dead. Normally, we get the chaplain for something like that, but he was in the back with the people who were really dying. When I told her about Jamie, she didn't believe me at first."

"Was this Jamie conscious at all?" Don wondered if he had moaned and thrashed and talked about the money. "Did he ask about my sister? See, if he said her name, then I'd know for sure that—"

She cut him off. "He never came to."

Don straightened up, as if inspiration had struck. "Say, did this Jamie guy come in with any possessions or anything? Like a suitcase or a bag? I'm wondering if he might have had an address book with my sister's name in it. Maybe another phone number we could try."

As he waited for the answer, Don watched the woman's face. Not her mouth, which was serious and helpful, but the upper part of her face—the eyes, the eyebrows and the forehead. That was the part of the face that people gave away their lies with, that and their feet. They could look at you with a smile on their face, unaware that their brows would be pulled down into a frown. And underneath the table their feet would be tap-dancing away. Paying attention to faces and feet had saved Don more than once or twice.

"Just him and his clothes, which we had to cut off him," the nurse said, with her feet still and her face clear. If there had been any talk of a Nike gym bag filled with cash, it hadn't reached her ears. "No wallet, no ID, no nothing. He was a good-looking kid. It was hard on the staff that they couldn't save him. I hear one of the accident reconstructionists eventually found his wallet along the side of the road. On the same day his parents came to get his body. So maybe you could try calling them. Although you know," she said, her words coming more slowly as she hesitated, "I heard they did find something on him, too. Maybe something you should know about before your sister gets into any trouble from hanging around with the wrong kind of people."

"What?"

She looked around the empty space before lowering her voice. "I heard they found a gun in a little holster strapped to his leg."

"Oh, God." Don covered his face with his hands, although the news was no surprise. Most people who worked as couriers figured out pretty quick that it was better to be armed. So Jamie had been brought in here with nothing but his clothes and his gun. The rest of his stuff—except the bag full of cash—had stayed in the car. And the only other thing that had left the car was this girl. Don figured he already knew the answer to his last question, but he had to be sure.

"My sister—she always carries around this bag. A black Nike gym bag. Did she have that with her? Because if she did, then I'll know for sure that it's Rachel." Don's voice tricked him when he said his wife's name, gave it a twist of emotion that he hadn't meant to put in there.

The nurse looked up, brightening at the thought of having some news. "Hey, she did have a bag. Like a gym bag, and a dark color." Her face fell again. "Only she said something about needing to give it to Jamie. So maybe that can't be your sister."

"Maybe she just had something that belonged to him," Don said, thinking that that was the understatement of the year.

twenty-five

The taxi hadn't even come to a complete stop before Craig was flinging open the door. Within seconds, he had grabbed a wheelchair from just inside the hospital entrance, helped Free into it, and thrown a bill through the cab driver's window. Moving so fast that he banged one wheel into the still-opening automatic door, Craig pushed Free into the emergency room. The half-dozen people waiting straightened up to get a better look at her.

A woman wearing a white blouse with a blue bow tie looked up from the desk. "Craig! What brings you in here?"

"Laurel, this lady's twenty-three weeks pregnant. She passed out about ten minutes ago, may have hit her belly on a mailbox when she went down, and now may be in labor. You need to get her back STAT."

"Okay," Laurel said, already halfway around the desk. "Let's see what's up."

A few minutes later, Free found herself in a tiny curtained cubicle, her dress pushed up above her waist, her feet in stirrups, and a gloved hand examining her. It was deja vu all over again, except this time there was no drape and she had an audience. In addition to the doctor who was examining her, there was a nurse, two men in green scrubs, and Craig, who was explaining to the older doctor exactly what had happened. The others all watched intently, as if the doctor might suddenly perform magic and pull a rabbit out of a hat or a baby out of her belly.

Free was too worried to be embarrassed at the number of people now viewing her most intimate areas. She panted as she again felt her belly harden. "Maybe you should contact my doctor, Peggy Davenport. She said I should page her if I went into labor."

The other doctor nodded without speaking. He had silver hair and looked like he was old enough to have retired ten years ago. He slipped his stethoscope into his ears and laid it on the skin of her abdomen, listening intently. The people behind him were quiet, although from another curtained cubicle Free could hear the sound of a confused old man querulously asking for his shoes.

The baby was still within Free's belly. There was something wrong with it. She had hurt it when she fell. It was dying. It was already dead. Free's thoughts chased each other, each one worse than the last. The doctor looked at his watch.

"One hundred fifty-nine beats a minute. I think it's probably sleeping." He ran his hands over her belly, his eyes intent. She winced when he came to her left hip, and he pressed lightly on the spot again. "You're already developing a hematoma here."

"What?" Free's anxiety returned.

"A bruise. And a nasty one, by the looks of it. Other than that, I see no signs of trauma."

"Am I in labor?"

"No."

Even though his answer was curt and without further explanation, Free found herself taking the first deep breath she had since witnessing the accident.

The doctor moved the stethoscope up further and listened to Free's own heartbeat without comment. He snapped off his gloves, revealing age-spotted hands, then dropped the gloves in the garbage.

"Can I sit up now?" Free asked. Without the doctor blocking the view, Free was now on full display. He gave her a distracted nod. She stood up and pulled her dress down into place, then sat back down at the edge of the table. The nurse had drifted away, and now the two men in green scrubs left, too. Only Craig stayed.

The doctor picked up a clipboard. "Okay, Lydia, tell me exactly what happened before you fainted."

"I was walking downtown when a car accident happened right next to me. I wasn't hurt at all, but it was very close. At first I felt okay, but then I started to feel dizzy."

"When did you last eat?"

"I had a pretty big breakfast."

The doctor made a little humming sound in the back of his throat. He put down the notebook. In silence, he took her blood pressure, then announced, "One-ten over sixty-five."

"What does that mean?"

"It's perfect. Not too low, not too high. Can you think of any reason you might have gotten dizzy? Have you been ill recently? Sleeping poorly?"

Free shook her head.

"Tell me exactly what happened just before you passed out."

"I had just seen the car accident happen, and then I started thinking about a car accident I saw once, a really bad one. One where people were killed. And when I noticed the pool of blood on the ground, that's when I really started feeling dizzy. And then I passed out."

"Blood!" Craig interjected. "That wasn't blood. That was transmission fluid."

The older doctor silenced him with a look, while Free felt herself flush at her foolishness. She should have realized there hadn't been any injuries, that this had been a fender-bender, not a fatal collision.

"Have you had these contractions before?"

"No. But I was just at my OB-GYN, though, and she warned me about how that was one of the signs of premature labor." She repeated her earlier question. "Isn't this what labor feels like?"

The older doctor didn't answer her. "How about this dizziness?

Have you felt lightheaded before today? Or have you experienced shortness of breath or a pounding heart?"

Free remembered sitting in the Chevette, feeling her heart race and the air disappear. "Yes. Why? What's wrong with me? Is there something wrong with my baby?"

He held up his hand, palm toward her. "And is this your first pregnancy?"

Free nodded.

"The contractions you're experiencing are normal. They are what are known as Braxton-Hicks contractions. Your uterine muscles are tightening and then loosening, exercising the uterus and preparing it to work efficiently during labor. Most women experience them long before they actually go into labor. It is a bit early, but if you're already under stress and then experience a serious shock—well, I'm not surprised."

"You mean, I'm not in labor?"

"No. But it's difficult for a lay person to tell." He glanced at Craig, and Free wondering if this was a wordless reprimand to his colleague for bringing her in. He picked up his chart again and began making notes. "If it happens again, wait until you feel five or more contractions in less than an hour. Then you can be pretty sure you're in labor, instead of just having false labor pains." He paused to write. "Or if you begin to bleed heavily. Or if you feel a gush of water. Just be sure it's really your water breaking, and not simply you losing control of your bladder." His tone implied that she couldn't be trusted to tell the difference between heartburn and a heart attack.

"But what about the dizziness or her passing out?" Craig asked. If he felt as embarrassed as Free did, he didn't show it. He must be some other kind of doctor if he didn't know all this.

The doctor shrugged. "Probably a panic attack."

"You mean it was all in my head?" Free asked.

The older doctor's tone softened just a little. "It's too simple to make that delineation. After all, your body and your mind are connected. Seeing the car accident reminded you of a similar, but much more stressful event. And you had just been alerted by your doctor to watch for signs of premature labor. As a primagravida, or first-time mother, you still aren't certain what is normal and what is not. When one combines stressful memories with hyper-vigilance, a panic attack may be the result. The self-monitoring and the fear become a loop that circles back on itself endlessly."

The doctor reached out for Free's right hand and moved it until it was on the bottom curve of her belly. "Close your eyes," he commanded. Free did as she said. "Now breathe in through your nose and out through your mouth. That's right. Exhale like you're blowing out a birthday candle. Exactly. And now when you breathe in, I want you to feel that hand on your abdomen moving."

"I felt like I was going crazy," Free confessed, her eyes still closed. "I felt like the baby was dying."

"And your body reacted to the perceived emergency. It's not real, but if you keep worrying that you might go crazy, or even die, then your body reacts to that."

Free opened her eyes again. "But it felt real."

"Of course it does. You were already in a heightened stage of vigilance, and your body was telling you that you felt out of con-trol. My advice is to practice that deep breathing for five minutes, twice a day, and stay away from stressful activities." He flipped her chart closed. "You'll need to arrange payment with the cashier on your way out."

Craig followed Free out to the cashier. An old woman dressed in an inside-out stocking cap and a dirty skirt and blouse was ahead of Free, arguing. One of her worn maroon pumps was tied on with a piece of twine that passed under her instep and wrapped around her ankle. "But I got that herpes from a limousine," she told the cashier impatiently, as if the cashier were being deliberately obtuse.

Free turned to Craig. "You don't need to wait for me. I'll be okay. I really appreciate your help."

"That's all right. I need to ask you a few questions anyway."

From the breast pocket of his corduroy jacket, he took a small tan notebook and flipped it open. "Could you tell me your full name and then spell it for me?"

"What?" Free wasn't following this at all. "Why do you need that?"

"You witnessed the accident, didn't you?"

"Yeah, but what does that matter?"

"We've got a hit-and-run driver out there, and we need to catch him. I'll need you to come down to the station house in the next day or two and see if you can help me identify the driver and his vehicle."

Free was starting to feel dizzy again. "Aren't you a doctor?"

Craig tilted his head, his expression surprised. "What made you think that?"

"You said you'd delivered babies in weird places before."

"Cops get called on to do all kinds of weird things."

"You're a cop?"

"Yeah. I had today off and came downtown to do some shopping. Then when I saw the accident, I stopped to see if I could give the guys a hand." He smiled. "Maybe it's better you didn't know. You might have been more freaked out."

Free managed an answering smile. This guy was a cop. A cop, not a doctor. Could it mean that they were on to her? Did the cops know about the missing money? Did they know Free wasn't really Lydia? Had he been following her and then seized the opportunity to make contact? She shook her head slightly. She was imagining dire scenarios instead of dealing with reality. Her mind was playing tricks on her again. Wasn't it?

Twenty-six

After Roy got out of the Monte Carlo, he got Pop-pop's hunting rifle from the backseat. He was parked on the edge of the pitted muddy field that served as a parking lot for guys who liked to come out here and target shoot. Twenty years ago, men had quarried gravel here, leaving behind pits with steep rock walls and pocked with deep pools of water that were said to be tainted with leached arsenic.

Roy looked around uncertainly. He saw Warren's big black Jeep, as well as a half-dozen other cars, but no Warren and nobody else. Roy walked back to the road, skirting the potholes, but the road curved out of sight as it dipped lower, and he still saw no one. He could hear the popping sound of firing not far away, though, even smell the sour tang of smoke in the air. The weather was a little bit above freezing, the sky a wash of pale gray overhead. Soon, the light would start to fade. Guys were taking advantage of one of the last long afternoons before daylight savings time ended next week.

Roy didn't know the last time he had slept, but even so, he was acutely aware of everything around him. The pine trees looked so crisp they could have been two-dimensional cutouts propped up on a movie set.

Warren stepped out from behind a tree to Roy's left, startling him. Roy was wearing denim jeans and a plaid quilted shirt, but Warren was wearing full camo. Warren had been in Special Forces in the Gulf War, and said he had killed more men than he could count. Once he had shown Roy a necklace strung with a half-dozen men's ears, shrunk down to tan curls that looked like dried mushrooms. Now Warren made good money working as a telephone lineman, getting double time and a half for overtime when the weather turned bad and the lines started to snap under the weight of the ice, which was pretty much all winter.

The two men nodded at each other by way of greeting. There was a knife on Warren's belt and an AR-15 with a 30-round magazine tucked under his arm. Shit, what Roy wouldn't give for a weapon like that, or to drive a Jeep like Warren's. Instead he had to drive Pop-pop's old car and shoot the old guy's hunting rifle. He had the Colt, but it was worthless at long distances.

"Heard you got fired from the plant." Warren looked at Roy with no expression on his face. When he wasn't working, Warren spent a lot of time in the woods. He liked to talk about how he could survive for months in the wilderness with only his knife and a twist of salt. Roy didn't know how true this was, but it sounded good. Maybe if he hadn't been kicked out of Cub Scouts for fighting he would have learned all that shit.

"This dickbreath was always on my case, so I had to teach him a lesson." The words sounded stupid, empty bragging, as they left his mouth. He knew that if Warren had been in his shoes, he would have killed Duane. Without even thinking about it, Roy turned and put the rifle to his shoulder and pulled the trigger. He saw a chip of wood fly out from the trunk of a tamarack about two hundred yards away. His whole body relaxed the way it hadn't since Lydia left. He turned back to Warren. "I need to find my whore of a wife. I think she's gone to ground in some shelter, even though they won't admit it."

"Yeah?" The word sounded like a challenge. A shaft of sunlight pierced through the clouds and glinted off the mirrored sunglasses Warren wore.

"And I was thinking that maybe Shari could help me. Lydia will have to deal with the system sometime. I thought Shari could keep an eye out for Lydia's new address."

Warren didn't ask what would happen then. "You know she charges a flat thousand for that."

"No discount for friends?" Roy tried out a smile.

Warren's answer was swift and emotionless. "No. Bring the money by the house this week and I'll tell Shari to start looking." Roy had met Shari only once, a skinny woman with downcast eyes who wore a long-sleeved turtleneck in the summer.

Roy wasn't too sure he had that kind of money. "Will you take a check?" He knew the question was dumb before it was even out of his mouth.

Warren snorted. "And leave a trail for the Feds? Shari only works for cash money. And she won't start looking until I tell her to."

"Okay, man, okay. I was only joking. I'll bring it by the house sometime this week."

A hundred yards away, two men pulled up in an old VW Beetle, the yellow paint splotched with red rust. They parked near Warren's Jeep. Warren and Roy watched them get out.

"Have you ever thought about just emptying your gun?" With his chin, Warren indicated the two target shooters.

"You mean, killing someone?" Roy felt a mixture of things— excitement and fear and a kind of stuttering anticipation. "Are you shitting me, man?"

"Haven't you ever wanted to?" Warren smiled, but Roy couldn't tell if he was joking or not. Roy thought about that necklace of men's ears. "Or are you too scared?"

The two guys came over before Roy could think of an answer. Their names were Vern and Howard. Both were about twenty years older than Roy, with beaten down expressions and flabby bodies. Howard had a long, narrow face and a careful comb-over. His mouth looked like it had too many teeth. He reminded Roy of that horse he used to watch on TV reruns when he was little. Mr. Ed. Vern was shorter and wider and looked like a bear, with thick brown hair he had tried without success to slick back with some kind of gel.

Roy thought he had seen Howard before, sitting at the end of the counter in the Red Barn Tavern, nursing a Bud, but he didn't mention it. Instead, he let Vern ramble on about how the two of them were starting a collection of ammunition and could they trade. All four of them did, although Roy didn't give a fuck and he could tell Warren didn't either. Then Vern and Howard said good-bye and began to walk down the road.

When they were far enough away to be barely out of earshot, Warren lifted the AR-15 and pretended to fire at them, making noises with his mouth like a little kid. That struck Roy as funny, as did the fact that dopey old Vern and Howard were oblivious, carefully picking their way around the muddy potholes. After they got about two hundred yards away, the two men stopped to light cigarettes, leaning against a tree and talking.

Warren had turned away from the two men, no longer interested. But Roy's brain was still occupied by Warren's suggestion. He wondered what it would be like to kill someone. Would it be different from shooting a deer, from what he had done to the cat? And these two guys were walking around, not knowing they could be dead. Oblivious. Not even realizing they were halfway dead already.

Roy looked back at the two men. Vern had produced a Thermos of coffee from the backpack, and Howard was tipping in something from a flask while the two men laughed. "Want to go shooting?" Roy asked Warren, not sure when he asked the question exactly what he was suggesting they go shooting at.

"Already been," Warren said, turning and beginning to walk away. "I'll look for you at the house this week."

Roy watched him walk away, climb into his Jeep, and start the engine. The Jeep had a deep, sure rumble to it, not like Pop-

pop's Monte Carlo, which wasn't even firing on all cylinders. He was angry with Warren, angry that he had acted as if Roy was stupid, angry that he had money and Roy didn't, angry that he seemed to think Roy was chicken. The Jeep drove up the road, around the bend and out of sight.

Without even thinking, Roy turned and brought the gun to his shoulder again. The two men were close together. The first bullet gouged chips out of a tree maybe three feet to their left. He saw them jerk, startled. They were still turning toward him when Roy adjusted his aim and fired again. Part of the head of the guy who looked like Mr. Ed was gone. He fell like a sack of potatoes. The fat guy turned and tried to run. Roy took aim again, his finger steady on the trigger. A dark spot blossomed on the back of his denim jacket, then another. He fell to the ground.

Roy saw that the one in the denim jacket was still alive. Was his name Vern or Howard? Roy didn't know anymore, and it didn't matter anymore. He walked up to him, closer and closer, until he was maybe fifteen feet away. The other man looked at him, just looked, his expression without hope or surprise like he knew exactly what was going to happen. Roy put the rifle to his shoulder again. The man jerked once and then was still.

The next thing Roy knew, he was out on the highway, behind the wheel of the Monte Carlo, doing eighty miles an hour and grinning like a maniac. What the fuck. All he knew was that it had felt good. It had felt better than the cat. If only Lydia could have seen what had just happened. She wouldn't have dared run away from him if she had known what he was capable of doing. No one was going to laugh at him now.

The whole thing was perfect. He had only been up at the old gravel pit for about half an hour. The only people who had known he had been there were the two dead guys and Warren. And he knew Warren would never tell.

It was to be nearly a week before Roy thought about the ammunition in Vern and Howard's pockets. The ammo with his prints on it.

Twenty-seven

Barry and Don divided up the town between them and then started the long job of going from business to business in widening circles around the hospital. Had this girl eaten at the In-N-Out Burger, bought first-aid supplies for her cut at the grocery store, spent the night in a motel?

It was nearly six o'clock when Don pushed open the door to the Stay-A-While Motel. Overhead, a bell jingled. The white Formica on the floor of the small reception area had turned ivory with age, and there were balls of dust and cat hair in the corners.

The space behind the counter reminded Don of those pictures you sometimes saw on TV, where a tornado or a bomb had torn one wall off an apartment building, leaving the contents exposed like a doll's house. Instead of an officelike alcove, it was really someone's living room, complete with a half-dozen cats. Don remembered staying in old motels like this one when he was doing courier work, where the person who ran the hotel lived on-site, in a unit where the living area also doubled as the space behind the front desk.

Behind the counter the floor was covered with a rust-colored wall-to-wall sculpted shag carpet. The only light came from a TV set. A couple of half-open doors presumably led to a kitchen or a bathroom or bedroom. In the far corner stood a small silver Christmas tree, unlit. No presents stood underneath, and Don wondered if the hotel's owner loved Christmas or simply lacked the will to pack away the tree every year. It made him uncomfortable, this glimpse into someone else's personal life, and a messy, lonely-looking one at that. What was it like to eat and sleep and shower only a few feet from customers, to sit down in front of the TV and know that anyone could walk in at any time?

There were cats every place—one on top of the TV, one sprawled on the coffee table, two sleeping entwined on the couch, and one in the lap of a large woman in a polyester muumuu who was watching the TV from the comfort of a lounger. At the sound of the bell, she swiveled the chair around and got to her feet, holding the cat against her chest. A smile appeared on her round, white face. She could have been any age between twenty-five and fifty-five.

"Good afternoon. Are you interested in a room?" She looked eager, as well she might. The parking lot had been empty.

"Sorry, no. I was just hoping I could ask you a question," Don said for the dozenth time. "By any chance, were you working the day of that big accident?"

She put her free hand to her chest and rolled her eyes heavenward. "Oh Lordy, yes. That was a terrible thing, terrible. All those poor people." A talker, Don could see. And so good and so helpful she wouldn't even think to attribute less stellar motives to anyone else.

Behind her, dramatic music swelled on the TV, which showed a stagey-looking hospital that bore no resemblance to the one Don had just left. The nurse was dressed all in white, with a cap perched on her head. The patient looked well enough to get out of bed and dance a jig. Instead, he grabbed the nurse as she bent over to adjust his IV, pulled her half on the bed and kissed her.

The soap opera gave Don the spin he needed. "What I'm doing is trying to find my sister. We got word from her that she was involved in the accident, but we haven't heard from her since.

We're real worried about her. See, when she called us, she told us she had hurt her head. Now we're thinking that maybe she has amnesia or something."

"Oh no!"

"I was wondering if you might have seen her. She's about twenty years younger than me, and tall, but probably the most distinctive thing about her is that she"—he began to put his hand near his ear.

"She's bald, isn't she? Just like you!"

So much for thinking that the ball cap hid his naked head. Still, this was pay dirt. Don managed to keep his voice calm. "You've seen her, then?"

"That poor thing! She come in here all covered in dirt and blood. There was a big cut on her head, so a lot of that blood was hers, but I think some of it belonged to other people. And her eyes were just—staring. I had to repeat everything twice. I asked her if she had been in that bad accident, and she said yes. And I said, 'Oh you poor child, let Darlene help you.'"

"Uh huh," Don said, in as interested and patient a tone as he could muster. He posed his own question before she could launch into her narrative again. "Was she by any chance carrying a bag? Like a black Nike gym bag? My sister always carries a Nike gym bag."

The woman's eyes got even wider. "Yes, she was. Darlene asked her if she had any clean clothes she could change into, but she said all the bag had in it was some paperwork."

Paperwork. Well, that was one thing you could call it, Don thought. The woman's words lit a cold fire in his belly. So this stupid girl with her buzz cut and her nose ring thought she could just run off with all of Don's hard-earned money and leave him hanging in the wind.

"So could I speak to this Darlene? Is she working today, too?"

The woman's face colored. "That's me. I'm Darlene. Sometimes I just talk about myself that way." She looked away, then took a file box from under the counter and pulled out a card. "See,"

Darlene continued, "see, here's where she signed her name. Free Meeker. Is that your sister?"

Better and better, thought Don. How many shaven-headed girls with silver nose rings and a name like Free could there be in the world? "Half-sister, like I said. But yeah, that's her." As he spoke, Don memorized the address. The girl lived in Medford, a good three hundred miles away in Southern Oregon. Had she gone home with her bag full of Don's money, or had she hightailed it off into parts unknown?

"So you're from Medford?"

"Not anymore," Don said. "I live in Portland now. My mom still lives down there."

"Her name was so unusual. She said her folks were hippies. She certainly looked a little different, what with no hair and all." Too late, she focused again on Don's head, as smooth as a billiard ball under the cap. "Darlene don't mean that in a bad way, of course. And she was sweet as could be. Darlene got her a first-aid kit and a clean dress and sweater, so she would have something to wear after she got herself cleaned up a little. Practically had to force them on her. So you think she might have amnesia?" On the television screen behind her, a commercial showed four women clustered around a toilet bowl, making admiring murmurs.

"The doctors we've talked to have said it's possible. In fact," Don decided to give this story another soap-opera worthy twist, "they're worried that there might be blood building up in her brain. It could be very dangerous. That's why we need to find her now, before it ruptures. Did she make any phone calls from her room? Did you see her talking to anyone?"

Darlene shook her head. "It costs extra to turn the phone on, but your sister said she didn't want it. Just the room. And as far as Darlene knows, the only person she talked to was her. The poor thing did seem confused." She gasped and put her hand to her chest. "Wait! Maybe Darlene knows where your sister went. Would that help?"

Don resisted giving his reply a sarcastic spin. "Of course it would."

"She asked me about Greyhound, since her car was totaled. She wanted to get to Portland. Maybe she was coming to visit you."

Portland, Don thought. So she had been in his territory all along. "Thank you very much, Darlene. You've been very helpful."

"Darlene hopes you find your sister. She was the sweetest girl. She was all worried because she had to leave here in my dress, since she didn't have anything else to wear, but I told her, 'Honey, Darlene orders those things by the truckload.'" She sighed. "Sure you don't want a room for the night? It's a long drive to Portland. And you could have your pick. We were full up for the first four days after the accident. Could have charged whatever we wanted. Now everyone's gone home."

"No, thanks. I really want to find my sister before it's too late. After all, we don't know how long she has. But if you think of anything else, please give me a call." Don pushed his card toward her. "Remember, it's a matter of life and death." Whose life and whose death, he didn't say.

When he got back home at midnight, Don went straight to his office and turned on his computer. He skimmed over all the articles posted on the Oregonian.com Web site about the accident. He was looking for Free's name, but he didn't see it among the list of injured or in any of the interviews with survivors. Finally he clicked on the "Find" button and typed in "Free Meeker." Obligingly, the computer highlighted her name, buried deep in the second story. But her name wasn't listed among the witnesses or among the injured.

Free Meeker was listed among the dead.

twenty-eight

"Hello, Mr. Black," the woman said, reaching out for Don's offered hand. Instead of shaking it, she folded her own over the top of his and squeezed it briefly. She had silver rings on every finger, including her thumb. "I'm Free's mother. Diane." The on-line version of the local paper, *The Medford Mail Tribune*, had said Free's mother was only forty-four, but to Don's eyes she looked at least a decade older. Her black hair was liberally threaded with gray, and she had the skin of someone who had spent a lot of time outdoors without sunscreen. Her dark eyes were shadowed, the lids red-rimmed. She had piercings all up and down her ears, and around her neck she wore a dozen strands of tiny multicolored beads.

"That reporter from *The Oregonian* is here," she called out over her shoulder. Which wasn't necessary, as Don could see the two men on the couch were craning their necks to get a good look at him. As soon as their gazes touched Don's, they both glanced away.

Don had spent Saturday finding out as much as he could about Free Meeker. There was only one week left until his deadline ran out. Deadline. He wondered if that would prove an apt term in this case. On *The Medford Mail Tribune*'s Internet story, he had found a picture of Free accompanying a story about her death.

Even though the photo was a couple of years old, it matched the descriptions he had been given of the girl who had been accompanying Jamie. Shaved hair, a silver ring in her nose, and eyes, that, in reproduction at least, looked dark. Even though she had looked actually very little like Rachel, while staring at the screen of his iMac, Don had been suddenly, painfully reminded of his former wife, with her flashing black eyes.

When Don had first seen the motel registry listing Free's address as Medford, he had been confused. Why had Jamie been dating someone on the other side of the state? But after he thought about it for a while, it made sense. Why have an extracurricular girlfriend in the same neighborhood as your main squeeze? If Jamie had been lonely when he was out of town, it made more sense that he would have picked up a local girl. A small-town girl who would be oh-so impressed with him, not an easy feat with the jaded Carly.

And Free probably hadn't been too hard to impress. According to the newspaper article, she had been a high school dropout working as a pet groomer for the local outpost of the Petorium chain. Don guessed that she probably would have been lucky if she made fifty cents above minimum wage.

The article also made brief mention of a boyfriend, Billy. A boyfriend. That gave him pause. But Free must have had her little secrets, the same way Jamie had his. There was also a sister, Moon Morton. Moon was described as a newlywed who lived in Pendleton, and the one who had identified the body. "Free's body was terribly burned, so we had her cremated," Diane Meeker was quoted by *The Medford Mail Tribune*. "We can't say we spread the ashes on the Applegate River, because that's against the law. Let's just say she is one with nature, where she always wanted to be."

The more Don thought about it, the more he realized there were a couple of missing pieces to the story. How had the police known that Free was dead? And why had her family agreed with them? Had Free's sister simply made an honest mistake when she was confronted with a charred corpse the police already thought was her sister? Or could she have been in on it from the beginning? Which led only to more questions. Even if this Free had had her eye on Jamie's Nike bag from the first day they met, it was beyond the bounds of possibility that she could have engineered a freak dust storm to get her hands on it. So it must have been a spur of the moment decision, Free seizing an opportunity that had presented itself.

But then where had this other woman's body come from? Had Jamie seen himself as such a stud that he had been traveling with not one, but two women? Barry had reported that Jamie had always seemed very businesslike, but if he had bent the rules enough to take along a woman, there was nothing to say he hadn't taken along two. Maybe the accident had left this other mystery woman dead, Jamie badly injured, and Free, despite her head injury, able to think clearly enough to plant her ID on the other woman's body before fleeing with Jamie's bag. But could anyone have really thought that fast on her feet, been able to twist misfortune to her advantage without a second thought?

For answers, Don needed to talk to the people who should have known Free best. He wanted to meet them face to face, weigh their grief and see how heavy it was. Watch their eyes and see if they betrayed guilty knowledge. And if her family and her boyfriend truly believed she was dead when she wasn't, he wanted to gather hints of what kind of person Free was and where she might have gone.

It was the article in *The Medford Mail Tribune* that gave Don the idea. He called Free's parents and told them he was Ken Black, a reporter with *The Oregonian*, one of a team assigned to do a more in-depth human interest story on the people who had died in the terrible multiple-car accident. It was a plausible story, so plausible that he was relieved Free's mother didn't say anything about his being the second *Oregonian* reporter to have called with an identical request. In fact, she told him unapologetically that they made it a point to never read any newspapers or magazines, or to watch TV. They viewed the media as corporate lackeys, with most of the content dictated by advertisers. Don supposed they were probably right.

As Don pulled up at Free's family's ramshackle house, he realized he could already solve one mystery. The paper had identified Free's parents as beaders and potters, occupations that seemed unlikely as a sole source of income. As Don got out of his car he caught sight of tinfoil on the small, dirty basement windows. He would bet any portion of the missing money that there was a grow operation in the basement.

Now Don followed Diane into the living room and back in time twenty-five years. Spider plants hung from the ceiling in macramé holders. A bead curtain separated the living room from the rest of the house. Above the sagging couch, covered with an old quilt leaking batting at one edge, was a batik print of an eagle flying over a mountain. In one corner of the room, a squat black woodstove did nothing to make it any warmer. Despite the chill in the air, Diane's feet were bare. Her delicate ankle bracelet of tiny royal blue and yellow beads contrasted to her wide, peasant-looking feet. She wore a short-sleeved man's T-shirt tucked into a long skirt made of different panels of printed fabric. From his younger days, Don remembered how girls had worn skirts like that to concerts, danced stoned in front of the band, twirling so that the skirts stood out like bells.

The two men stood up. The older of the two said, "I'm Bob, Free's dad, and this is Billy, her boyfriend." Bob had a narrow face, a scruffy goatee, and long, thinning hair pulled back and tied with a leather thong into a scanty ponytail. He wore a faded denim shirt and cream-colored corduroy pants tucked into homemade-looking knee-high moccasin-style boots. Don put his hand out, and the other man shook it briefly in a conventional manner. Then he surprised Don by twisting his hand so that his fingers grasped the base of Don's thumb, then pulling back a little so that only their fingers gripped each other before he finally released his grip. A soul handshake, they had called them back when Don was fifteen, and his hand had remembered and followed the moves better than his startled mind.

Billy offered Don nothing more than a limp handshake, for which Don was grateful. Looking at him more closely, Don saw that Billy was nearer Don's age than Free's. He, too, had long hair, but more of it, worn loose, black and silky and flowing over his shoulders. Jesus hair, they used to call it. Don always noticed men's hair. Billy wore old Levi's and workboots and a scratchy-looking Guatemalan sweater stretched out at the cuffs. There was something about his demeanor that struck Don as odd. A little off. His dark, depthless eyes looked into Don's for too long. It was Don who finally had to look away, his gaze dropping to the floor and the green army-surplus backpack at Billy's feet. A "Legalize Marijuana" patch was sewn on the flap.

They were all of them standing now, the three of them looking at him expectantly. Don wasn't sure where he should sit. In addition to the couch where the two men had been sitting, there was only a denim-covered beanbag chair.

"Why don't we sit at the dining room table," Diane said, solving the dilemma. "That's where we've got all the pictures you asked for."

Remembering his role, Don slipped out of his shirt pocket the narrow tan notebook he had bought that morning. Taking the pen from behind his ear, he flipped open the notebook. He was wearing clear half-glasses and the only toupee he owned. It had been breathtakingly expensive, hand-knotted from human hair—and it still looked like he had a dead marmot strapped to his head. The one advantage it had was that people who saw it tended to remember it, not him. "I'd be very interested in seeing the photographs." While he only wanted current pictures, he figured a real reporter would want more than that. He'd dump the remainder in the first public trash can he came to.

Diane held the amber strands of the bead curtain to one side for Don. Her gaze brushed over him, sad and dark, focused on nothing.

They each took one of the four mismatched wooden chairs that stood around the rough wooden table. The table seemed old enough to be an antique, or maybe it had just been well used. What Don could see of the surface was gouged with the black lines of old knife cuts, but much of the top was covered with dozens of photos. A few were fading Polaroids, but most were color photographs. All were of the same girl, ranging from a babe in arms to nearly an adult. The only other thing on the table was an open clear plastic tackle box. Each of the small compartments was filled with different colored glass beads. Diane sat down in front of the box and began to stir her finger in the blue beads without looking at them. Her eyes were drifty and Don wondered if she was high on something.

Don took a seat opposite Diane. Bob sat down on Don's left and Billy on his right. Don picked up the photo nearest him. In it, a girl about two years old stood in a muddy yard next to a chicken. Her hair was a tangled mass of brown curls, and she wore nothing except streaks of mud on her legs. Hands on hips, she looked straight at the camera.

"She looks"—Don tried to think of the right word—"determined."

The two men nodded, smiles flitting across their mouths, while Diane continued to poke at the beads, expressionless.

Don put the photograph down on the table and laid his open notebook next to it. "I really appreciate your allowing me to talk with you at this difficult time. As you know, we're planning an in-depth story that will run later in the year, focusing on the people who were killed. As I said on the phone, the story won't dwell on them as victims, but rather it will be a celebration of their lives and what they meant to those around them. Perhaps you could begin by telling me about what Free was like as an adult?" Don wanted to avoid spending too much time wandering around memory lane, talking about her childhood. "Are any of these photos more current? Did she have any particular interests or aspirations?" Aspirations she could fill now that she had her hands on his money, was what Don was thinking. He wanted to know all he could about her. The more he knew about this girl, the quicker he could find her. No one could shed their old life completely. He knew that.

Diane's voice startled all of them. "I remember the night she was born." Her words were stretched out and dreamy and she swayed back and forth in her chair. "There was a full moon out that night. Our friends were there, beating the drums and burning the incense, giving me the strength to push her out. And after she slid out of me, Bob helped the midwife put her on my chest and we waited for the afterbirth to come. Then we wrapped her up and took her outside to show her the world. I remember looking down at her and seeing the moon reflected in her eyes. And you could tell by the look in her eyes that she already knew everything, that she had been someplace that adults had already forgotten about. And her eyes were like, like molten metal. They say all babies' eyes are blue—well, hers were never blue. And she was just looking up at that moon like she recognized it, like maybe she had been there before."

One of the things Don remembered from reading the baby books when Rachel was pregnant was that newborn babies couldn't focus on anything more than eighteen inches away. Even so, for some reason he couldn't shake the image of the newborn baby staring up at the moon. The other two men must have been feeling the same way, because they sat staring in silence at the kitchen table.

Abruptly, Don remembered that a reporter would probably be writing everything down. He scribbled some words—"molten," "eyes," "moon"—in his notebook. In the hope they might pass for shorthand, he made them as illegible as possible.

"Let's go back to what Free was like as an adult," Don said. "What would she have done if she had won the lottery?" In a way, Don guessed she had.

"That's an odd question." Bob looked hurt, and Don realized he was slipping. He had to remember that to these people, Free was dead, not off living the good life someplace, spending Don's money. To these people, asking about a dead girl's dreams might come across as insensitive.

"Oh, sometimes in these interviews I like to ask that question because it reveals people's dreams, their true selves. I mean, we are all in a way forced to enslave ourselves to earn money. But what would a person be like if they were freed from that burden?"

"But we are free," Diane said. "Don't you know that, Mr. Black? You don't have to sell yourself for money. You don't have to live by others' expectations, by society's rules. What would you do if you could do whatever you wanted?" He thought of the baby he had never been allowed to hold, imagined cradling the warm, sweet weight of it against his chest. With difficulty, he pushed that thought away, made himself focus on what was in front of him. These people thought they were free, but they didn't see how they must have freighted their daughter with their expectations.

Don acted as if he had never heard her question. "Your daughter worked at the Petorium, right?"

"Yeah, down at the mall," Billy said. For a man, he had an oddly high-pitched voice. Something small and furry poked out of the back of Billy's shirt, then disappeared. It was there and gone so quickly that Don decided he must have imagined it. "That's where we met, in fact."

"Do you work there, too?" Don inquired politely, while writing down the word "pets" and underlining it. Maybe he could find this girl through her affinity for animals. Too bad pretty much everyone in America had a pet.

Billy rolled his eyes as if Don should know better. "I raise ferrets."

"You're a ferret breeder, then?"

"People never understand this, but I don't like to sell them. In a way, they're like my children." Billy dropped his head and put his hand over his eyes. The little furry something appeared again, popping its head out and then climbing out to sit on Billy's shoulder. Billy raised his head, smiled sadly, and reached back to stroke what Don realized now must be a ferret. To Don it looked like a slightly fluffier rat. "See, I like to have one with me wherever I go. I was looking for some new toys for them, and I took Princess into the Petorium. She was hiding in my sleeve. But then she jumped out, I don't know why. There were three dogs there. They were all on leashes, but they jerked free when they saw Princess. She tried to hide, so she ran into the grooming area. I ran after her, slammed the door closed, and there was Free." He took something from his wallet and handed it to Don. "This was from our first date."

It was a strip of photos from a photo booth, creased where it had been folded in half. Each of the four showed Free and Billy. In the first, she offered an artificial smile, but in the rest her head was turned slightly away from the camera, her eyes looking at Billy's proprietary hand that now lay on her shoulder. In these three photos, as in *The Medford Mail Tribune* photo, her expression was tentative and somehow defeated. Don wondered what had happened, where the little girl with a will of her own had gone. In the photo strip, Billy had the same dreamy expression in every picture, neither happy nor sad. There was something childlike about him, but not in a good way. They made quite a contrast, the girl with a buzz cut and the man with more than enough hair for both of them. Don found himself sympathizing with Free. Maybe she was well shut of him. As if he could hear Don's thoughts, Billy took the photo strip back and slipped it in his wallet.

Don made a show of looking at the other photos Bob began to hand him. Even though they weren't in chronological order, he could discern a progression. In the earlier photos, Free lived up to her name, her head high, her eyes bright. Once she was old enough for school portraits, her eyes no longer looked straight at the camera, and her face looked blank somehow, as if she was denying that she occupied her body at all. The change was especially marked in the five or six photos that showed Free with a buzz cut.

"She had beautiful hair. Why did she cut it all off?"

Diane seemed to stir at that, but it was Bob who answered. "I don't know. She just came home from school one day—this was in seventh grade—and when she came out of the bathroom she had hacked it all off. Then she went and bought a pair of clippers and finished the job. I thought it was kind of strange, because she was always after me to let her fit in. To let her be, quote, normal. Like the other kids." His voice betrayed what he had thought of that idea. "She always wanted me to get a TV set or to let her buy white bread and cow's milk from the grocery store. When she knew that cow's milk gives you mucus."

Don thought he could guess what had happened. Free had given up. If the whole world was going to insist on treating her as different just because her family was, then she would be different. Really different, to prove she didn't care when they teased her. To prove that they couldn't take her any further than she could take herself.

"Do you have any other current photos of her?"

"I've got one more," Billy said.

He had carried in his backpack, and now he bent over it and rummaged around, coming up with a photo of Free wearing a blue smock leaning over a large black dog. Her scissors were a silver blur. She looked as if she had been unaware of the camera, her brows drawn together with concentration. Despite the silliness of her nose ring and her naked scalp, this was the first photo of Free Don had seen where he would have described her as pretty. He reached for it, but Billy pulled it back. Underneath the table, Don became aware of Billy's feet, bouncing up and down in place. "I'm not sure I want to give it to you. Will you promise to give it back right away? I must look at that photo a dozen times a day. Right before," he stammered, "right before, before she died, we were talking about getting married."

"Married?" Bob echoed. Even Diane, who Don had thought wasn't listening, lifted her head.

Billy's feet were jiggling faster than ever. "I know it's kind of old-fashioned, but lately I'd been thinking about it."

Marriage? Don wrote in his notebook. Was that what had inspired Free to run off—the prospect of marrying this empty-headed boy? "What did you two like to do for fun?" Don asked. "Did you ever travel?"

Billy shrugged. "We went to the coast a couple of times."

"What did she dream of doing? Did she ever talk about wanting to travel overseas or down to Mexico?" The three of them were shaking their heads. "Or did she speak any foreign languages?"

"Free?" Billy echoed, incredulous. "She dropped out of high school in eleventh grade."

Bob looked up. "They were feeding her head with all their phony expectations."

Don resisted the urge to roll his eyes. His own mother hadn't had much use for formal education, but at least she hadn't openly mocked it. These people were so firmly mired in the past that they didn't realize it had hardened around them like a carapace.

"She told me once," Billy said, "that she was tired of people teasing her because she didn't fit in."

Bob looked angry. "You create your own reality. I tried to tell her that, but she didn't understand."

Don wondered if her parents would have accepted Free's reality if it had included shaving her underarms instead of her head. He tried to steer the conversation back on track. "This might be a little awkward to ask about, but this boy's car she was found in—"

Bob cut in. "What are you talking about, man?"

"Jamie Labot. The boy whose car your daughter was found in."

"You must be thinking of someone else. Free's body was found in her car. That's how they knew it was her, even though she was so, so . . ." Bob's words trailed off.

"I'm sorry." Don's words came slowly as his brain rapidly recalculated things. "I'm doing so many follow-up stories, sometimes I get a little confused. But that's no excuse. Now just so I'm sure I've got everything straightened out, was she traveling with any one?"

"No." Billy shook his head. "She just took her Impala and went to visit her sister. Man, she loved that car. The radio didn't work, but she said it just gave her time to think."

Maybe Jamie's parents had been at least halfway right when they insisted Jamie didn't have a girlfriend. Free hadn't been the other woman. The only other woman in this story was the woman who had been found dead in Free's car. Don was getting more confused. If Free had been traveling by herself, then how had she ended up with Jamie's bag, known to ask for him by name? But still someone else must have died, someone the police didn't know was missing. Free must have found the money after the accident. Even so, she was someone who thought fast on her feet, fast enough to know that when she found a bag of money it was best to keep her mouth shut, best to take the money and run.

"Are there other friends of hers I could interview?" Don said, meaning were there other friends of hers she might have told the truth to.

They all thought about it for a minute. "She had friends in high school, but I don't think there's anyone else close now," Bob said slowly. "She got along well with people, but she was always, you know, quiet."

Don was getting a picture here. Free had been a woman sur-rounded by—even overwhelmed by—other, stronger personalities. Now that she was on her own, what would she do? Who would she be? Would she even be the person they had known?

"Are you a beader, Mr. Black?" Diane asked him, breaking into the conversation, her question from left field.

"No," Don said, humoring her. It was pretty clear she had checked out, either from grief or from drugs.

"You should try it. Beading requires you to sit down, slow down and do something with your hands. These are skills we can all benefit from." Diane's eyes were empty, her words sounding as if she had said them so many times the meaning had leaked away long ago. Her fingers moved over the compartments of beads as she talked, unerringly choosing one color and then another without looking at them, threading each bead onto a clear plastic thread that Don thought might be fishing line.

"Do you know what the beads mean?" Her words were flat, each equally accented.

This time Don just shook his head.

"Each color has a meaning. Purple, for example, stands for wisdom. Red for cheerfulness." She selected and threaded each color as she spoke. "White for peace, orange for strength, pink for tenderness." For a moment, her hands paused, hovering above the tray. He wondered if she were thinking about pink's other, more traditional meaning, about blue being for baby boys and pink for girls. Although probably these people had just wrapped Free in a homemade piece of tie-dye. Diane's head began to fall forward, and then she jerked it upright again. She blinked twice, and Don could tell she was back behind her eyes now, fully alive, as she looked at him with some emotion he could not name. "Black stands for protection, dark blue for courage, light green for knowledge. And these clear beads here, do you know what they stand for?"

Bob cleared his throat. "Honey, I don't know that Mr. Black is interested in beading. It's not like we're at the country fair. He came to talk about Free."

Diane continued as if he hadn't spoken. "They stand for the truth, Mr. Black. They stand for truth."

And suddenly Diane's eyes weren't drifty anymore, but focused on him. Was it his imagination, or did they hold an accusation? Finally, he had to break away from her stare. The other two men seemed to have noticed nothing, not even paying attention to her talk about beads, let alone hearing any deeper meaning. Don's mind whirled. Did she know that her daughter wasn't dead? Did she know that Don's only wish was to track down her daughter and get back his money? And that getting back his money would probably lead to the death of her daughter—for real?

All Don knew right now was that he had to get away from this woman with her witchy eyes.

Twenty-nine

Monday, OCTOBER 23, 5:35 P.M.

Free had bought a thirteen-inch TV for the living room, and she and Lexi were watching NBC Nightly News when she began to feel the baby kick in earnest. Free pressed her hand against the spot, feeling it both from the inside and the outside. She pulled up her shirt and tugged down the waistband of her pants, and then she saw it, the skin rippling up for a minute and then going back into place. Feeling a mixture of delight, amazement and fear, she began to laugh. Lexi looked over at her with a shocked expression, and Free realized she had laughed at the exact same moment as Tom Brokaw was describing how a man had shot his wife, son and newborn daughter.

"I can see the baby kicking," Free explained. "Look—look right here." She pointed at a spot a few inches below her ribs.

"Are you supposed to be able to *see* it?" Lexi looked like she thought they should call Peggy to make sure something wasn't terribly wrong.

"I guess so. I never thought about it before."

The phone rang, cutting off whatever Lexi had been about to say. She answered it, her tone already combative. Her soon-to-be ex-husband had taken to calling every night, each time with a new demand. Gene wanted Lexi to keep him on her dental plan. Gene wanted to dig up the flowering quince in the backyard. Gene was hoping to drop by to pick up the silverware, which he was now sure had been a wedding present from his side of the family. Each time she hung up, Lexi would calm herself with a cigarette in the backyard while Free listened to her rant.

But tonight, rather than launching into another rebuttal, Lexi just said, "Yes, she is. Just a minute," and handed the phone to Free. "It's for you."

"Hello?"

"Lydia? Lydia Watkins?" A man's voice, low. Free felt a spurt of fear. Who thought that Lydia Watkins lived here? Had someone tracked her down, thinking she was the real Lydia?

"This is, um, this is Lydia."

"This is Sergeant Craig Cole. You know, from the hit-and-run on Friday?"

"Oh, hi!" Free told herself that the emotion that arced through her body was relief.

"One of the reasons I called was to see how things are going for you. Are you and the baby still doing okay?"

"We're both doing fine." It felt weird to talk about herself in the plural. "I have a bruise the size of a softball near my hipbone, so I guess I know for sure where I hit myself when I fell. But other than that I'm okay."

"Good. I'm really glad to hear that." He paused, and when he spoke again, his tone sounded clipped and official. "The other reason I was calling is that I need to follow up on Friday's accident. We haven't been able to locate the driver who fled the scene. I need to get a better description of the vehicle, as well as a detailed account of exactly what happened. As far as we can determine, you are the only witness who saw the whole thing from the beginning. Would you be able to come in tomorrow?"

She hesitated, but what else could she say? "Sure, I guess so." Free didn't really want to be in a place where she would be surrounded by cops, but she couldn't think of a good excuse. And refusing to cooperate might draw more attention than simply going in, providing the little information she remembered and leaving. They arranged to meet at eleven o'clock at Central Precinct, which turned out to be only a few blocks from the scene of the accident.

When Free put down the phone, Lexi said, "What are you so happy about?"

"What do you mean?"

"You've got that cat-that-ate-the-canary look."

"No, I don't. It was only that cop who took me to the hospital on Friday. He's just a nice guy, that's all."

"Mmm hmm." Lexi looked back down at her paper.

As she got ready to go to the police station, Free washed her face and began to apply makeup, trying to emulate the expert application of the saleswoman who had sold her $149 worth of cosmetics at Nordstrom two days ago. Slowly, Free was learning not to start when she caught sight of her own reflection in a shop window, complete with hair and brightly colored lips.

Pausing on Lexi's top step, Free took a deep breath. It was a perfect fall day. The snap in the air belied the patches of bright blue sky. A couple of days before she had bought a pregnancy tape at Baby Togs, and now she pressed the play button on her Walkman. One of her legs felt numb and the other achy. The pregnancy tape described this as "ligament discomfort." The narrator was a man with a cheerful, overly articulate voice. Free imagined that if it had been him feeling it, he wouldn't have labeled it anything so half-hearted as "discomfort." The tape came to an end, then switched to side two. This side was narrated by a woman. "Most women have very few problems in pregnancy," she crooned, "but in the last three months it's not unusual to have heartburn, constipation, sleeping problems, nose bleeds, varicose veins, headaches, abdominal pain and swelling of the feet and ankles." Free guessed this was the same woman they hired to do voice-overs in pharmaceutical commercials, the one who was able to say things like, "Side effects may include fainting, nausea, vomiting and kidney problems," and make them all sound desirable. Free switched off the tape and stuck the headphones in her purse.

As she walked through downtown, a breeze scudded red and orange maple leaves ahead of her. People with briefcases marched along, talking on their cell phones, seemingly oblivious to the beauty around them. Despite the faint ache in her legs, Free walked briskly, swinging her arms, feeling light on her feet even though her belly seemed to have popped out an inch further overnight. On such a day, she told herself, it was only natural to feel full of energy, completely alive and aware.

Everywhere downtown were reminders that there was only one more week until Halloween. The store windows showed masks, costumes, strings of pumpkin lights and gauzy fake cobwebs. Even the clothing stores had managed to work Indian corn, scarecrows and hay bales into their displays. Free was reminded of her dad with a longing so painful it made her throat close. Bob loved Halloween with its pagan roots. Every year he made elaborate papier-mâché masks for himself and Diane. More often than not, they had left Free and Moon to deal with the traditional trick-or-treaters while they went off to an adult party that usually featured Wiccans, Druids and a strange mix of pagan rituals and modern drugs. Last year, Bob and Diane hadn't made it home until dawn because they accidentally took Quaaludes thinking they were speed and ended up falling asleep on someone's couch. "Never," Free had scolded them, "never take anything unless you are absolutely sure of what it is."

As she waited on the corner across from Central Precinct for the light to change, Free wiped her hands on her jacket in case they were sweaty. In the parking lot next to her, a dark-skinned man was bustling around a permanently parked white catering van with a sign reading INDIA TANDOORI OVEN. The front seats of the van were stacked to the ceiling with boxes holding plastic utensils and paper plates. On the side, a tiny metal awning sheltered three green plastic lawn chairs.

Central Precinct's lobby was a circular soaring space, empty except for a green granite directory. The floor was laid out in alternating squares of pink and white marble, set on the diagonal. On both sides of the room, a set of stairs curved upward in perfect symmetry, flanked by shining silver handrails. Blue-uniformed cops walked quickly past Free, their steps echoing. Posted on the wall was a warning that visitors had to check in at the front desk. She found it in a narrow, low-ceilinged hallway tucked behind the lobby. Behind a thick sheet of Plexiglas, three clerks waited. Free leaned close to the round silver grill. Next to her, a Hispanic man pressed a torn scrap of paper against the glass and said, "I need to talk to this guy."

"I have an appointment to see Craig Cole," Free said.

After checking a list, the woman slid over a pen and a red-and-white badge that said *Visitor* with a line underneath. After a second's hesitation, Free filled in Lydia's name.

The microphone buzzed and snapped when the clerk spoke. "Go to the end of the hall and wait by the door."

The door opened and Craig stepped out with a smile, his hand outstretched. She had been expecting him to be dressed in a blue uniform, like the other cops, but he wore a black long-sleeved polo shirt and black dress slacks. The long stretch of a single color made him look formal, reserved and in control. A few dark hairs curled over the edge of the white T-shirt he wore underneath the polo shirt. Free scolded herself for noticing, then wondered what he saw when he looked at her. A matronly blob? A silly girl who fainted over the sight of transmission fluid?

"I really appreciate your coming down." Craig's hand was warm and dry, his grip firm.

"It's no problem. Besides, it gives me another chance to thank you for taking me to the hospital and making sure I was all right." Free found herself flushing as she thought about just how much of her he had seen, which was kind of silly. In her family, everyone had showered together in order to conserve water. This had included any overnight guests.

"I'm just glad everything turned out okay." He turned all business. "Let's go back to my office." He walked ahead of her with an easy stride, nodding or saying hello to the half-dozen people they passed. It was clear Craig was on his own turf. After leading her through a rat's nest of cubicles, he finally stopped at one that held a desk and two cheap-looking office chairs with orange upholstery. He took the one nearest the desk, and she took the other. Free looked around his cubicle with interest. In contrast to many of the desks they had passed, Craig's was neat. Instead of blizzards of paper, there were orderly piles. Instead of walls covered by push-pinned photos of what she supposed were perps and victims, children and wives, he had a single framed reproduction of an old painting, a portrait of a young woman. Wearing a dangling pearl earring, she looked at the viewer with wide blue eyes.

"She's beautiful," Free said, nodding at the painting.

"What? Oh, the Vermeer? It's called 'Girl with a Pearl Earring.' I was lucky enough to be back in D.C. for a conference in 1992 when they had the big Vermeer show at the National Gallery." Craig took the top file folder off his desk and opened it, then picked up a pen. "Okay, I was wondering if you could tell me more about this truck that took off. The driver of the Camaro has turned out not to be too good with details. He's still in shock about what happened to his quote-unquote classic car."

Free closed her eyes. She saw the scene unfolding in front of her. "Well, the truck was definitely a Dodge. I remember staring at the name stamped on the tailgate after it passed me. A red Dodge. New, I think, or fairly new. And it was one of those over-size trucks—what do they call them—three-quarter ton?"

Craig made a note without answering her half-question. His fingers were long and slender, with nails so short she wondered if he bit them. "What shade of red was the pickup? Dark? Light?"

"Bright red. I guess I would say blood red, only it's kind of embarrassing to say the word blood after that fainting spell."

"I've seen civilians make that mistake about transmission fluid before. And didn't you say something about having been in a bad collision recently?"

Free had planned all the lies she would tell, and she offered him one now that served the dual purpose of answering the question of where the father of her child was. "My husband was killed in a car crash a few months ago, before we even knew I was pregnant."

Craig's eyes widened in sympathy, and Free couldn't help but feel a little guilty. "I'm so sorry. Were you with him?"

"Yes, but I wasn't hurt." She straightened up, trying to indicate that she didn't want to talk about it anymore.

He went on to ask her about whether the pickup had had any bumper or window stickers (none that she could remember) or whether she recalled anything about the license plate (only that it had been the ubiquitous white Oregon plate, the one with a green tree in the middle). Her description of the driver felt equally useless to her—a guy in his early twenties, with short blond hair. It became clear that Craig was just going through the formalities as he brought the interview to an end.

"I'm sorry I didn't pay more attention," Free said. To her intense embarrassment, her stomach sent out a loud rumble.

Craig's mouth quirked into a smile. "It's sounds like I'm keeping you."

"No, no, that's okay. There's no place I have to be."

"That's good, because I'd like to take you to lunch to thank you for all your help."

Free colored even further. "Oh, no, really, that's okay."

"I insist. And I'll warn you, you don't want to argue with me."

"That's really not necessary. Thank you all the same."

"I told you, I'm not taking no for an answer."

Could Craig be interested in her? Free's belly loomed in her peripheral vision. There was no way this straight-arrow cop would hit on a widow with a belly out to there. He probably felt sorry for her. She didn't say yes, but she stopped saying no.

Taking a dark-colored zippered jacket off the back of his chair,

Craig slipped it on. On their way back through the main lobby, they walked underneath a hand-carved wooden eagle, six-foot wings outstretched in flight, mounted above the door. She had expected that they would go to a nearby restaurant, but instead Craig headed right for the India Tandoori Oven catering van she had passed an hour ago as the owner was setting up. Now he was efficiently dealing with a long line of customers, many of them cops. Most nodded at Craig, or said hello, and all of them seemed to be looking at her with curiosity. Mentally Free kicked herself again for not having wiggled out of his unexpected offer.

As the line inched forward, Free started to fumble with Lydia's purse.

"My treat," Craig said. "What do you want? The mutter paneer is good."

"What's that?" Only a few of the items listed on the white board menu sounded familiar, but the air was filled with the savory smell of seared meat and unfamiliar spices.

"Fresh green peas with cheese and spices. The vegetable korma is good, too—that's assorted green vegetables with raisins and cashews. I'm going to have the Goa lamb curry."

Lamb. Free had eaten meat on the sly when she was away from home, particularly Chicken McNuggets from the McDonald's next to the Petorium, and now Lexi was introducing her to exotic meats like pancetta or basil chicken sausage. But to Free, lamb still meant little lambs gamboling in the fields. Her parents' philosophy had always been not to eat anything with a face.

As far as Free was concerned, though, chickens didn't count. When Free was growing up, she had been in charge of feeding the chickens and gathering their eggs. They were stupid, nervous birds that pecked her bare feet and insisted on laying eggs in places even they forgot about. "I think I'll have the tandoori chicken." Feeling adventurous, she added, "And a can of guava nectar."

After getting their order, Craig said, "Come on. Let's go sit by the river." They walked a couple of blocks and then waited at Naito Parkway for the light to change. When it did, he took her arm protectively, swiveling his head to make sure people turning left didn't run into them. "You wouldn't believe how many pedestrians have been killed on this street. People think they can jaywalk, but they don't realize that some of these cars have just gotten off the freeway and are still going fifty miles an hour."

After crossing the street, they faced a long swath of green, as wide as a city block, that bordered the river as far as she could see. "Oh, this is beautiful," Free said in surprise. There was something about the stretch of open space that she found immediately calming. Now that she knew about it, she would walk over here more often. Free would be glad when she could saunter through the city like a native, know the names of the neighborhoods, identify the mountains, anticipate the weather.

"You haven't been down here before?"

"I just moved from Pendleton about two months ago." Following him past the fountain, Free pushed the date back so that there would be no way he would connect her with the chain-reaction accident.

"You know, you don't live that far from me. I just live in the John's Landing area—it's less than a mile from your house. There's a nice park along the Willamette River down there, too. You should check it out. This is Waterfront Park. There are events here nearly all year—Cinco de Mayo, a big carnival for Rose Festival, the Bite. My favorite is the Waterfront Blues Festival over the Fourth of July. People put their blankets out on the grass and listen to blues and picnic all day, then watch the fireworks at night." As he spoke, Craig sat down on a bench facing the fountain and perpendicular to the river and began to spread out the food.

Free sat and turned to face the river. She hadn't realized how tense she was until her breath let itself out as a sigh loud enough that Craig looked up and smiled. The jumbled buildings of downtown were to her back, a stretch of green to her left, and the fountain to her right. Directly in front of her was the river, bordered by an ornate metal fence.

"You can see why they sometimes call Portland Bridge City,"

Craig said. There were two bridges upriver from them and two down, each cutting the cloudy sky into a different and pleasing pattern of arches and curves. The other side of the river looked a lot less pleasant, mostly windowless industrial buildings surrounded by the loops of exits and overpasses. The steady traffic was far enough away that it looked like toys, and Free was reminded of her one plane ride with her sister, when they had looked down at the tiny cars.

Craig turned and pointed behind him at the fence along the river. "During the 1996 floods, the water rose so high that they thought downtown was going to be flooded. The mayor asked for volunteers, and hundreds of them came down and bolted plywood along that seawall, hoping to stop it."

"Did it work?"

"We never found out. The river ended up cresting about a foot below, so we got lucky."

They began to eat, and Free found that she liked everything. With both of their mouths full, neither of them attempted conversation for a few moments.

Free pretended to watch the passersby, while stealing glances at Craig. He seemed like the all-American guy, the kind who still had a baseball glove and could lope quickly around the bases, the kind who held the door for little old ladies and coached his kid's soccer team on weekends. The kind of guy who never talked to her in high school, the kind she had lusted after from afar. But that kind of guy dated the cheerleaders, or very occasionally one of the quiet, smart girls. That kind of guy had never really looked at her, never seen past the buzz cut and the nose ring. She wondered what Craig would see if she took off her wig, twisted a silver ring back into her nose. Would he look at her the same way he was now? Every time their glances met, she imagined she felt a little hum of interest coming from him. And she couldn't help but notice that he didn't have a wedding ring, although that didn't mean anything.

She found herself thinking of her parents again. They would

be horrified to see her sitting companionably with a cop. Cops were jack-booted thugs on power trips. They hauled you in for smoking pot, which everyone knew was harmless, and they weren't above planting hard drugs in your pocket to make for a better arrest. The fuzz tapped your phones, stole your mail, infiltrated your meetings and beat you up when they arrested you. So why did she feel so comfortable with Craig? It must be, she decided, that she was no longer so much Free Meeker, but more Lydia Watkins, a woman who had probably always trusted the cops.

"Were you a jock in high school?" Free spoke around a mouthful of chewy naan bread after a middle-aged jogger huffed past them, she and Craig sharing a repulsed smile at how his mesh T-shirt showed off his pot belly and hairy back.

"Hmm—not really. I ran track, but that was about it."

"You just remind me of the guys who were on the baseball team."

"What do you mean?"

Unable to put it into words, Free smiled, shrugged and used the last bit of bread to mop up the final teaspoon of sauce. It was something about Craig's tanned face, or the way he walked, with a bounce in his step as if he was always ready to steal a base or leap for a fly ball, or the way his green eyes continually seemed to be scanning the distance.

"Why did you move to Portland?"

Free found an answer that was true, word to word, even if it wasn't the whole truth. "I couldn't keep living where I had been. Too many memories."

"It must get lonely being in a strange city, though. Isn't it hard, not knowing anyone?"

"I'm meeting people. I mean, I have my roommate, Lexi, that woman who answered the phone. And I see my doctor once a week. I probably talk to people too much in the grocery store." Not wanting him to ask her any more questions, she turned the tables. "So, why did you become a cop?"

"You know, to be the good guy. The guy in the white hat.

The guy with the 'S' on his chest. When I was a kid, I always wanted to be that guy." Craig seemed to be laughing at himself, but Free thought he couldn't hide that part of him that still believed in what he was saying. "And the guy who lived next door was a cop. He was the best. My dad wasn't around much when I was growing up, so in a lot of ways he was like my dad."

"Do you work with him now? Or is he retired?"

He pressed his lips together and she guessed the answer before he spoke. "About five years ago, he was killed by a runaway with a stolen gun."

"I'm sorry." Free changed to a lighter subject. "So is this what you do all day? Interview people about traffic accidents?"

Craig looked down at the takeout container, then back up at her. "Actually, it's not. I have a confession to make. I used to be a patrol officer, but I'm not anymore. Now I'm a criminalist. I investigate crime scenes, not traffic accidents. I asked if I could do your follow-up interview instead of the traffic division. There's only four of them, and they deal with twenty hit-and-runs a day, so they were happy to say yes. I just wanted to see you again, find out how you were doing. At the hospital you just seemed so totally alone. I was worried about you."

Great. That was all she needed. A cop worried about her welfare. Fate offered her a way out when a big drop splashed on the end of her nose, followed by another on her cheek. Free looked up at the rapidly darkening sky. "Looks like it's time to get going. Thanks so much for buying me lunch."

"No problem. And if you remember anything more about that truck, give me a call. Let me give you my card. He took one from his wallet, and wrote on the back with a pen from inside his jacket pocket. "Here's my beeper number. Sometimes it's easier to reach me there."

"Sure," Free said, intending on throwing it away as soon as he was out of sight. "I'll do that."

Thirty

Tuesday, OCTOBER 24, 4:37 P.M.

Roy peeled his tongue off the roof of his mouth. When he raised his head from the couch, it was like lifting a stone. Eyes half-closed, he stumbled into the kitchen, turned on the faucet and stuck his mouth under the water. It tasted brackish at first, but he didn't care, swallowing and swallowing. He had been asleep since sometime early Saturday morning, and he wasn't sure how long it had been before that since he ate or drank. With his head tilted, Roy had to hold on to the edge of the counter to keep from falling over, but finally he had drunk enough.

He was scrubbing the sleep from his eyes when he remembered. Those two guys! He had offed those two doofuses. Thinking again of how that big one had tried to run away sent a thrill down Roy's spine. He had been so cool, so calm. Sighting an imaginary rifle, he fired again, making "pow" noises with his mouth.

He was suddenly, ravenously hungry. In the back of the cupboard, he found a box of Lucky Charms. He grabbed it off the shelf, but the fucking thing was empty except for some cereal dust. Not even a goddamn marshmallow. He threw the box on the floor, stamped on it, then picked it up again and tried to rip it in half. It refused to tear. With a snarl, he threw the box behind him, where it landed on top of the broken stuff that had once belonged to Lydia.

Maybe there was something good in the freezer. A venison steak or maybe a frozen dinner. He opened the door and then jumped back. The sour taste of vomit rose in his throat.

Shit. He'd forgotten about that damn cat. Wrapped in a once-white dishtowel, it stared at Roy with its remaining eye. He slammed the door shut.

In the refrigerator, the milk had gone sour, but he found some square cheese and ate piece after piece, so hungry it was hard to be patient enough to unwrap the plastic. Behind a melting blob of what had once been lettuce, he finally found two of the micro-wave burritos he liked. Not bothering with a plate, Roy put them in the microwave, then burned his fingers and tongue while he wolfed them down.

If Lydia hadn't left, the refrigerator would be full. If Lydia hadn't left, the house would be swept up. If Lydia hadn't left, everything would be so neat a man wouldn't know where he could sit down without risking getting something dirty. But she had left. If Lydia were here now, he'd beat her so bad she couldn't show her face at the grocery store, so bad she couldn't walk away from him again, so bad she would never tell another soul what wasn't their business.

After what had happened at the gravel pit, Roy had spent three hours at Jiggles, buying lap dance after lap dance from some chick named Darcy, finally throwing in an extra fifty for her to join him at a little private party in the parking lot. And then he'd come home and crashed. Now he didn't even know what day it was. He turned on the TV and flipped around through the channels until he finally found a cable news show that told him it was Tuesday. Roy counted on his fingers. He'd been asleep for nearly three days.

He flipped through the channels again, looking for *Baywatch* reruns, but he couldn't find any. He was about ready to turn off the TV when he caught a local newscaster, all prissy in a collar buttoned up under her chin, saying something about the killings at the gravel pit. Up above her shoulder was a photo of the gravel pit and some yellow crime-scene tape. The words *Badger Ridge Killings* ran across the bottom. The woman on TV said they were looking at all available leads, but Roy didn't feel too worried. No one but Warren and the two dead guys had seen Roy or his Monte Carlo that day. And Warren could be counted on not to talk. Pop-pop's rifle was now at the bottom of the river, in a spot deep enough where it would never see the light of day. When the woman started yammering on about county budget shortfalls, Roy turned off the TV. What he had done, he figured, was what they called the perfect crime. The cops would fall all over themselves trying to figure out who had known those two guys, who had had reasons to kill them. They'd look at their coworkers and friends, they'd look at their current and ex-wives, and they'd look at their kids. They'd spend weeks chasing their own tails before finally giving up.

Thinking of Warren reminded Roy that he had to get Warren the money before he would tell Shari to start looking for Lydia. He checked his wallet. Three fives and two ones. He maybe had two or three hundred in checking. Wasn't he due some kind of severance check from Dri-N-Fresh? Roy walked out to the mailbox. It was jammed full, but only with bills. He searched through twice. Nothing. He walked inside the house and let the useless pieces of paper fall to the floor.

You couldn't sell blood for that kind of money. He looked around the living room. Nothing he owned would bring it either. He needed some Benjamins real bad. He was also out of meth, and he could feel the need for it beginning to seize him up.

He thought about the biddy who lived across the street, the one who had called the cops on him. There had been rumors for years that she didn't believe in banks, that she had squirreled all her money away in hidey-holes all through her house.

Roy thought about it and thought about it. Then he put on his coat and walked out the door, determined to get what he needed.

Thirty-one

Wednesday, OCTOBER 25, 3:07 P.M.

Four more days. Don had four more days to get his money back. He had turned Free Meeker's life upside down and shaken it, and come up with nothing. Nothing that meant anything, anyway.

If you were willing to pay for information, you could have it. They didn't call it the Information Age for nothing. You no longer needed some grubby private investigator wearing a dirty trench coat, wafting whiskey with every breath. Instead, you E-mailed a business that called itself an information broker. In turn, it could access a thousand databases, both legal and not so legal, depending on how much you were willing to spend. To keep the transaction at arm's length, Don used both a dummy E-mail account and a credit card that was ultimately billed to a shell company in Costa Rica.

The first thing Don bought was Free's parents' telephone records, as well as those of Moon and Billy. But the only out-of-town phone calls in the last three weeks had all been among themselves. The only exception had been a phone call at nine o'clock at night to Free's parents from the state police. There were no calls from pay phones or cells.

As he traced his finger over the various printouts, figuring out the sequence of events, Don could imagine what lay behind each call. First came the devastating phone call from the state police that their daughter might be among the dead. Then Free's parents had called Moon and asked her to identify her sister's charred body. Next they had called Billy and broken the news. A gap of about two hours probably reflected everyone waiting while Moon completed her grim errand. Then, dread suspicion turned cold reality, came the calls from Moon, first to her parents and then to Billy. The next flurry of phone calls had come the day after the accident. It was easy to guess that these calls had been to work out the details of returning the body and arranging for the funeral. And in between and around and always there must have been the exchange of tears and memories. Don knew all about how that worked, too.

In addition to getting phone records Don purchased bank account information. There had been no recent influx of money. Billy's checking account had a current balance of $335.13. Deposits were made regularly by his father. He had no savings. Free's parents, whom the paper had pointedly called "life companions," had paid out nearly nine hundred dollars for funeral expenses, leaving them with a little less than a thousand in their account. According to their banking records, neither one of them had income from a regular job. Instead, there had been a steady trickle of small checks. Most of them had been written on the weekends to Starshine Beading Supply.

The only real surprise had been eighteen-year-old Moon Morton, who had recently married a seventy-three-year-old who owned a chain of auto-supply stores. On the surface, it was hard to guess who was getting the short end of the deal—the seventy-three-year-old who now had an eighteen-year-old in his bed, or the eighteen-year-old who now had her name on a joint checking account containing $544,916.37.

Don had worked every nook and cranny in Free's life, investigated the people she was friendly with at the Petorium, had even had her family and friends' comings and goings monitored. About all he had figured out was that Billy had a skirt on the side, a Taco

Bell counter girl who was as beautiful as she was dumb, and that Moon's new husband had made a few shady deals back in his salad days, thirty years before. But there was nothing, absolutely nothing, that led him to believe that Free's friends and family thought she was anything but dead.

Whatever this Free Meeker had done, it seemed she had accomplished it without their complicity. And whatever sympathy Don had felt for her when talking to her parents had dwindled away and vanished altogether as the days passed with no sign of her. Because by stealing his money, this girl had signed Don's death warrant.

Thirty-two

Wednesday, OCTOBER 25, 7:32 P.M.

"So what did Peggy say today?"

Free's mouth was full so she had to wait to answer. She and Lexi had fixed chicken breasts covered with a sauce made from chanterelle mushrooms sautéed in butter, thickened with cream and flavored with rosemary. Free kept dragging forkfuls of rice or steamed broccoli through the sauce, determined to eat every last drop. It was so good she figured she could have boiled one of her Birkenstocks, covered it with the sauce and happily eaten every bite.

"Peggy says everything seems like it's progressing just fine. Oh—I'll be going to birthing class this Saturday. It's an all-day class, so I won't be around much that day."

"Aren't you supposed to have a, um, partner for that?" For just a second, Lexi's gaze met hers.

"I suppose most women are going to be there with their husbands or boyfriends, but Peggy said it was okay if I came by myself."

"If you want," Lexi said, not looking directly at Free, "I'll be your labor coach."

"Really?" Free didn't want to get her hopes up. "That's asking a lot. I mean, there's not only the class, but they say a first labor can last twenty-four hours or even longer." This was another fun fact from her pregnancy tape.

"Well, I don't think it would be fair for you to leave me sitting at home, wondering about what's going on, while you go waltzing off in a taxi or something. Besides, I'm nosy. I don't want to have to wait up until you finally get around to calling me and telling me what you had and how it went."

"You're sure?" Free felt a warm glow of friendship. How long had it been since she had had a close friend who would do such a big thing for her?

"Of course I'm sure, Lydia."

And Free was reminded that Lexi wasn't really friends with her, but with some woman named Lydia.

Thirty-Three

Two days. Don had two days until the money was due. And he was no nearer to finding that money than he had been in the beginning. He had paid dearly to have the flight lists for both domestic and international flights checked, but no Free Meeker had flown anyplace under that name in the last two weeks. He had dispatched searchers throughout downtown Portland, but while there were a dozen girls in Pioneer Square who resembled her, thanks to a certain sameness granted by a buzz cut and a nose ring, none was actually her. He had chased down every lead, and he had come up with nothing.

After the next two days were used up, what would happen then? He didn't really think they would do anything right after the deadline expired. At least Don told himself that. That would be like killing the goose that laid the golden eggs. If they eliminated him, then they eliminated their ability to turn dirty money into clean.

But if he was wrong, then he might be dead in two days. Don wondered what would happen to him then. Would he just be dead, be nothing? Maybe it would be good to be quiet, to finally be at rest. But if that wasn't how it worked, if there was a hell, he would probably go to it. He had never intentionally hurt an innocent person, but there were too many people he had dispatched from this earth. And if there was a heaven? Would he be there with Rachel? With Rachel and their child?

Sixteen years before, Don had come home after a long day to find Rachel lying in a lake of blood on the floor of the bathroom. She was curled like a comma around the bulge of the baby that still weighted down her body. There was so much blood Don could smell it, an oily sweetish smell. So much blood Don could taste it in the very air. And even as he ran to Rachel, he saw it was old blood, turning brown, so thick and tacky it sucked at his shoes. There was blood running down the sides of the toilet seat, blood soaked into a towel discarded on the floor, blood saturating her gray maternity pants. And there was not the least bit of human warmth in Rachel when Don kneeled by her side and howled, howled for the woman and the baby he would never hold.

He didn't know how long he pressed her against him. Finally, his eyes focused on the smeared handprints on the cream-colored wall, about waist high. Had Rachel tried to get up, or had she staggered as she fell?

Placenta previa, the doctor who did the autopsy had called it. The placenta had been attached over Rachel's cervix, then ripped away. "Did she ever have an ultrasound?"

Don shook his head.

The other man shrugged. "If she had had one, it probably would have caught it. But there are still some old-time doctors who don't think it's important in a first pregnancy, with an obviously healthy mother. Placenta previa is quite uncommon in a primagravida, a first-time mom. But when it does occur, time is of the essence."

Don heard the words as a personal accusation, even though he knew the doctor wasn't making one. But there was no denying the fundamental truth. He had left Rachel alone, to die alone. "Does it hurt?" His voice so strangled he didn't recognize it.

"No. The bleeding occurs suddenly and without pain. Some women delay seeking help because of that absence of pain. And there's the element of surprise. She probably bled so fast she didn't have time to change her mind. She had at most ten minutes before she passed out. Death occurred within half an hour." The doctor guessed what Don was thinking. "Even if she had been brought in during those first few minutes, it would have been touch and go. The veins simply collapse from blood loss."

In the first few months after her death, Don's thoughts would obsessively return to what he had been doing while Rachel lay on the floor, the life blood gushing from her. Had he been laughing? Sharing a hit with Barry? Driving, singing along with the CD player? Yawning, eating lunch, filling out paperwork to show that money had been someplace it hadn't? If he and Rachel had really loved each other as much as they said, if they had really been connected the way Rachel had promised, then why hadn't his own heart stopped beating when hers did?

The obstetrician who had treated Rachel had a little hobby: woodworking. One day, about six weeks after Rachel's death, he had a most unfortunate accident with a saw, severing his right hand. Death from blood loss had been almost immediate. The suddenness and the horrific nature of the accident, it was theorized, had prevented him from realizing he needed to go upstairs and phone for help. Instead, he had staggered around his basement hobby shop, blood fountaining from the stump, until finally he lay down and died.

That night, Don had washed the red stains from a yellow rain slicker and matching pants, flushed the drains with bleach, then wrapped the rain clothes in brown paper and deposited them in a Dumpster behind an Albertsons in SE Portland. A few weeks later, driving through the same area, he saw a homeless man with a beard and hair so long they had matted and tangled together, wearing the blindingly yellow outfit, even though it was eighty degrees outside.

Thirty-four

Free had plenty of time to feel anxious as she waited in the long line at the DMV office. The two clerks refused to be harried or hurried, plodding stubbornly along. When one of them went to lunch, he turned his sign around to CLOSED — USE OTHER WINDOW, paying no attention to the groans.

She had chosen this time of day deliberately. Her goal was to get more than a sticker listing a new address for the back of Lydia's driver's license. She wanted a whole new license—one with her picture on the front. The couple of times she had had to hand the license over, like at the hospital, she had been nervous the whole time. Someday someone would look at Lydia's face, then back at Free, and realize that while they looked something alike, the woman in the picture and the woman standing before them were not the same person. Getting a new license was a risk, but a risk Free would have to take just once. And it was a risk she had finally decided was worth it.

When she got to the front of the line, she handed in her change of address form and offered the clerk a flirtatious smile. "Can I get one with a new picture? I don't like the way I look in this one." It truly wasn't the most flattering photo of Lydia. Her chin was dipped down, her eyes were shadowed, and there wasn't the trace of a smile on her face.

Free had been afraid the clerk would scrutinize the photo, but instead his only answer was a grunt. Twenty minutes later, Free had a brand-new license in her wallet—with Lydia's name but Free's address and photo. She walked out of the office with a little bounce in her step. With the acquisition of the driver's license, it felt like she had crossed over a threshold. Now she had proof that she really was Lydia Watkins. The first thing she would do would be to get a library card. And after that, maybe she would open a checking account, and dribble in money a little bit at a time, but never enough to attract the IRS. Still, it would be easier than always paying cash for everything. Clerks tended to look at you a little too closely when you paid for everything with hundred-dollar bills.

Thirty-five

Don's private line rang, startling him. He hadn't been asleep, just somewhere else, resting his head in his hands, his eyes closed. The Caller ID display read *Private Caller*. He was sure it was a reminder from the syndicate. His hand, he was glad to see, was steady as he reached for the phone.

"Hello?"

"May I speak to Don Cannon?" A woman's voice. Hesitant. He allowed himself to relax a fraction.

"Speaking."

"This is Darlene Sherman. From the Stay-A-While? With your sister's address, at least part of it. Your sister must have addressed it with a felt-tip pen, and then the whole package looks like it got wet, so Darlene's address was smeared too. It took them a while to track me down."

Don did not let his tone betray his impatience. "Well, what can you make out?"

"She's definitely still in Portland. And the zip code is nine-seven-two-zero . . . seven? No, it's a one."

Somewhere near downtown then. "How about the street address?"

"It's on something called Southwest Arnold." Darlene's words were infuriatingly slow. "The first two numbers in the address are definitely a one and a three. But I can't make out the last two at all."

"But that's wonderful, Darlene. That means it narrows it down to just a block. We'll be able to find her and get her to a doctor right away. Our mother will be so happy to hear this." Don had a quick flash of his mother, dead at forty-four when her liver gave out. "You don't know how much I appreciate your calling me." He briefly considered offering to pay Darlene, but discarded the idea as being out of character with his original story.

"Can you just let Darlene know how she is? Darlene's been worrying about her, what with that amnesia and all. But she must not have forgotten everything, right? Because she remembered to return the dress to old Darlene. That was sure sweet of her."

"Yes, it certainly was," he agreed. "And I'll let you know how it turns out. You've given me the first real hope of finding her." And the first real hope of finding the missing money. And once he did that, well, any loose ends would have to be taken care of. As Don exchanged a few more pleasantries, not betraying his eagerness to get this woman off the line, he wondered what Darlene would think if she knew she had more than likely just marked Free Meeker for death.

Don drove to the Central Library in downtown Portland. The grand old building had been recently restored, although the gray granite walls were still an irresistible target for the city's graffiti artists. Faint ghosts of tags still glowed on the walls, sunk down into the pores where even the highest-powered steam cleaner couldn't reach without wearing away the rock.

At the reference section, Don requested the city directory for Portland. A city directory had nothing to do with the telephone company. The city directory was organized into two sections. One was alphabetical by name and the other was indexed according to street location. It was the second directory that had brought Don here. This was the kind of search he could do cheaper, quicker and better on his own. He saw that there were four houses on SW

Arnold Street that began with a 13. No apartment buildings, which made his search infinitely easier. Each listing showed the full name of the person who lived at each address, and if it was rented or owned. A code detailed how long the person had lived there, the person's marital status and the name of the spouse, as well as the names of the other people occupying the dwelling. Sometimes even the person's job title and employer were listed.

The four houses, according to the city directory, were occupied by a married couple in their twenties with three children and a Hmong last name, a retired couple in their late seventies, a married couple in their late twenties, and a single man in his fifties who lived with a male roommate, also in his fifties. Nothing obvious jumped out at Don, but still, he knew he was closing in on Free Meeker. He would find her, take back his money, and then do whatever he needed to do.

Thirty-six

Since she had arrived in Portland, Free had avoided being in a car. When she needed to buy groceries or to go downtown, she walked. A few times when her legs had gotten tired, she had taken the bus home. Buses didn't cause her heart to race and the hairs on her scalp to rise.

Of course, she had ridden in the taxi to the hospital, but that was when she was already in the grip of a full-blown panic attack. Before that, the last time she had been in a car was when she freaked out just sitting in the rusted-out Chevette. And the time before that—Free could still feel the impact of each vehicle striking her Impala. She had been slammed against the door, the steering wheel, the window, the seat, until she lost count of the blows. In her dreams, Free still saw the way Lydia had looked at the end, her mouth slack and her eyes empty.

Free had suggested they walk to the birthing class, a distance of about a mile and a half, but Lexi had looked at her as if she were crazy. "It's freezing out there. And to walk there and back would take an hour. I'll warm up the car so we'll be nice and toasty." Not wanting to bruise their tentative friendship, Free didn't press the issue. Besides, she told herself, she was going to have to get used to being in a car again. Someday she was probably even going to have to drive one.

As Lexi drove to the birthing class, Free concentrated on breathing slowly. But that didn't stop her from realizing that when the other woman looked over, she didn't see Free, with her shaven head, nose ring and tattoo. Instead, she saw demure Lydia, with her carefully made-up face and her conservative clothes. Basically, Lexi was seeing what Free had seen a couple of weeks before. It was like some kind of reverse déjà vu. Panic began to build up in Free. Intellectually, she tried to remind herself that was what it had to be. A panic attack. But she felt like she was about to die, go crazy—or both.

Putting her hand on the curve of her belly, Free tried breathing in through her nose and out through her mouth, just as the gruff doctor had told her to at the hospital. She hadn't been practicing the way he had said she should. It had been easier to simply avoid being in a car. Now, as her scalp prickled and her stomach seized up, she realized she should have forced herself earlier to get past the fear. Her chest felt so heavy that it was impossible to take a deep breath.

"Count backward from one hundred by sevens," Lexi said suddenly. Even though she was sitting right next to Free, her voice sounded far away.

"What?" Free could barely hear her.

Lexi put her hand on Free's knee and shook it. "Count backward from one hundred by sevens. Just do it, Lydia. Out loud."

Lexi wasn't making any sense, but Free complied, grateful for any thought, no matter how small, on which she could focus. "One hundred. Ninety-three. Eighty-six. Seventy-nine. Seventy-two. Um, sixty-five . . ." When Free got to "three" and couldn't go any farther, Lexi instructed her to go back to one hundred and do the same thing, only by nines. Thus occupied, Free managed to make it to the medical office building where the class was being held.

But as soon as Lexi pulled into a parking space, Free bolted from the car. Lexi turned off the motor and came around to where

Free stood, her breath coming in pants, her skin wet with cold sweat. Saying nothing, Lexi embraced her. It was odd being comforted by someone who was a couple of inches shorter than she was.

"I had them, too, right after Gene left. Panic attacks are awful, aren't they? I'm sorry, I should have listened to what you were trying to say and remembered about what happened to your husband."

Free was barely able to nod, her chin brushing the softness of the other woman's hair. After a few minutes, the two of them went into the class.

Just before the afternoon break in the birthing class, the instructor held up a short piece of metal duct work in one hand. In the other she held the plastic doll that was serving as a stand-in for a newborn. "Now remember," she said, "that even when you're fully dilated, your cervix is only ten centimeters wide. And the baby has to fit through that space." Unsuccessfully, she butted the baby's head against the metal ring. Then her gaze fell on her wristwatch. "Oops, everyone, it looks like it's time for our break. Let's meet back here in ten minutes."

Lexi broke for the front door, with Free following. Along with a sheepish-looking expectant father, they stood under the building's overhang. Lexi sucked her freshly lit cigarette so hard the end glowed bright red.

"I'm not sure what I was supposed to learn from that last bit, but it wasn't exactly reassuring," Free said.

"Women have been having babies for millions of years. Besides, you never hear about a situation where the baby just gets stuck. And even if it did, they could always do a C-section." Despite her reassurances, Free noticed that Lexi looked a bit green.

The last part of the class concentrated on what life would be like after the baby was born. They each got their own doll and practiced diapering it, burping it and holding it for breastfeeding.

Then the instructor dimmed the lights and showed the fourth video of the day. The class stressed the importance of breastfeeding, and this video was designed to teach women who were going back to work how they could manually express breast milk.

The odd thing was that it reminded Free of the porno movies that Billy sometimes rented, only this video was like a strange cross between something from the amateur rack and a cooking demonstration. It began with about five minutes of credits, listing such things as "Hairstyles by . . . ," "Makeup by . . . ," "Edited by . . . ," all accompanied by canned sprightly music that Free swore she had heard in one of those videos from the Castle Super Store. It was like a cartoon spoof she had seen once on TV, *Bambi Meets Godzilla*, which had lengthy credits ("Bambi's wardrobe furnished by . . ."). Once the credits were over, the movie consisted entirely of Bambi standing in the forest for about two seconds before he was squashed by a huge scaled foot.

Finally, this video cut to the chase—a white studio kitchen. In it, a woman wearing a black-and-white harlequin sweater stood next to a woman in a blue business suit who was seated on a stool. The woman in the sweater introduced herself to the camera as the instructor. When she turned back, the other woman, Marilyn, had spread open her jacket and undone her white blouse. Next the instructor demonstrated how to massage the breasts. Free felt awkward, sitting bolt upright in a hard chair, surrounded by strangers, watching one woman place her thumb and finger on another woman's nipple, demonstrating the proper way to milk the breasts. As the instructor laughed in delight, fine streams of pale liquid shot out, presumably staining Marilyn's skirt, although by this time the camera had moved in for a closeup and all the audience could see was Marilyn's breast and the four hands on it. Later, when the camera pulled back to look at the two woman's faces, it was out of focus for a minute, again giving Free the impression of a bad amateur sex video.

Then the instructor came up with a variety of containers for Marilyn to try expressing into: a Pyrex measuring cup, a funnel, a bottle, a plastic bag liner for a baby bottle, a plastic bag liner for a preemie bottle. As the instructor searched for more containers (a plastic bowl, a wineglass), Marilyn waited patiently, her hand in position on her nipple. Free found the whole thing bizarre. Even when the instructor wasn't actually touching Marilyn's breast, she leaned close, her head nearly on Marilyn's shoulder, as she breathed admiration for her technique and the amount of milk she produced.

Free had to bite her lip to keep from laughing.

Chirty-seven

Saturday, OCTOBER 28, 5:07 P.M.

Warren looked down at the envelope Roy had pressed into his hand. It was so fat Roy had had to close it with a rubber band.

"You can count it if you want." Behind Warren, Roy could see Shari teetering around on black five-inch heels that fastened over her ankles with what looked like little locks. She was putting away groceries from six sacks that filled the dining room table. In the living room, the TV was tuned to a football game. God, Warren had the right idea about life.

"I know you wouldn't be dumb enough to short me," Warren said, holding Roy's gaze a second longer than he felt comfortable with. The other man sniffed, and Roy knew he was probably smelling the stink that clung to him, a smell like cat piss that all meth cookers simply got used to.

Roy had realized he could kill two birds with one stone: make some money for Warren and satisfy the craving that had begun to gnaw at him almost as soon as he woke up. At Newberry's he got some aquarium tubing, and a new Pyrex pot to replace the one that Lydia had thrown out that one time, then pretended that she hadn't known what she was doing. While he waited in line, he rubbed the thumb of his left hand over the knuckles of his right, thinking about how he had taught her a lesson.

Roy had first tried his hand at making meth three years ago, but an arrest—later thrown out on a technicality—had scared him off dealing. Now he didn't care about the law anymore. The whole idea made him smile. He was a stone-cold killer, and the newspaper he picked up at one of the grocery stores said that police had little to go on in what were being called the Badger Ridge thrill killings. He guessed that made him the Badger Ridge Thrill Killer. Roy kind of liked the sound of that.

He had spread his purchases over four grocery stores, buying three bottles of allergy medicine at each, along with a little food and the other supplies he needed. At the Safeway, Roy thought the clerk tipped him a knowing wink while he rang up the allergy medicine, a package of cotton balls and a box of coffee filters, as well as three Hungryman dinners, but he couldn't be sure.

Back home, he taped towels over the windows and got to work. You had to be careful when you were making meth. It was nasty shit—it smelled rank, and the fumes could and did catch on fire. But in less than twenty-four hours, what you got was what you needed, only for a fraction of the price the dealer wanted to charge you. Not only did you end up with more than enough for yourself, but best of all, you could become a dealer yourself.

The next day, Roy was waiting at the edge of the parking lot for shift change at Dri-N-Fresh. A lot of people who worked the line used crank. And it wasn't long before Roy had the money he needed.

"Did you hear about those two guys they found up at Badger Ridge?" Warren asked now. "The ones that were shot to death?" Was it Roy's imagination, or was Warren looking at him with a new respect?

"Yeah. Poor fuckers." He tried, and failed, to hide his grin.

"Yeah, poor fuckers," Warren echoed. Roy wasn't sure, but he thought his tone might be sarcastic. "Aren't you afraid of what's going to happen when they look at those bullets?"

Things were turning, Roy knew that, but he didn't know in what direction. "I don't have that rifle anymore. And they're never going to find it, neither. I dumped it in the river."

Warren shook his head impatiently. "No, I mean the ammo in their pockets. Or did you suddenly get smart and remember to take the ammo back?"

"What?" After the shooting, Roy hadn't done anything but run as fast as he could back to his car, only able to take a deep breath when he realized no one had seen what had happened.

"You dumb fuck. The ammunition that we traded with them. I was wearing gloves Saturday, but that ammo had your prints on it. You didn't take it back off them, did you?"

"No." Roy felt frightened. He felt like he had to take a shit. "But, but—you're the one who said I should—"

Warren grabbed the neck of Roy's sweatshirt and twisted until the air dwindled in Roy's throat. "You'd better not be saying that. Or even thinking that. Because I could take you out in a minute. And I wouldn't even blink." Roy had a crazy sideways view of one of Warren's eyes, the white all yellow, and past that he could see Shari standing stock still in the kitchen, her mouth half open, before she turned with a jerk and picked up a big plastic bag of generic Cocoa Puffs.

Finally, Warren released him. Roy staggered back, gasping for breath. "Sorry, Warren, sorry. I don't have the best memory, you know, because sometimes I slam my head into things. Keeps it quiet up there." He tapped on his temple, wondering frantically whether Warren was now going to kill him.

The other man eyed him for a long time. "It's good to know that. You'd better go slam your head against the wall a couple of more times, so you forget all about who was or wasn't at Badger Ridge that day." Warren looked down at the money in his hand, and Roy didn't know whether he was going to throw it back at him or keep it and never do anything. When he looked back up, his eyes were narrowed down to slits. "Let me just give you one piece of advice. When you get your hands on Lydia, you'd better leave her where no one will find her." He turned to go back into the house. "I'll call you if Shari finds out anything."

Thirty-eight

SATURDAY, OCTOBER 28, 5:08 P.M.

By mutual agreement, Lexi drove home from the birthing class while Free walked. A half hour after she got in the door, the doorbell rang. "Can you get it?" Lexi called from the bathroom.

Free opened the door expecting to see Gene, Lexi's ex-husband, who had said he planned on stopping by today. He had already come by the night before, finally leaving with a framed photograph of their old dog, a colander, and a half-used tube of toothpaste. Even though he was the one who had left Lexi, he seemed to be bent on extracting some kind of protracted revenge.

Craig stood on the steps. Something shifted deep in Free's belly, and she tried to tell herself it was just the baby doing a back flip.

"Oh, um, hello."

"Hey, I was just driving home from work and wondered if you wanted to sample some of Portland's finest cuisine."

"I don't—" Free began, when Lexi came up behind her. Free made introductions all around. Craig wore a dark blue Columbia Sportswear parka over a wine-red shirt and black pants. His cheeks were ruddy from the cold. Lexi took advantage of a moment when Craig was looking elsewhere to shoot Free a meaningful glance. Lexi could communicate more by raising one perfectly arched eyebrow than most people could in an hour's worth of conversation.

"Would you like to come with us? I was just asking Lydia if she wanted to sample some of Portland's finest cuisine—AKA McMennamin's fries."

"I don't think—" Free began again, when Lexi's voice overrode hers.

"I think that sounds like a great idea. But I'm afraid I can't go with you guys. My ex-husband called a few minutes ago, and he needs to come over and pick up a few more of his things." Lexi's bemused glance took in the denuded living and dining rooms. "If I don't stick around, he'll take anything that isn't nailed down. And maybe a few things that are."

Free put her hand on the door. "I really appreciate the offer, Craig, but I'm afraid I can't. I'm just not ready to be in a car again. I tried to go with Lexi someplace today, and it was just too much."

"That's okay. It's walking distance from here. And it's a beautiful night."

"I think you should go," Lexi said, giving Free a little push on the shoulder. "You don't want to hear me and Gene arguing." Another quirk of the eyebrow, only this one seemed to be asking for some privacy. The night before, Free had stayed in her room, pretending not to hear the vituperative shouting match going on between her roommate and her soon-to-be ex.

"All right." Free gave in. "Let me just get my coat." She pulled it back out of the closet, along with a pair of red gloves and matching Polartec earmuffs. A hat would keep her ears warmer, but she didn't wear a hat anymore, for fear of pulling off her wig along with the hat. When they said their good-byes to Lexi, Free felt oddly like a character on one of the TV shows she had avidly watched at friends' houses, as if Lexi were her mother and she were the slightly rebellious—but good-hearted—teenage daughter.

The air was crisp, a few degrees above freezing. Stars sprinkled the clear sky. They walked down the stairs, past the overgrown laurel hedge, and then down the sidewalk past what Free presumed was Craig's car, a newer model dark-colored sedan. He said, "Do you mind if I give you a piece of crime-prevention advice?"

"What?" Free had learned to be wary of advice.

"You guys should think about trimming your hedges. I have never been called out to work a burglary on a home where the hedges are squared off. I don't know that the bad guys even know that they're thinking it—but subconsciously, I think they believe that if your hedges are all even, you're probably not going to be sloppy about your home's security, either."

"Lexi's husband did all the outdoor stuff—and he took all the tools with him when he left. She's been renting a lawnmower from Barbur Boulevard Rentals—maybe I can ask her to pick up a hedge trimmer, too."

"How about if I bring over my hedge trimmer and ladder tomorrow?"

"No, that's okay. I'm sure we can handle it." And sure that she didn't want this guy inserting himself any further in her life. At the same time, part of Free couldn't help being intrigued. Craig was like a different species. Free had never known a man who owned power tools, or even a ladder. If something broke, Bob was hard pressed to find a screwdriver. In her parents' house, anything that required elevation was accomplished by climbing on a chair or table. Despite her interest in Craig, Free decided to make it clear that this would be the last time she would see him. He was clearly every inch a cop, the kind of cop who couldn't stop thinking about his job even when he was away from it. She wondered what it would be like to care about a job so much that it just became part of who you were. "Do you have to go to school to be a cop?" She now had half a dozen career books from the library, but she had never looked at the sections on law enforcement.

Craig detoured around a small puddle where the sidewalk sagged. "I went to Portland State during the day and worked nights as a reserve officer for a year before I was hired. You do that at your own expense."

"You mean, for free?" It was hard to imagine loving something so much you would be willing to do it for no money. But wasn't that the same position she was in? She had so much money now that she might never need to work. Still, Free found she wanted to do something with her life. Eventually this baby would need to go to school, and she couldn't imagine spending six hours a day cleaning and baking cookies and waiting for a child to come home. She was beginning to realize that work offered so much more than money. It was a chance to do what you were good at, a place to have friends, a way to shape your day.

"For free," Craig echoed. "Every now and then, if you're lucky, they pay you to fill in a shift when a regular officer is gone. Of course, they pay you a lot less money than they do a regular officer. After I got hired, I spent a couple of years as a patrol officer in Hollywood before I became a criminalist." He noticed the look on her face. "Not Hollywood, California. Hollywood is a section of Portland." He turned and pointed across the river, a broad black band amidst all the lights. "It's on the Eastside, near I-84, not too far from downtown."

"Why did you want to change from being a cop-cop?"

He shrugged. "First, there's the politics of the whole thing. You are doing a job where you can expect to get whipped by the public and the media. You're working your tail off, and then people put unrealistic expectations on you. At the same time, a lot of the public act like all cops are country boys or hicks. Rednecks. People think all cops go out hunting on the weekends, or that we all own big trucks. They act like cops have no interest in the arts or culture. Like a cop would never read a book. That kind of attitude was even worse when I was a patrol cop. But the main problem with being a patrol cop is that it's basically like being a babysitter. You're mostly dealing with parents who can't handle their children, so they call the police. I spent a lot of time giving out advice and phone numbers for places where they could get help. And the next week I would get called back to the same address, and the week after that. It felt like you never made any progress."

"Is that why you became a"—Free stumbled on the word—"a criminalist?"

"When I got hired, I got to tour each division. I spent a week in ID, and I thought forensics were cool. So when an entry-level position opened up, I applied for it. The great thing about this job is when you pluck a bad guy out of thin air when no one else could catch him. I get to work at my own pace, and I'm learning new stuff all the time. I think of it like being a fireman. Everything you do is training for the big one. Only in my case, it's a homicide instead of a four-alarm fire."

They walked past a small shopping complex. Most of the stores were dark and the parking lot was nearly empty. The only other person they had seen on foot was a man walking a golden retriever. Both sides of the street were lined with eighty-year-old single-family homes, most set back and up from the street. As well as listening to Craig, Free was covertly observing the people in the houses, walking, talking, eating or watching TV in the warm spills of light. No one seemed alone. There were families and old couples and friends.

"Isn't it hard, though, dealing with dead people all day?"

Craig's laugh was unexpected. "Portland doesn't have that many murders! Most of the time I'm looking for twelve- to seventeen-year-old burglars who don't even have the sense to wear gloves when they break a window." As they turned down a side street, he sobered. "There are days when it is hard. The worst is when it's child abuse. I've seen infants that have been burned and scalded. Last week I worked a case where an eight-year-old girl was brutally raped, so bad she had to have surgery. And the only thing I can do for that girl is to do the best damn crime-scene investigation I can so we can nail the bastard who did it to her." He pointed down the street. "Here's where we're going. The Fulton Pub." It was an unprepossessing wooden building with two picnic tables out front. Inside, there wasn't much room to move, with six booths on the left, bar stools and a counter on the right, and a few tables crowded in between. Nearly every spot was taken, but just as they walked in the doors another couple stood up from one of the booths. Craig and Free snagged it.

While they waited for the waitress-slash-bartender to wipe their table down, Free looked around the small space. A blackboard ran the length of one wall just above their heads. Along with the day's food and microbrewed specials, it had elaborate chalk drawings of Superman and the Powerpuff Girls. The rest of the walls were decorated with handpainted murals, old road and advertising signs and a display of Pez dispensers. No one paid attention to the small TV playing soundlessly on a wall high above the bar. Craig took the laminated menus from their permanent place on the table behind the ketchup and mustard bottles, and handed one to her. When the waitress came back, he ordered a pint of ale, a small order of fries and a steak sandwich with sautéed peppers and onions.

"I'll have the Wilbur Jumbo Deluxe," Free said, ignoring Craig's raised eyebrow. By its description, the Wilbur was a heart attack on a plate, a hamburger that came topped with cheese, a fried egg and strips of bacon. Free didn't care. All she knew was that it sounded really good. She didn't know whether it was the baby or just being able to eat what she pleased, but lately just the thought of meat made her mouth water. "And a glass of milk and a small order of fries."

Both the waitress and Craig smiled at that. "How about if you just make it one order of fries for both of us," he told the woman. They exchanged knowing smiles. "She's never been here before so she doesn't know how big a small fry is."

After the waitress left, Free asked, "Why were you dressed all in black when I saw you the other day? Was that like a uniform?"

Craig shook his head. "I do have a special black jumpsuit I keep at my office to wear if it's going to be really messy. But normally I wear dark-colored civilian clothes because black powder and khaki don't go together. And then I have a dress A uniform, the blue uniform, but I usually only wear that on ceremonial occasions."

"Do you wear a bulletproof vest?" Free wanted to keep him talking so he wouldn't ask questions about her and her life.

He shrugged. "Sometimes. I wear it under my shirt. It can come on and off, depending on whether it might be needed."

"How about a gun?"

"When I'm on duty. I try to keep it low key. I have it on a holster on my belt. It's just another piece of equipment, and I'd rather most civilians didn't notice it. But I'm a sworn officer. I may get asked to cover another officer. And I've had bad guys return to the scene of a crime." Their food came, including a huge basket of shoestring fries, and for a moment they busied themselves with squirting ketchup and deploying napkins. Free knew it probably wasn't very nutritious, but the combination of grease and salt, set off by the sweet tang of ketchup, was wonderful.

Craig shifted a bite to continue talking. "The vest and the gun aren't what get the job done. Mostly, it's just me and the evidence. And if you pay attention, the evidence can tell you everything you need to know. Last year, I worked a crime scene where the victim was found with her hands tied behind her back. There were no fingerprints at the scene, and she was strangled, so there was no blood spatter and no bullet. And she wasn't raped, so there weren't any body fluids, and there was nothing under her fingernails. And no witnesses—nobody heard anything, nobody saw anything. And it was the third killing like that in six months. Everyone thought we were looking at the work of a serial killer."

"But what did you think?" Free realized she was honestly interested in the answer.

"It all came down to the knot. There's a lot you can tell just from the way a knot is tied. Every day, everybody uses knots to tie their shoelaces, or to wrap a package or to tie down a load in the back of a pickup. And different hobbies or professions use certain kinds of knots—sailors, people who do macramé, fishermen. That woman I was talking about, the one found with her hands tied behind her back? The kind of knot her killer used was a special kind of knot that only rock climbers use. Her boyfriend was a rock climber on weekends. It was a copycat killing. What the boyfriend didn't know was that the knot he tied his girlfriend's hands together with was nothing like the knot these two other women had. But if that had been overlooked, then he might have gotten off scot-free."

"Oh," Free said, and pressed a hand on her ribs. She still wasn't used to the idea that she could be kicked from *inside* her own body.

Craig paused in mid–French fry. "Was that the baby?"

"It's so big now that it's like having a five-pound carp flopping in my belly."

He cocked his head to one side, his expression quizzical. "Is it weird to feel something inside your body moving by itself?"

"Very. Sometimes I feel it's like my liver decided that it wanted to be in a different place and is now wiggling into position without my say-so."

"It must be hard, having to deal with all of this by yourself." Craig waved his hand, presumably indicating her imaginary husband's death as well as the pregnancy.

Free nodded agreement, thinking of everything that kept her awake at night. Lydia's flat gaze. The screams from the injured. Jamie's eyes, as bright as blue flames about to be snuffed out. The look and feel and smell of seventy-four stacks of used bills. And her own not-always-easy transformation from hippie child to soft-spoken grown-up. Free was succeeding in becoming the person she had always wanted to be—so why did she suddenly feel so lost?

"You must really miss your husband."

This was a road Free didn't want to travel. "I would really prefer not to talk about that."

"I'm sorry." Craig made a ring on the table with his beer glass, then wiped it away with his napkin. "I dated this one woman for five years. We were living together and planning to get married. Pam was an accountant. She worked in an office building." He picked up his beer again, took a sip, then blew a sigh from puffed cheeks. "She ended up having an affair with the guy who worked in the next cubicle over. I knew something was going on, so finally I asked her about it. She said she was tired of me coming home late, tired of hearing about people who had been hurt and killed, tired that I didn't have a nine-to-five job. Oh, and by the way, she was moving out. She got married to him last June. The weird thing was that Pam ended up getting married on the day she had picked for our wedding. She wore the same dress and everything."

Free watched Craig's face as he told her this. She expected to see pain, but instead his green eyes were as cold as cat's-eye marbles. He drained the last of his beer, then wiped his face with his napkin and started counting out the money for the bill.

"Put your money away," Free said. "You paid last time. Now it's my turn. I want us to be even." She also didn't want either one of them thinking this was a date. They went back and forth a few times before Craig finally put his wallet back in his pocket.

As they began the walk home, he asked, "What kind of work did you do when you lived in Pendleton?" His question reminded her again that he saw her not as Free Meeker, but as Lydia Watkins.

"Nothing that was like a career. Now I think I want to go to college. I keep going to the library and getting books about different kinds of jobs."

"What do you think you want to do?"

"I'm not sure. I have enough money that I don't need to work right now. Sometimes . . ." She looked away from him, feeling an urge to be honest to counteract the many lies that stood between them. "Sometimes I've thought about being a writer." She had half filled a notebook with scenes, ideas and the beginnings of a few short stories. In a way, she figured she already was a storyteller.

Craig nodded, seeming not to find anything incongruous in her idea, and Free felt heartened. She liked this man and she liked who she was with him. But she had to face reality. There was no way she could hook up with a guy who made a living looking for clues and figuring out the truth. As they walked up the hill that led to Lexi's house, she said, "Look, Craig, I had a nice time tonight. But I have to tell you I'm not ready to be in any kind of relationship. And I won't be for a long time." More to the point, she was never going to be ready for a relationship with a cop.

Craig drew back. His tone was chilly. "I'm afraid you've misunderstood me. I wasn't thinking of this as a date. That's not the way I feel about you. After the accident the other day, you just seemed very . . . vulnerable. You've recently lost your husband, you're alone, and you're new to Portland. I was just trying to reach out to you as a friend."

Every word he said just made Free feel smaller and sillier. Of course Craig wasn't interested in her, except as a charity case. She was an ungainly six months pregnant, and now she had become the overly emotional kind of woman who panicked at every opportunity and misinterpreted every situation. "I'm sorry if I misunderstood you. I just had to make things clear. And while I appreciate your offer of friendship . . ." She let her sentence hang unfinished.

"No problem. I hear what you're saying." There was a moment of awkward silence, then he said, "Thanks again for taking a walk with me. I'll just watch you get safely inside, if you don't mind."

"No, that's okay. Thanks again for everything, from taking me to the hospital to showing me the sights of the city. It may not seem like it, but I really appreciate it." Free's chest felt heavy, but she told herself it was just heartburn. She started up the steps, then turned halfway up and waved. When she had first discovered the money, it had felt like a magic key that would set her free. Now it was beginning to feel more like a prison.

thirty-nine

Don Cannon shook his head as he watched the guy drive off in the dark blue Honda. This guy was cop or military. He didn't know which, but he was sure it was one or the other. He could practically smell it. It was more than just the neatly barbered hair. It was the way he had stood, ramrod straight, and the way he had talked to this girl with his hands clasped behind him, as if he were on parade rest.

Since Darlene had called him with Free Meeker's partial address, Don had spent most of his time in a van with specially tinted windows that he had parked in front of a house for sale. The empty house was a few doors down from the four houses that started with the same two numbers as the address on the envelope Free Meeker had sent Darlene. One of these houses must contain Free Meeker. But which one? The retired couple didn't seem to have any guests or visitors, and neither did the two gay guys. People came and went from the Hmong family's house, but Don hadn't seen a single non-Asian face among them.

That left the married couple in their late twenties. The Ashburgs. But if this guy was the husband, Gene Ashburg, why had he knocked on the door when he arrived and why was he leaving now? And, according to the city directory, the husband worked at a local dot.com, not in the service or for the police. There was another guy who had come around last night and again for a few minutes tonight, but he had knocked on the door too. Each time he left with a paper grocery sack, but carrying it so carelessly that Don knew there was no way it could be holding the money.

The two women were a puzzle, too. One was a knockout with black curly hair, a great figure, and a cute little BMW. The other was pretty, not beautiful, with shoulder-length brown hair—and she was pregnant. Whenever one of the two women appeared outside the house, he would look back and forth from her face to Free's picture. The black-haired woman's face was too angular to ever have belonged to Free, so was she Alexis Ashburg? The brunette was closer, if you supposed that the blunt cut was a wig and tried to imagine Free's photograph with the addition of hair and makeup and minus the nose ring. But the fact that this girl, whoever she was, was pregnant completely threw Don off stride. If Free had been pregnant, he was sure her parents or boyfriend would have said something, if only to mourn their double loss. And certainly the parents would not have kept quiet out of shame, since they themselves had never bothered with a marriage license.

But this girl, whoever she was, seemed the only possibility on the block. He could kidnap her, Don supposed. It wouldn't take long before she would tell him what she knew, who she was. But if he was wrong, if she knew nothing about the money, then he would have to kill her to keep her quiet. Well, he would have to kill her if he was right, too, but that seemed trifling compared to the idea of killing a stranger who had never done him any harm.

No, kidnapping was too drastic a step, at least right now, when he wasn't even sure who these women were, when the only resolution would be a cold-blooded killing. He would explore a few other avenues first. Earlier, he had called Metro, the regional authority that oversaw waste disposal and recycling. "I'm going to be house-sitting for a few weeks," he told the clerk who answered, "and they forgot to tell me what day to put the garbage out." Then he gave the address that belonged to the two women. The answer was Monday. Which meant they would more than likely put their garbage out tomorrow night, Sunday, on the eve of his deadline. His luck, Don told himself, was turning.

The old saying was that you are what you eat. But Don knew you are also what you throw away. Which is why he had a top-of-the-line cross-cut shredder in his office and wasn't above making "deposits" in other restaurants' Dumpsters.

So tomorrow night he would snatch not the girl, but her garbage. And then he would see what he would see.

Sunday, OCTOBER 29, 11:47 A.M.

From somewhere far away, the phone was ringing. It had been ringing so long that Roy had already answered it a million times in his dreams. But no matter how often his dream hand picked it up and his dream mouth said hello, it refused to stop ringing. Finally, the real Roy pushed the upper part of his body enough off the couch to grab the phone. He didn't even say hello.

"You still looking for your wife?" Warren's voice, irritated-sounding. The tone of it trumped Roy's own irritation. One thing you never wanted was Warren mad.

"Yup."

"She's in Portland. Get a pencil and I'll tell you the address."

Roy finally found a pen, but no paper, so he wrote on one of the ripped pieces of the photograph of Lydia's parents. When he finished and turned it over, her mother's fisheye stared at him. She had never liked Roy, and she'd brought her daughter up to follow in her footsteps. Now, wherever she was, he hoped the old bitch was sincerely sorry. Because he was going to take his own sweet time at teaching her daughter a lesson. He'd make Lydia crawl, he'd make her beg, he'd make her do things she would never have done in a million years. And when he was done with her, maybe he would offer her around to whoever would have her. Put her on a pool table in the back of the Red Barn and let anyone have a go. Or maybe he'd just—finish her off. In private. Or maybe he would do first the one and then the other.

Roy grinned, his head awhirl with possibilities.

Forty-one

On Monday, at three in the morning, Don drove down the block where the two women lived. He had spent all day yesterday watching the same four houses—but turning up no more possibilities than he had originally. Each time it came down to the pregnant girl as the only possible choice. He had watched her walk right past him three different times. There was a bounce to her step and her eyes were lively. Once she looked straight at the van, straight into his eyes, if only she had known it. Lucky for him, the neighborhood was often used by people who didn't live there but who did want a free place to park ten minutes from downtown or Portland State.

At this time of night, all the houses on the street were dark. Good. He didn't want to meet anyone else. For a while, when newsprint values had been high, a few enterprising souls had turned into scavengers, grabbing up the sorted newspaper from the curb before the garbage men could get to it. But prices for recycled newsprint had dropped, and Don didn't expect to meet anyone else. Just in case, he tucked his Walther PPK with the silencer into his shoulder holster. It had been so long since he routinely went armed that that he was acutely aware of the holster's presence every time he turned the wheel.

Driving down the street, he saw lines of trash cans that had been trundled out to the curb, each with one or two yellow plastic recycling bins next to it. Portland prided itself on the percentage of trash that got recycled. Don just hoped that the two women followed the example of nearly all of their neighbors and put the trash out the night before.

His headlights picked out a cylindrical shape flanked by two squat rectangles. Behind it, the women's house sat dark and quiet. He was in luck. Don turned off the dome light so he wouldn't illuminate himself when he opened the door. He didn't want to light up like a Christmas tree. He was wearing dark clothes and a black knit cap so the light wouldn't shine off his bald head. Aside from the dark clothes and his shoulder holster, he hadn't taken any other precautions against being seen. Only the rankest of amateurs would blacken his face. You might as well get a sandwich board that said *Up to No Good* and walk back and forth in front of Central Precinct.

Leaving the engine running, he eased open his door. He left it open for the same reason he left the car idling—because it was quicker and quieter. Working briskly but calmly, he opened the trunk and then picked up the garbage can and upended it. He had lined the trunk beforehand with a blue plastic tarp. He didn't know where Barry had gotten this car, or if he planned on returning it, but Don figured it was probably better if he did what he could to minimize the smell. The bag of paper recycling he set on top of the garbage, with the bag of newspapers right beside it. He left the bin filled with plastic and metal containers. He didn't rush, he didn't cast guilty glances at the house, he didn't drop anything. The trick was to act as if taking trash from the curb and stuffing it in your car was a normal routine.

Don gently closed the trunk so that the sound of the latch was almost inaudible, then looked at his watch. Less than a minute had elapsed since he drove up in front of the house. He smiled. Fifteen years since he had done any field work, but he still had the touch.

A woman's voice made Don nearly jump out of his skin, although he managed to control his startle. "Excuse me, but what are you doing?"

He turned. The voice belonged to an old lady in a pink satin housecoat and foam rollers. A red handknit scarf was looped a million times around her neck. At her feet sat some kind of bored-looking mutt on a leash.

Uncertain of what to do, Don took a step closer toward his open door.

"I said, excuse me, but what are you doing?" The old lady's voice was louder, more pointed. A light blinked on in the upstairs of the house next to the target's. He couldn't let this happen, let everything turn to shit because of some noisy old biddy. Slipping his hand inside his jacket, Don turned toward the woman. He had to get her to be quiet.

Forty-Two

Don sat back on his haunches, exhausted. In his hands, which were encased in bright yellow Playtex gloves, he held the pair of chopsticks he had used to probe the chicken bones and sodden broccoli, all of it covered by the sweepings from a dustpan. He didn't want to risk cutting himself on a tin can lid. He had tied around his face a bandana that he had dipped in vanilla extract. He had also sprayed around an air freshener call Berried Treasure, which showed pictures of forested mountains on the canister and promised to smell like candles. Neither of these measures had worked to mask the fug of garbage. His nose ran continually—one of the side effects of total alopecia. No hair anywhere on his body meant no hairs in his nose to screen out dust and dirt. After Barry took the car away, he was going to have to open the doors and hope that the stench dissipated before Margherita arrived for the morning.

According to a lawyer Don had once talked to, there were technically two types of refuse: trash and garbage. Garbage consisted of the remains of food: wilted lettuce, corn cobs, meat trimmings. Everything else—broken thermometers, Styrofoam meat trays, cardboard boxes—was trash. And legally, both garbage and trash were fair game. The Supreme Court had ruled that once something was thrown away, it wasn't protected by privacy laws.

When he had been confronted by that busybody neighbor, Don hadn't said anything about the Supreme Court. Instead he had said quietly, his voice nonchalant and his eyes looking directly into hers, "I'm a researcher for the Department of Health. We're doing spot checks to determine what percentages of recyclables people are really sorting."

"Oh," she had said, sniffing as if the very idea of recycling was foolish, "in my day we didn't have these fancy yellow bins. We just put our garbage out back and let the pigs and the goats have at it. And what was left, we burned." But then she had pulled her old dog to its feet and walked away, and Don had let his hand drop to his side.

If he really were a Department of Health researcher, Don thought now, he would have to give the two women high marks for their recycling skills. He himself was a stickler for it in his businesses as well as at home. He knew that frozen entree boxes had to be put in the garbage, but Post-It notes could be recycled. He knew that wire hangers went in the same bin as the tin cans, and that a cardboard box had to be deconstructed into pieces that didn't exceed thirty-six inches in length in any direction. Unless the material was highly sensitive, Don was always careful to put the contents of his shredder into the bag of paper recycling.

Uncertain of where he might find a clue, Don had paid attention to everything the women had discarded, overlooking nothing. He had gone through the stack of *Oregonians*, looking for a note scribbled in a corner, an article clipped out, a piece of paper that might have gotten folded inside. Zip. The newspapers were larded with magazines and catalogs, following the new and somewhat confusing system recently adopted by the city of Portland. All the catalogs and magazines had Alexis Ashburg's name on the mailing label. Don leafed through a couple. She seemed to be the kind of woman who shopped frequently and didn't balk at paying $300 for a cardigan if it was hand-loomed.

He poked through the contents of the blue tarp, carefully sorting it into neat piles. The largest pile was kitchen scraps—long curls of potato peelings, apple cores chewed down to the seeds. He wondered why they weren't putting stuff like that down the garbage disposal. The house was old, though, and maybe the kitchen hadn't been updated or the plumbing couldn't handle a garbage disposal.

Don had to give the two women credit, though. He had read that most Americans reported healthy diets to researchers, glossing over the Lays potato chips and Ben & Jerry's that they really ate behind closed doors. These two, though, were paragons of virtue. They ate cantaloupe, prewashed salads, organically grown oranges. They drank nonfat milk and properly rinsed and flattened the waxed containers and put them in the paper recycling, along with the labels for peaches and pears and pineapple canned in their own unsweetened juice.

There were only a few interesting things from the garbage can. A crumpled pack of Merit Lights surprised Don. He hadn't seen either of the two women smoking. A secret smoker, then. He found himself hoping it wasn't the pregnant one. There was nothing worse than seeing a woman with a baby in her belly and a cigarette between her lips. The other interesting thing was a broken dark blue Faberware cup. Had it been thrown in the heat of an argument? Or had it simply slipped from someone's hands? Don shook his head. He was starting to tell himself stories, but he was only here to get his hands on the facts—and, ultimately, on his money.

The bag of recycled paper was much more promising. He looked at every scrap of paper, every bill, every receipt, every letter. Nothing was shredded, which made his job easier, although it was a stupid move on their part. They must not know how many tweakers were out there, trolling people's garbage for unopened credit card offers and cancelled checks, using the information to open their own accounts or even create their own checks with the help of a computer, a scanner and a color printer.

Most of the paper was packaging, empty boxes of Shredded Wheat or Ronzoni pasta, which Don needed only to glance at and then pile to one side. The little bits and pieces of paper were more tricky. You never knew when you might run across a telephone number or a note or a lock combination scribbled on a Post-It, an envelope, a napkin, a piece of scrap paper. He found the itemized portion of their telephone bill and set it aside for later investigation. No calls into the 541 area code, though, which meant if this girl really was Free, she wasn't calling anyone in the southern part of the state. There was a sheaf of credit card statements for Alexis, all showing that she carried balances, some of them substantial. A lot of the charges were to the same catalogs he had found with the newspapers.

In the end, Don kept fewer than a half-dozen pieces of paper that interested him. The first was a note in what he thought of as a woman's handwriting, half-cursive, half-printed, all loops. "Lydia—next time you go to the store, could you get me a half-pint of nonfat sour cream? Thanks! Lexi." That fixed the names of the two women. Lexi must be short for Alexis. And the mystery woman, whoever she was, was calling herself Lydia. Or maybe, Don thought, maybe she really was Lydia and not Free at all.

Next was a note that said, "You are being totally unreasonable and selfish. You act as if I did this to hurt you. I wasn't even thinking about you when I did it. I had to be true to myself." Not addressed to anyone, not signed, but written in all capital letters, so not from Lexi. From Lydia or from someone else?

In a third kind of handwriting, printed again, but in smaller, messier letters, there was a list of things for the baby, each one with a line drawn through it. Lexi hadn't written this note. So it must be Lydia who was pregnant. And Lydia wasn't the one who had written the accusing note. Instead, she had just made a careful list of everything she needed. Onesies, crib sheets, baby shampoo, baby soap, thermometer, booties, stroller, high chair, car seat. Don had a memory flash of Rachel sitting with her black eyebrows pulled together like two wings, carefully checking off item after item on just such a list.

From the receipts in shopping bags for various suppliers of baby products, he saw that Lydia always paid in cash, even when the total was over two hundred dollars. Not many people routinely carried around that kind of money, but she seemed to, and she certainly seemed to be spending it. Was she just being free with it because it wasn't her money? Or maybe there was a simpler explanation, that she was buying a lot of things because having a baby required a lot of specialized stuff. Don remembered Rachel laughing at his horrified expression when she showed him a bristly nipple brush, then explaining that the brush was meant for a bottle's nipples, not hers. He pushed the thought away. He didn't know why he was thinking about her so much lately. If he remembered the happy times, then that meant he had to remember what had come after, too, and he wouldn't let himself do that.

But the most interesting thing, Don thought, was what he hadn't found. Once more, he sorted through the various envelopes, catalogs and mailings, checking to see to whom each was addressed. There were a few things addressed to Gene Ashburg, the seemingly absent man of the house. But there was nothing at all with the name of this other girl, this Lydia. It was as if she didn't exist.

A breeze blew in through the garage door, which was open a couple of inches, releasing a fresh wave of stench that penetrated though his vanilla-soaked bandana as if it weren't even there. A piece of paper went skidding, and he grabbed it. "I had to be true to myself," he read again before putting it with all the papers he wanted to save and weighing them down with a trowel. Don sneezed, then got the shovel and began loading everything else into fresh trash bags.

Forty-three

Monday, OCTOBER 30, 9:32 A.M.

From the van where he had been parked since four that morning, Don Cannon had watched as Lexi left at 7:25 in the morning, backing out of the driveway at a good clip, with only a cursory tap on the brakes before she shot out into the street.

Most of the neighboring houses had emptied out as well. No one really stayed at home anymore. Kids went to school, moms and dads both went to work. You couldn't count on having a bored housewife or elderly shut-in call 911. The world didn't even have any bored housewives or elderly shut-ins left. They all had careers or lived in retirement communities or had taken up golf. If there was anyone left, they were bundled up inside, staying warm by the glow of their TVs.

With his binoculars, Don could track the other girl's progress from room to room, even though she was not much more than a shape passing by a window or a shadow on the curtains.

The girl who called herself Lydia left the house at 9:30 A.M., her back arched a bit as she carried the compact weight of the baby in front of her. Don wished this girl, whoever she was, weren't pregnant. The baby complicated everything. No one who had known Free Meeker had mentioned a baby. Was this simply a child they hadn't known about? He remembered how Rachel's belly had suddenly popped out, right about her fifth month. Of course, she hadn't been built anything like this girl here, who was tall and full-figured. This girl would have had an easier time of concealing a pregnancy, at least for the first few months.

Again he studied the picture of Free Meeker as the girl walked by his van. The facial shape was the same, the eyes, but hadn't Don met people before who looked so much like someone else? What if he were making a mistake? What if he had to kill this girl and she didn't know anything? He felt like a man about to step over a precipice.

Ten minutes later he walked briskly to the back of the house. On his head, Don wore an orange safety helmet and in his hands he carried a clipboard. He was dressed in a denim shirt and khakis, neat enough to pass for a uniform. If you looked official, people tended to not even see you.

It was another ten minutes before the window into the daylit basement yielded to his folding pry bar with a squeal. He stopped for a minute, listening, alert for the slightest change. Don was kneeling in the window well, mostly hidden from any neighbor's curious eyes by the thick green loops of a garden hose. He found himself thinking that they should really drain the hose and put it away before winter. When the temperature dropped below freezing, the water would swell into ice, splitting the hose. And why hadn't they put a grate over this window, instead of leaving it winking an invitation to the first would-be burglar who wandered by? Annoyed that his interior voice was more homeowner than bad guy, Don shook the thought away.

He squeezed his way inside, scraping his shoulders and abdomen. *I am way too old for this*, Don thought sourly. Maybe all those kids who wanted a piece of him were right. He was getting too old, too soft, for the realities of how the game was really played. Before he began moving around, he paused and listened again. Even though he had watched both women leave, you couldn't rule out surprise. Maybe one of them had brought someone home who was still asleep upstairs. Maybe a relative had shown up from out of town and was even now sitting at the breakfast table, spoon halfway to mouth, wondering what the hell they had just heard in the basement.

Don heard only silence. After a moment, he began to move around the basement. Sets of heavy-duty black plastic shelving took up one corner of the room. There was the white wavy mark of a waterline two inches around the base of each of the units. In a hole in the corner, a sump pump squatted. Half of Portland would probably qualify as a wetland if it were zoned today.

The shelves were stacked with Rubbermaid boxes. Each one was labeled. "Christmas ornaments," "candles and flashlights" (good luck finding that one when the power went out), "textbooks." Don reached out a gloved hand and smudged it through the dust on top of one of the boxes, thick enough that it predated Jamie's death or even this year. Here and there were gaps in the rows of boxes where someone had taken something away. Don didn't care about things that were missing. He was looking for something that might recently have been added, but after two minutes he was certain that hadn't happened here.

He went up the steep wooden steps, worn as soft as corduroy, then slowly turned the knob on the door at the top. He was in a laundry room, with the back door opposite him. Holding his breath, Don was again met with nothing but silence. On rubber-soled shoes, he walked out into the main part of the house.

It was clear that the missing boxes in the basement had their counterparts up here as well. Someone had made a raid on this place recently. Not a burglar. This was an inside job. What furniture was left was good, but there were a lot of bare spots where furniture and paintings used to be. He noted that whoever had done it hadn't taken any of the books or cookware. Maybe this girl Lexi was better off.

The note he had found in their trash made more sense now. "*You are being totally unreasonable and selfish. You act as if I did this to hurt you. I wasn't even thinking about you when I did it. I had to be true to myself.*" The husband must have taken off. And taken a few things with him, by the look of it. A guy so self-involved he could walk off with all the choicest bits and still complain.

So what were these two women to each other? Were they lovers? Don had watched Lexi and Lydia Sunday evening as they took a leisurely walk. From what he had seen, there had been no exchange of private smiles, no hand that lingered on the small of the back, no arms brushing companionably. Now he realized what he had seen was two girls acting like what he guessed they were— polite strangers, roommates sharing a house to save money.

Don's gut told him anything of interest was not hidden in the common areas. He went upstairs to the bedrooms, careful not to touch any more than he needed to. Glove marks were nearly as interesting to a fingerprint specialist as prints, and Don wanted to leave no trace of where he had been.

The first door revealed a bedroom with adjoining bath. In the next room, a crib stood next to a changing table. At the end of the hall was a large master bedroom, again with an adjoining bath. This room had odd gaps in its decor, and a king-size bed. Lexi's room, he guessed. Before going back to search the other woman's bedroom, Don found himself stopping in the nursery. The changing table was so new that the mattress was still sheathed in plastic. The crib had been made up, though, in a cheerful genderless turquoise fabric patterned with cartoon moons and stars and suns. It was filled with a zoo of large stuffed animals. On top lay a C-shaped pillow that matched the crib sheet and bumper pad. Don trailed his fingers across it, wondering what it was for. He didn't remember Rachel bringing home anything like that. It must be some new contraption, the latest in baby accessories.

Some things never changed, though. On the bottom shelf of the changing table stood a row of baby products, including the curved shape of a bottle of Johnson & Johnson baby shampoo. He found himself unscrewing the cap and inhaling deeply. It was more than a smell, but something visceral, the distilled essence of babyhood. Had his own mother used the same stuff on him when he was a baby? Rachel had brought home a bottle as part of the legion of supplies that her books had said were absolutely essential for having a child. He had wanted to ask his own mom, but June had been dead by then, her liver having finally given out under her continued assault. She insisted on drinking even when the doctor told her it would kill her, because she said it was the only thing that gave her pleasure. She had said this right in front of Don and it didn't even bother him.

Back in Lydia's room, he started with all the obvious places, taking care not to leave any traces. He could rip the room apart, but that would only serve to alert this girl if he came up empty-handed. In the back of her panty drawer he found what he was looking for. In an unsealed envelope were a driver's license, a library card and a Visa card. All of them bearing the name Free Meeker. And a Pendleton library card with the name Lydia Watkins. Don should have felt happy, but instead it felt like a weight pressing on his chest. He told himself it was because he still didn't know where the money was, and then he began to hunt for it.

As he worked, he wondered who the real Lydia Watkins really was. Or, he amended the thought, had been. After all, somebody's body had been cremated and sprinkled on the Applegate River, and that somebody must have been Lydia Watkins. His search turned up nothing more. Nothing of interest to him, anyway. Nothing else tucked in that same panty drawer, or in any of the other drawers or underneath them. Nothing in her pillowcase, or between or under her mattresses. Her suitcase held only air, the bathroom cupboards held only towels, and her shoes and the pockets of her clothes were empty. A notebook next to the bed was filled with scraps of poetry, lists, and descriptions of weather. Don got down on his knees and checked the wall-to-wall carpet around the room's perimeter, looking for a loose spot where the carpet might have been taken up. There were none.

Maybe the money wasn't in this room. Maybe it wasn't even in this house. Had she rented a safety deposit box, stuffed it in a locker down at the Greyhound depot, buried it in the backyard? Don didn't know. And the only person who could tell him the answer was this Free Meeker. Free, who had more than one secret to keep. Free, with her dark gaze and the baby inside her. He would have to snatch her and get her to tell him where the money was. And if she didn't want to talk, he would have to make her tell him. He didn't have any choice. And Don didn't let himself think about what would have to happen to her after that.

And maybe even then it would be too late. Today the deadline the syndicate had given him would expire. But his bosses were business people first and foremost. Killing him wouldn't net them anything. If he could just get his hands on the money in the next day or two, they would wait while he made his wire transfers, finished his paperwork, waved his magic wand and finally made a deposit for three-quarters of a million in one of their numbered accounts. Don tried to tell himself that there was only one last bit of unpleasantness to get through, and then his life would be back to normal.

He was still on his knees when he heard tires crunch up the driveway. Crawling forward, he twitched the curtain. Down below, Lexi sat in her car, gathering some papers from the passenger's seat. And standing on the sidewalk, watching Lexi from twenty feet away, was some strung-out-looking skinny guy with dark greasy hair and a heart-shaped face.

Forty-four

Free put her soup bowl in the dishwasher. Lexi must have stopped by the house before Free came home for lunch, because Free had found the mail on the table and a plate with crumbs on it in the sink. She rinsed off Lexi's plate and was putting it in the dishwasher when the doorbell rang. She was surprised to find Craig on the other side. His expression was serious, nearly severe.

"I know you said you didn't want to see me, but there's something important I need to talk to you about." Not waiting for an invitation, Craig stepped inside. He closed the door behind him, then leaned against it, crossing his arms.

It was suddenly hard for Free to breathe. He must have found out somehow about the money.

"I know about what happened to you."

"You do?" She tried to rewrite her reaction. "I mean, what are you talking about?"

"In fact, I have to confess that I did something I shouldn't have. I'm a cop. I look into things. It's my nature." His green eyes were unreadable.

"And?"

"I know about what happened to you and why you're living

here with Lexi. I know why you haven't told me the truth." His voice softened. "You're afraid, aren't you?"

Slowly, without a conscious decision, Free found herself nodding. She took a deep, shaky breath, feeling her chest ease. It would all come out in the open now. Craig knew, but he wasn't judging her. He knew, but he could still hold her gaze and not look away. Together, they would find a way out of this mess.

Craig's next words didn't make any sense. "I talked to the station in Pendleton, Lydia. Officers were called to your house on three different occasions by the neighbors. Each time, you denied anything was wrong, even when questioned separately from your husband. All three times, your face or body showed evidence of bruising."

Free was silent. Her heart began to hammer again, so loud she could scarcely hear what Craig was saying. And what was he saying? Lydia's husband was dead. She remembered sitting in the Impala beside Lydia, listening to the other woman recite her losses. Mother, father and husband, all dead and buried. Now Craig was saying Lydia had lied. And then Free had pretended to be Lydia, piling lies on top of lies.

"Your husband's not dead, is he, Lydia? You're not even divorced."

Craig reached out his hand. Brushing aside her bangs, he ran his thumb lightly across the fading scar on her forehead. "When you were at the hospital, I saw the bruises up and down your arms and legs, this cut on your head. They were from Roy, weren't they? That's why you didn't want me to see you anymore. You're still married." He hesitated, then looked at her directly, his green eyes sharp as glass. "Do you still love him, despite everything?"

"You saw me fall," she said stubbornly, stupidly. "That's where I got those bruises from."

"Lydia, I'm not dumb. I know what fresh bruises look like. Those were old." Craig shook his head, his expression disappointed, even angry. "You sound just like my mom. When I was growing up, I used to lie on my bed and put the pillow over my ears, but still I could hear them in the bedroom, I could hear him yelling and the sound of him pounding her with his fists. I felt so helpless and angry. I wanted to protect her, but she wouldn't let me. She wouldn't let anyone."

Free ached for the pain in Craig's eyes, ached enough to push away her own confusion about what he had told her about Lydia. "What happened? Do they still live together?"

The silence dragged on long enough that she could guess at the answer. "Six years ago my mom had a stroke and died in the hospital. They said the stroke was caused by a clot from a fall she had taken. Fall! I knew it wasn't a fall. My dad's still in town, but I haven't talked to him in years. A couple of years back I saw him at Fred Meyer, but I just looked through him like he was nothing. Because he was." He put his hands on her shoulders. "I'm a cop, Lydia. I know what these guys are like. They won't let it go. They won't let you go. Let me help you file a restraining order against him. Then you can get a divorce and you'll be free of him. You don't want him coming after you, hitting you again, or even fighting you for custody of this baby. I can help you get the protection you need. Please, let me help you."

Free wanted so much to answer the appeal in Craig's eyes. But how could she tell him the truth? And if she did, wouldn't he despise her? She had to find a way to push him away, hurt him so that he wouldn't keep coming around, picking at all the inconsistencies in her story.

"Is this what happened with Pam?" Taking a step back, she threw his old girlfriend's name at him like a challenge.

"What do you mean?"

"Did you poke around in Pam's life, spy on her without her knowing about it? Is that how you found out about her affair? Did you use all your cop tricks to get information on her, have your buddies stake out her house, interrogate the people she worked with, go over every scrap of paper in her purse?" Free threw out as many accusations as she could think of, and when a muscle flickered under his eye she guessed at least one had found its mark.

"I'm not proud of what I did. But what happened with Pam has nothing to do with this. Your life is in danger and I want to help you."

"I've got a news flash for you, Craig. Stay out of my life. Stop poking around where you're not wanted. Because if I had needed your help, I would have asked for it."

"You'd rather be dead than ask for help? Fine." His voice was brittle. "You know where to find me if you change your mind." He turned on his heel, opened the door, and then Free watched him walk out of her life. It was all she could do not to run after him. But how could she tell him the truth?

Forty-five

Free went up to her room and lay down on the bed, her belly rising before her. She stroked it absentmindedly. Her thoughts were so jumbled she couldn't follow one of them for long. She thought she had known everything she needed to know about Lydia, but Lydia had lied to her. Lydia had presented Free with the face Free had wanted to see. By now, Free had told enough tall tales of her own that maybe she shouldn't be surprised that other people shaped the truth until it reflected what they wanted rather than what was.

Had Lydia lied about other things? Were her parents really dead? Where had she really been going? To a lover who even now wondered where she was, unable to call her husband and ask? Or to a lawyer, as she had said, but to a divorce lawyer?

Free shook her head. How could it be the way Craig said? Lydia's voice had gone all soft when she talked about her husband. Free shook out the contents of Lydia's purse, which she now used for her own, onto the bed. She had never removed the little cloth-covered photo album, and now she slowly paged through it until she came to the wedding-day picture of Lydia and her husband. In the picture, Lydia's face glowed. There was no hint that one day her husband would beat her and she would lie about it through swollen lips. And what about the husband? What had Craig said his name was? Roy? In the beginning, Roy must have loved Lydia. There must have been love there, and maybe there had even been love right up to the last—or else why had Lydia refused over and over again to press charges?

Now Roy must be frantic, wondering where his wife was. Was it fair that he might go through the rest of his life thinking he saw Lydia on every street corner?

When she picked up the purse to put everything back, it still felt oddly heavy. When she shook it, something rattled. Holding it toward the light, Free opened the purse wide. The bottom was made out of a separate piece of leather. She pressed on it and found that it was firm on one side and gave on the other. The bottom, she realized, had been separated from the bag and moved up. What had Lydia been hiding? Despite her square appearance, had she been smuggling drugs like Jamie?

With her fingernails, Free managed to lift up one side, revealing a flat hidden object. Whatever she had thought she would find, it wasn't this. A little book, bound in black cloth, about three inches by two inches and a half-inch thick. The cover was stamped with the word *Addresses,* but when she opened it up the pages were filled edge to edge with a tiny cursive handwriting. The letters were so small and crowded together that Free at first thought it was all in code.

Then a phrase leaped up at her. *He hit me again today. For nothing.*

Jamie had looked like a college kid, but in real life he had been a drug dealer. Lydia had said she mourned a dead husband, good and kind, but instead she had been fleeing him. And Free herself had turned into someone other than who she really was.

She began to page through the diary, reading an entry here and there. The entries were undated.

In public, he kisses and hugs me. People like to be around him because he is funny. Whenever we go out, I don't want to come home, because I want him to stay the nice Roy, the sweet Roy, the Roy he was when we first started dating. No one knows what is happening and they probably wouldn't believe it. My stomach hurts all the time. I would be so ashamed if people knew the truth.

My life will end if I call the police. I know that. They make it sound so easy in the women's magazines. Press charges. Teach him a lesson. But even if they could keep me safe for a while, he would probably get out on bail. And even if he went to jail, he would still eventually get out. And then what? I know Roy. He has the patience of Job when he wants to.

I have to get out of here or I will end up dead. Even though I am afraid that if I leave he might still kill me anyway.

But how can I go? I don't have any money of my own. Just the money he gives me for groceries, and I have to account for every penny of that. He is the only one who can sign checks or withdraw money from savings.

I thought of it today. Or really, two things. Bottle return money and coupons! They're the only things he hasn't figured in. I can get maybe two dollars every week from his beer and pop cans and bottles. And today I asked the cashier to ring the coupons up separate, after she had already totaled it. I told her it was so I could see exactly how much I saved, but really, I just tore the slip off after that first total. Roy doesn't know that with coupons and bottle money, today I got $2.60 back. I hid it in my shoe. Even though he took off all my clothes when I got home, I knew he would only check my underwear. My shoes he doesn't care about.

I feel happy today for the first time in months.

———

The diary ended there. Free sat back, surprised to notice the wet-ness of tears on her face. Now she understood the crumpled one-dollar bills in Lydia's purse. How many weeks of saving had those thirty-two dollars represented? How many times of being forced to take off her clothes while her husband sought proof of an imaginary lover?

Forty-six

Tuesday, OCTOBER 31, 5:07 A.M.

His bedside clock said 5:07 when Don rolled over in the dark to answer the phone. Instead of sleeping, he had been thinking about what today would bring. The deadline had officially expired. Yesterday, he'd managed to slip down to the basement before Lexi walked in the front door, then left the way he came in after she had gone. The twitchy-looking guy had taken off, too, after Don gave him what Barry called Don's "don't fuck with me" look. Don figured him for some guy who had been ready to troll through any empty houses, looking for something to support his habit. Don could have told him he would find no ready cash in the house.

At first, the voice on the other end of the phone was insubstantial. Don had to ask its owner to repeat herself.

"He's dead!" A woman's voice. High-pitched. Breathless. And on the verge of totally losing it.

"Who's dead?" Don asked, although part of him already knew the answer. Who else would they call him about? Everyone else he loved was already dead.

"Barry."

"Where are you?"

"At the Java Jiant."

"What's your name?" This woman sounded like she was about

to launch into full-blown hysterics, and he didn't need that now.

"Heather."

Don remembered Heather, tall, thin, stick-straight hair dyed an unconvincing shade of orange-red. She and Barry always opened the store. He forced himself to speak slowly. "Are you sure he's dead, Heather?" Maybe the girl had gotten all flustered. Maybe they had just beaten Barry up really, really bad. "Did you try CPR? Did you call an ambulance? You should call an—"

She cut him off. "His brains are all over the wall. And he's got a knife in his chest with a note stuck on it. And the note's got your name on it."

"What does it say?" The world was falling away from under his feet. In his mind's eye, Don saw Barry laughing in the storage room down in the basement where they used to hide out to share a bong, back when they were eleven.

"It says, 'When will we get it, Don?' What does anyone want that would be worth this?" Heather's tone was one of shock but not surprise, and in some other part of his mind, that worried Don. Had Barry been talking to her, bragging on his relationship to Don, hinting and whispering about the real source of Don's income? It was probable that Barry had been screwing this girl, just like he had half the other baristas. Barry was—had been, Don amended—still the same guy he had been in high school, still smoking pot and dating eighteen-year-olds. Only he had gotten older and the pot had gotten stronger and the girls had stayed the same age.

"Who else have you called?"

"Nobody." Her voice flat.

"Do me a favor, would you, Heather?"

"What?" The word was a challenge. "I'm not going to touch him. I can't touch him, so don't ask me to touch him, okay? 'Cause I'm not gonna."

"Would you just do me a favor and wait there and not call anybody until I come? I can be there in ten minutes."

"I can't"—her voice stumbled at the thought—"I can't go back in there with him. I'm out in my car on my cell phone. I only stayed long enough to get your number off the bulletin board."

"Just hang tight, then, please? I'll be there in ten minutes."

All the way there, screaming down Vista in his Porsche Boxter, going sixty-five in a zone marked thirty, Don's mind pawed over Barry's death for its many meanings. They had picked his weakest spot and literally driven a knife into it. Enrique was trying to show Don that he meant business, that Don and anything he might care about would not be safe until the money was back where it belonged.

But there was another message Don could read in the spilling of Barry's blood. Don was now expendable. You didn't make a statement of this nature and expect that you would continue to have a good, long-term relationship with the employee who was on the receiving end.

No, this message was simply designed to make Don cough up the money, real quick. And then they would kill him, too. One day, Don would turn the key in the Boxter and a bomb would blow his legs off. Or a new gardener would drop his hose and pull a gun from his waistband and shoot Don through his study window while he was checking his E-mail. Maybe they would even get to Margherita, pay or threaten her until she agreed to slowly poison him. Although that wasn't like them. They liked showy things. They liked to watch their work turn up on the nightly news. They fancied themselves the new Mafia, killing a turncoat and then stuffing his throat with his own cut-off dick.

The parking lot of the Java Jiant was empty except for a beaten-up brown Volkswagen Rabbit sitting in the far corner of the lot. Barry's car. Don didn't know how many times he had laid down the rule that staff were not to park in the lot. Don got out of his car and took a deep breath. The door to the shop was standing open. Through it, he could see Barry sitting with his back against the counter, his legs splayed out on the floor. Don turned sideways and walked in, careful not to touch anything, although he was wearing black leather driving gloves.

He squatted down in front of his old friend. Barry's blue eyes were open and dull. Don didn't know if he only imagined the expression of surprise. There was a neat round hole in his forehead, but most of the back of his head was gone and there was a hell of a bloody mess running down the white wall behind the counter. Don wondered if Barry had let them in, or if the door had already been unlocked for Heather. He supposed he would never know. It looked like Barry had been shot where he stood, without time to run or even to realize what was happening.

The knife that stood in Barry's chest was big and ornate and not to be missed. It had a black-and-silver handle that was five inches long, at least. The note was in cursive handwriting, pretty penmanship for such an ugly setting. It said what Heather had said it did. *When will we get it, Don?* The paper was all white, except for a few spots of blood around the hilt of the knife. So Barry had been dead when they had done this to him, his heart no longer pumping blood. Don was glad of that. He hoped his old friend had never really known what was happening, had had no time to feel fear or pain or anything else but the beginnings of surprise.

Don tried to weigh everything. This was going to come back to him, one way or another. Because he was Barry's employer and his friend, the police would come sniffing around. Thorough scrutiny might reveal a few loose ends that might then be pulled, causing the whole careful setup, the one he had labored on for years, to unravel. They were crazy to do something so public that would only draw attention to Don. Then again, he knew that his bosses no longer cared about what he did or what he could do past their getting their money one last time. Don thought about taking the knife, but decided against it. Instead he reached down and yanked the paper up, so that it was sliced cleanly by the edge of the knife. He folded up the note and slipped it in his jacket pocket. Then he went around the counter and turned the key for the till, pressed the button so it popped open. It held about $200 in small bills. One by one, he snapped open the spring-loaded metal latches that held the money in place and cleaned out the till.

Then he carried the money to where Heather sat waiting in a blue Toyota Tercel station wagon parked at the curb. Her face was blanched so white that her skin was almost translucent. Maybe she really was a redhead. She didn't move when he opened the door, but she flinched when he put the money on her lap. Her mouth drew down at the corners while she regarded the money the way she might look at something rotten.

"Why did you call me instead of the police?" Don asked.

She didn't answer him, and that was answer enough. Damn that Barry! Don took out his wallet and peeled off ten one-hundred dollar bills and added them to the pile. "If I ask you to, will you go back in and call them now?"

"I saw you take that note off him. Am I not supposed to say anything about that?"

Smart girl, this Heather. "If you wouldn't mind."

"Still, how long will it be until they come looking for you?"

"You mean the cops? Maybe never, if they think it's a robbery."

She looked up at him with eyes the color of ashes. "I meant the people who did this to Barry."

Forty-seven

The girl came out of the house. She stood on the front porch, taking deep breaths of the crisp air, steam rising from her mouth, her cheeks reddening. She wore black pants, white tennis shoes and a red quilted jacket he hadn't seen before. The color suited her.

Don sighed. He knew what he was doing. Killing time, wasting it instead of mentally preparing himself to do what had to be done. As soon as she left, he would break into her house again, hide himself and then wait for her to come home. Even if she managed to scream once before he put the gun in her ear and got the gag in her mouth, it wouldn't make any difference. There would be no one around to hear it.

And then he would ask Free where the money was. He'd give her a pen and paper so she could write it down. And then he would have to hurt her to make sure she was telling the truth. And then he would kill her. It was as simple as that. The baby she carried in her belly, the way she somehow reminded him of Rachel—all of that didn't make any difference. She had taken what wasn't hers, and she had to pay for that.

Part of Don wanted to be weak, to tell himself that he might let her live. If he could extract a promise from her that she would never tell anyone what had happened. If she gave up the money without a struggle and swore on the life of her unborn child to keep her silence. That family of hers had raised her up not to trust cops. The guy who had come around that one time was a cop, Don knew that for certain from having his plates run, but he had watched the way Free stepped away from him whenever he got close. Maybe there really was a chance she wouldn't tell.

But he couldn't count on that. Kill her and—he forced himself to think it—maybe stage it afterward to look like an uncompleted rape and the cops would be looking for some sick perv who got his jollies savaging pregnant women. If he let her live, he would be taking the chance that she wouldn't go yakking to the cop, and that the cop couldn't draw a line from A to B, from a million dollars to the syndicate. Once they learned the size of what Free had had and then had taken away, the cops would be anxious as hell to figure out who had done it. They would conjure up futures for themselves filled with news conferences, attaboys and career advancements, knowing that any find of that magnitude was a lot farther up the scale than some dealer on the corner. And Free would be able to detail Don's size and his build, guess at his age, give them clues by describing how he walked, talked and spoke. Even with long sleeves and a ski mask, she might still notice that he was as hairless as a naked mole rat, and how many men were there in town who met that description?

Free started down the flagstone steps, bouncing at every one. No earmuffs or hat, he noticed, even though it was cold. That wig probably kept her warm. Then to the corner, ready to cross the street. She waited patiently for a huge old black Monte Carlo, as big as a boat, to cross in front of her. It turtled along, the square shape of a blue handicapped parking pass dangling from the rear-view mirror. The pass served as a kind of unofficial warning that the driver, a hunched figure wearing a gray watch cap, was slow and couldn't be counted on to see well or react in time.

Don watched the power window slide down on the driver's side, the old man lean forward to ask Free a question. He must have asked for the time, because Free looked down at her wrist and then back up. Don watched her lips move. He saw the driver cup his left hand around his ear. Alarm bells were beginning to ring in Don's brain. Free leaned closer.

The driver's hand shot forward to clamp around her wrist. Then two things happened at the same time. The trunk was released just as the driver's door flew open, hitting Free in the abdomen. Don watched the girl's lips part in a shocked, soundless cry, her free hand flying to her belly. Still with a hold on Free's arm through the open window, the driver stepped out of the car. He didn't look old at all now, although Don couldn't see his face. He had pulled the brim of his watch cap down over it, turning it into a ski mask. Don guessed that the driver and Free were about the same size, but the man had a gun, which tipped the balance. Even a half-block away, Don recognized it as a shiny nickle-plated Colt. The one with the ivory grips, for godssake. A big gun, way too showy for Don's taste. A bullet from that gun at that range would tear a fist-sized hole through a man. Or a woman.

Faster than Don could think of what to do, the gunman pulled Free back against him and put the gun against her temple. This time she did make a noise, the beginning of a scream that he quickly stifled with the palm of one gloved hand. With no memory of taking his gun from his holster, Don found himself sighting at the man, but the two were so close that there was no way Don could risk it, not with the distance and not with a window between him and them.

Free was struggling, then suddenly went as still as a child playing freeze tag. Don saw where the gun was pointed. Not at her head, but pressed against the bulge of her belly. Don started at the sound of his own, unthinking moan as he saw the gun press hard enough to make a dimple.

With his free hand, the gunman reached inside the car and came out with a strip of duct tape that he must have stuck on the inside of the door. The tape went over Free's mouth. The sight of her pleading eyes wild above that silver tape inflamed Don. The man produced another, longer strip, and muttered something in her ear, pushing the gun against her belly again for emphasis. Obediently she held her hands behind her where her assailant taped them together. Then he marched Free to the back of the car, keeping as close as a shadow, offering Don no target. He tipped the girl in, slammed the trunk closed, ran back to the open door, slid behind the wheel and drove away.

From start to finish, the whole thing had taken about sixty seconds.

What in the hell is going on, Don wondered as he fumbled the key into the ignition. He could think of only one reason why someone would snatch this girl Free. Someone else knew that she had three-quarters of a million dollars. Someone who was fast and professional. Even the threat against her unborn baby had probably been professional, the same way Don's decision to stage a rape scene would have been the work of a professional. Nothing personal, you know?

They already knew that Don didn't have the money, although he didn't think that they knew—or probably cared—why. Had Enrique decided to skip Don and cut out the middleman? Or was this guy the new middleman? As for that big gun, well, maybe that was the only sign of a weakness in this whole scenario. Someone who had a piece like that probably relied on it a little too much.

Forty-eight

Tuesday, OCTOBER 31, 11:42 A.M.

Free tried to climb into the trunk, but with her hands bound behind her back the only way in was to fall. Arching her back, she
twisted as frantically as a cat about to be plunged into water, trying
to avoid landing on her belly and hurting the baby. With a thud,
she landed half on her back and half on her side, knocking the air
out of her and wrenching her shoulder. Tears of pain sprung up in
her eyes.

Her thoughts a crazy jumble, Free listened to the slamming of
the trunk and then the driver's door. Her kidnapper, whoever he
was, hadn't said much more to her beyond "Don't make a sound
or I'll kill you" and "Get in." He hadn't pushed her into the trunk,
but he hadn't helped her in, either. All she knew about him was
that he was a man about her own height, but wirier. She guessed
he was not much older than she was, certainly nowhere past fifty.
A smell had clung to him, something rank like cat urine.

Just the memory of the smell made Free want to vomit. She
forced herself to swallow back the nausea. With this piece of tape
stuck over her mouth, if she threw up right now she would probably choke and die. She tried taking deep breaths through her
nose. The urgency receded a little bit. Free had never liked en-
closed spaces, and here she was, doubly caught, stuck in a pitch-

275

black trunk and trapped again inside her own head. Not being able to breathe through her mouth made her feel like she was being slowly smothered. Thank God she didn't have a cold.

What was going to happen next? She'd read in a dozen women's magazines that you should never go with a kidnapper, that it was better to be shot or stabbed in your own neighborhood than to wind up a corpse in a shallow mountain grave. That advice had never addressed the issue she had faced, though. This guy had been willing to shoot her in the stomach, willing to kill her baby at the same time as he injured or even killed her. Again, Free suppressed the gag that shuddered through her.

Concentrating on taking slow, deep breaths through her nose, she tried to calm herself by reasoning out what had happened. Like most women, Free had thought herself well-versed in the calculus that allowed her to deduce how much danger she was in whenever she walked down the street. You factored in what the person or persons approaching you were wearing, how many of them there were, what their car looked like (if there was one), how old they were, if there were any women with them and whether or not they were smoking or drinking beer.

Now it was clear she couldn't add two and two. She had seen the handicapped sticker and taken it for a sign that she was safe. She had known that she had $740,000 of someone else's money, and she had stupidly figured they wouldn't be able to track her down. The guy driving this car must be Don, Jamie's contact. The same guy who had scared Jamie so bad that he had kept trying to walk on dead legs.

Oh, there was probably some small chance that the guy up front could be just your average crazed serial killer. Somebody looking for any girl with a pageboy haircut. Someone who might have taken Free because she reminded him of some girl who had stood him up at the ninth-grade prom. Free didn't think so, though. There could be only one reason this guy had taken her—the money. He knew she had it and he wanted it. Or he guessed she had it and he wanted it. Either way, she knew that whenever he finally popped open the latch, he wouldn't do it next to a crowded city sidewalk, someplace where she might escape. No, when he finally stopped and opened the trunk, they would be alone, with no witnesses. Just Don and the ivory-handled gun, and Free with her hands bound behind her. Lamb to the slaughter. Because once he had the money, or even just knew where it was, what would he do with her? She remembered Jamie's words, chilling as a prophecy: *"Don'll kill me if I don't give it to him."*

Even over the throaty rumble of the car engine, Free could hear her own breathing, a panicked panting through her nose. She forced herself to take deeper, calmer breaths, trying to distract herself by wondering about the car. This was the kind of older model car with quite a bit of horsepower under the hood. An old man's car driven by a young man. Where had he gotten it and the handicapped tag that had dangled from the rearview mirror? She hoped he hadn't killed some old man for the protective coloration of the car.

Presumably the Don guy was running the heater up there. Here in the trunk she figured it was freezing or worse. The air seemed stuffy. Did car manufacturers even bother to shield the contents of the trunk from the exhaust fumes, or was she slowly being poisoned to death back here? She had to continually swallow to keep herself from throwing up. Maybe it didn't even matter if she were breathing carbon monoxide. Strangling on her own vomit would probably kill her first.

An even stronger wave of nausea rolled through her. The tape itched and pulled at her cheeks, over her lips. Overcome by an unreasoning panic, Free forgot and breathed through her mouth, sucking the tape back until it touched her tongue. A bitter taste filled her mouth, and she gagged again, even more strongly.

She had to get rid of this tape over her lips, or that Don guy was going to find her already dead whenever he stopped and opened the trunk. And the baby would be dead inside her.

Rolling forward, Free scraped her head against the thin carpet covering the floor, hoping to catch the edge of the tape and roll it off. Over and over, she rubbed until her cheek felt raw, but the tape didn't seem to move. Her wig came off, but the tape stayed put. Free's mouth filled with water again, and she could tell that she was seconds away from vomiting.

Water. Saliva. She tried licking the tape, forcing herself to ignore the terrible taste. Chewing her tongue, trying to make herself drool even more, she turned her face down so that all the spit would land right on the tape in front of her lips. She stretched the muscles of her face and began to force open her jaw, feeling the fine hairs around her mouth pull loose. Lexi visited her beautician once a month to get her upper lip and her bikini line waxed. If and when Free ever saw her roommate again, she was going to have to tell her about the power of duct tape.

Finally, the tape popped away from her lower lip, although it still clung stubbornly under her nose. The effect was like breathing behind a curtain. At least her nausea had abated. And she no longer had to worry that she would suffocate on her own vomit.

Now for the tape around her wrists. When her kidnapper had bound her wrists together with a strip of duct tape, Free had done the only thing she could think of. She had held them apart a fraction, tensed her muscles in the hope that later her bindings would be loose. Turning her wrists and stretching her hands apart gained her a bit of wiggle room, but not enough to slide one hand past the other. She let her head sag back down to the carpet. It was hopeless. This Don guy hadn't whacked her on the head, he hadn't drugged her, but she was as helpless as if he had.

Maybe if she could find the edge, she could gradually peel the tape loose. Curling her already numb-feeling fingers, she tried to locate the edge of the tape. Nothing. Finally, by twisting her wrists, she found it. By painfully torquing her hand, she was able to touch it with two fingers. But she didn't have enough leverage or flexibility to peel it back.

She thought about what would happen when he finally stopped the car. She imagined this Don guy leaning in, and her as helpless as a baby in a crib. Spurred on by a new burst of fear and energy, she managed to twist her hands even further. In twenty minutes or thirty or an eternity, she succeeded in peeling back the edge. It was another endless stretch of time before she freed her hands. The first thing she did was to rip the rest of the tape off her face. The next few minutes she spent trying to massage the feeling back into her fingers, without much success.

Even the inside of her mouth was cold. The air was so chilled that it felt like it was pulling her lungs inside out with every breath. Within her, the baby was still. She hoped it was sleeping, warm and quiet, that all of this had been only a lulling rocking to the baby. Free's legs ached and her feet were numb. She tried moving her legs back and forth like a pair of scissors, but they responded only sluggishly.

Clearly, she wasn't going to be able to spring up and overpower this guy when he opened the trunk. Was there something in here with her she could use as a weapon? Starting at the nearest wall, she began to methodically sweep her hands back and forth, exploring every nook and cranny, looking for something she could use as a weapon. What she wouldn't give for a heavy metal jack! Even a first-aid kit would be useful. She could hide the tiny pair of scissors somewhere up her sleeve or in her cleavage and then try to stab this guy in the eye. The smallest thing might give her an advantage. If only she hadn't dropped her purse on the sidewalk when he grabbed her. She could have threaded her keys between her fingers and raked his eyes, or tried to cut open his throat with the sharp new edge of her driver's license. Something. Anything. Because Free was pretty sure that any encounter that started with some guy pushing a gun against her belly and throwing her in a trunk was probably going to end with her dead.

There was something in the back corner of the trunk. Something small and icy cold and wrapped in cloth. Something firm that still yielded to pressure. Before she could decide whether she was doing the right thing, her fingers found their way inside. Something hairy and sticky with ice crystals clinging to it. For a minute, Free thought she was touching a head, a human head, and she almost lost it. Then she realized that what she was touching was some kind of small dead animal, like road kill, something so dead that most of its insides were now on the outside. A guy who would pick up road kill and wrap it up was probably not the most stable kind of guy.

Behind the dead animal, though, was something more promising. Her hand grasped a round wooden shaft. A handle of some sort. She ran her fingers one way until they met only air, then back down again until she was at the business end. She moved her hand slowly, worried that it might be an axe or something sharp.

In the dark, her eyes widened. A shovel.

Why would someone put a shovel in the car—unless he had plans to do some digging? Was it a shovel for burying the animal? Or a shovel for digging Free's grave?

Her numb fingers closed tightly around the shaft and she dragged it to her chest. She wasn't going to let that happen. Underneath her the tires made a constant thrum. Free lost track of time. She prayed a little, and it felt like someone might be listening. After a while, she got so cold her teeth stopped chattering, so cold that she tugged the rag from around the dead animal and wrapped it around her torso. Whatever it was, she could smell it now, a sweetish smell like rotting potatoes. Free's nausea returned.

Was this it, then? Her baby would die before it was even born. And her own life would be cut short before she had ever settled on who she was. She would never have a career, a home of her own, a husband. She would never watch her baby grow up to have more babies.

In the darkness Free found that nearly everything fell away. What was important was love, she decided. To do something you loved, to be surrounded by people you loved. She had still been groping her way toward both of those.

She had abandoned her family and Billy. Their only crime had been that they hadn't seen her, exactly, just seen their own reflections. But the lesson she had taught them was too harsh.

She and Lexi had been edging toward being true friends. And

Craig—she had turned away from her heart and toward her lies, pretended to herself that there wasn't something about him that drew her.

Not just for herself, but for this baby, Free had to live. Whenever the car stopped, she would have to draw upon every bit of her cleverness, act as brave as she wished she were. Because she was alone. No one was going to get her out of this but herself.

As she shifted her numb hands on the handle of the shovel, she realized maybe there was something she could do right now. Maybe there was a way to help herself.

Forty-nine

As he followed the Monte Carlo down the merge lane and onto I-84, Don kept his eye on the other car, noting the dimple in the back passenger fender, the NRA bumper sticker, the place where the antenna stuck up from the hood and the angle it made. He memorized the taillight design, in case this thing lasted after it got dark. His mind automatically recorded the information, but another part of him couldn't help thinking of what it must be like inside that trunk. Had she hit her head? What if she got sick to her stomach?

One time Don had heard about a kidnap victim who threw up. With his mouth taped closed he choked on his own vomit and died. In about ten seconds flat, his captors had gone from would-be rich guys to wanted killers.

So what did this guy want Free for? The money? That was the only thing that made any sense. But how could anyone besides Don have connected this girl with the money?

He was so tired it hurt to think, so tired that the skin on his face felt stretched over cheekbones as heavy as balls of lead. He had been awake for more than thirty hours. Don didn't know that he ever would sleep again. What was it they used to say? *I'll sleep when I'm dead.*

He dialed a number from memory, his fingers finding the buttons on his cell phone without his needing to look. "This is Don Cannon. I need you to run a plate for me and call me back at this number."

The phone rang less than five minutes later.

"It belongs to a Roy Watkins from Pendleton."

Roy Watkins. Where had he heard that name? Then he remembered. Not Roy Watkins, but Lydia Watkins. So he must be related to the woman whose name Free had taken. This changed everything, but Don didn't know how.

"Can you do a quick and dirty check on him? Place of employment, any criminal record, financial history? I only want what you can dig up in fifteen minutes." He didn't know where Roy Watkins was going, but he wanted to know a little bit more about him before they got there.

"It will be sketchy. And expensive."

"I know that." Don clicked the off button without saying anything more and concentrated on his driving. Following someone required a delicate balance. Too many shield cars made it extremely difficult to maintain visual contact with the car and increased the chance of losing it. Too few cars, though, and Don would get burned for sure. At the same time, he had to make sure that he stayed close. He was certain that he was Free's only chance at coming out of this alive. You didn't tie someone up and throw them in a car trunk as a prank. He told himself that it was important to keep her alive so he could get the money back.

Was she even still alive? Had she hit her head when she tumbled into the trunk? Was there even air back there? The sky was a blanket of solid white. Don thought it looked like snow. If she stayed back there too long, would she freeze to death?

As soon as Roy came to a stop, Don could shoot him before he even walked to the trunk. Then he could free this Free. For a minute, he imagined lifting her from the trunk, the way she would chafe her numb hands after he cut them loose, looking up at him through her lashes, her eyes dark and smiling.

He shook his head, realizing he was so exhausted he was close to dreaming. That was the only excuse for his fantasy. Because that's what it was, a fantasy. This guy was heading someplace he could be alone. He wouldn't stop if he could see Don was right behind him. And by the time Don caught up, Roy would have the girl again.

They were passing Gresham now, heading toward the mountains. Where were they going? Don was a good driver, and he had spent a lot of his time behind the wheel when he was young, both as a courier and running various errands, including tailing people. Old habits continued to come back to him. This Roy guy drove a little too fast, which meant he was easier to follow than someone who drove too slowly. Speeders paid attention to the road ahead, looking for openings in traffic and keeping an eye out for cops. People who dawdled spent a lot of time looking around them— including in their rearview mirrors.

Earlier Don had kept just two or three cars between him and the Monte Carlo, automatically making adjustments based on the density, speed and flow of traffic. Here, where exits were limited and fewer surprises could happen, he let as many as six or seven cars come between him and the old car.

Easing off gave him time to think, which wasn't entirely welcome. Barry was dead, and Don's life was on the line. The truth was that even if he brought the money back, they would still kill him. Maybe not today, maybe not tomorrow, but someday it would come. But if he didn't come trotting back and lay the money at their feet, then what?

More than seven hundred thousand dollars was still quite a bit of money. Enough to go and live someplace on a Third World beach, drinking rum and watching the sun sink into the sea. And if he took this money and ran, then he could play by his own rules. Let this girl live. Heck, maybe she would want to come along for the ride. It wasn't a realistic plan, Don knew that, but it was a plan nonetheless.

The phone ringing made him start. He fumbled it up to his ear. "Hello?"

"Okay, you ready? Here goes. Roy Watkins. Twenty-four years old. Lives in Pendleton. His mother was a stripper, father unknown. Went to live with his grandparents when he was three after his mother was charged with neglect. They both died a few years back, and Roy inherited the Monte Carlo from them. Until recently, he was an employee of a factory that made disposable diapers under the brand Dri-N-Fresh. He was fired a couple of weeks ago. He's got no savings account, he's got a Discover card that's run up to the max, and a checking account with $160 in it. Roy has one bust for meth manufacturing, but he got off on some technical glitch to do with how the evidence was processed. Local cops have rolled on his house three times in the last couple of years after neighbors reported domestic violence. Each time the wife, Lydia Watkins, age twenty-three, maiden name of Pearce, refused to press charges. She is unemployed and they have no children. No other information available on her without a site visit.

"Now I've got a little bonus for you, Don, just because you're such a good customer. Did you hear about the Badger Ridge thrill killings? Two guys out target shooting found dead, shot down while they were drinking from a Thermos? A little bird tells me Roy Watkins is considered to be a person of interest in that case. His fingerprints were found on bullets in the deceaseds' pockets. He's wanted for questioning in connection with the case, but when the cops dropped by for a chat, he was not at home. So if you're planning on messing with him, you'd better be prepared."

"Thanks for the tip. I owe you one."

"No, you don't." Don could hear the grin through the phone line. "I took an extra little bite out of your Visa."

So Roy was a tweaker, and quite probably a killer. Back in Don's dealing days, he mostly sold pot and coke. Some mushrooms, some hash, very occasionally some heroin. And sometimes black beauties or cross tops. Back then, speed had been more legit, diverted on its way to a drugstore, going to college kids who wanted to pull an all-nighter or women who wanted to be slim without effort. It wasn't this cheap shit that people made in trailer parks and by-the-hour hotels.

There hadn't been much demand for crank, not back then. Not that there was much margin in it. It was too inexpensive to make to be truly profitable. Most of it was homemade, cooked up in little meth labs set up in trailers all over Oregon. The ingredients could be purchased at Rite-Aid. They called it the poor man's cocaine. But unlike cocaine, it was physically addicting. Casual users quickly turned into slaves.

The state had an outpost of Services for Families and Children near the Burnside Java Jiant, and over the years Don had come to know a number of the social workers who worked there. They told him that most of the kids getting yanked out of their homes for abuse and neglect had parents hooked on meth. Sometimes they cried as they talked to him about the numbing parade of kids, all bones and bedsores, bruises and black eyes. They saw infants with cracked skulls and ribs. Toddlers with missing hair and cigarette burns. "Homes" where there was dog shit on the bare mattress and chemicals cooked on stovetops while the refrigerator sat empty. At best, meth users were irritable. At worst, they were dangerous.

So that's what Don was up against. An angry, hopped-up guy with a gun who had probably killed before. And Don would have to stop him before he killed Free.

His shoulders sagged. Who was he kidding? He was in good shape, but it was the kind of shape that came from mornings at the Multnomah Athletic Club with a personal trainer. Not the kind of strength that came from having to be the biggest, baddest guy on the street. He hadn't done any dirty work for years. These days, he seldom had to order it done. His people knew that he wanted them to take care of problems without him having to bother about every little thing.

Without signaling, the Monte Carlo took the next exit. Don followed, hanging as far back as he dared. They were the only two cars on the road, which meant whenever the road curved, Don lost sight of him altogether. His heart would pause until he again saw the now-familiar shape of it.

Something was happening at the back of the Monte Carlo. Don wished he dared get closer. As the other car rounded a bend, he saw that one of the taillights had been broken. From inside. He felt a rush of exultation. Free was alive. She was alive and she must have gotten her hands loose. And there was one of them. A little white hand waving out the back.

And Don the only one to see it.

Tuesday, OCTOBER 31, 1:39 P.M.

Her right hand was so cold that Free could no longer feel the deep scratches braceleting her wrist. She couldn't tell if her wrist was still bleeding from having forced it through the broken taillight. At one point, she had pressed her face against the hole, but the only car she had been able to see was a battered white van with tinted windows, too far back on the narrow, winding road, she thought, to even spot her silent call for help. The next time she looked, even the van was gone. Free had to face the fact she was all alone.

After bumping over the uneven road for about half an hour, the Monte Carlo lurched to a stop. Free readied herself as best she could, her hands gripping the shaft of the shovel two feet below where it attached to the metal blade. She tensed her muscles, ready to swing it like a bat. If she were lucky, she might be able to take advantage of a momentary surprise.

But she wasn't lucky. As the trunk lid opened, Free swung the shovel. But her captor was as quick as a cat, jerking his head to one side so that the blade of the shovel only scraped hard across his ear. With one hand, he twisted the shovel out of her grasp, then knocked her on the side of the head with the shaft for good

289

measure. Pain bloomed inside Free's skull, and she fell back into the trunk.

"Hey, psycho bitch, if you want to live a little while longer, you'd better not try anything like that again." He held the gun in his right hand, and the shovel in his left. "Now get out of the car and don't try anything or I'll gut shoot you."

Free took her time about getting out of the car, her eyes darting everywhere, looking for something with which she could save herself. But there was nothing. No other tool was revealed in the trunk by the gauzy light, only the clump of her wig and the body of a cat so mangled that at the sight of it her stomach threatened again to revolt. The driveway they stood on was paved, so there weren't even any stones she could pick up and throw at him. Scarves of fog draped the tall pines that pressed all around this little clearing with its tiny cabin and the narrow road that twisted away from them. There was no other evidence of human habitation. Except for her captor's rapid breathing, there was no other sound. Free was completely alone.

"Do you want the money back? Because I have almost all of it. Jamie asked me to get his bag, and by the time I found him again he was dead. I'll give it all back to you, and I promise I'll pay you back whatever is missing."

In the shifting light of dusk, she thought that this Don guy looked somehow familiar with his dark eyes, slanted brows and heart-shaped face. She must have seen him following her, waiting for a chance to snatch her off the street. He also seemed extremely anxious, jittering from foot to foot, with bloodshot eyes and skin so pasty it practically glowed.

"I don't know what the hell you're talking about. All I want is my wife back from that shelter you all run."

"Your wife?" Free echoed. Time seemed to have slowed to a crawl, the way it did when a glass fell from your hand and your brain had plenty of time to watch, even as your body reacted too slowly. She had figured everything out, and again she had figured it wrong.

This wasn't Don, but Roy. Dead Lydia's not-very-dead husband.

"Yeah, I forget, I'll bet you've got so many of them that you can't even keep them straight. My wife is Lydia Watkins. And before she started getting brochures from you people, we had a perfectly happy marriage."

"What are you talking about?" Free asked, stalling for time. Even though she bet the shovel in his hands had originally been meant to dig Lydia's grave, Free didn't think Roy would like it if she told him Lydia was already dead. Chances were, he would probably kill Free right now if she told him the truth about what had happened to his wife. Better to lie and buy time for something to happen.

"Don't play dumb with me. Lydia's got herself hooked up with a bunch of rich do-gooder lesbians running a shelter for"—he hooked his fingers—"battered women." Lesbians? Free realized Roy thought she and Lexi were lovers.

Something about Roy was familiar. Bob and Diane stayed away from needle drugs, or anything that took a bathtub full of chemicals to manufacture. That didn't mean that there weren't people on the periphery of their circle of friends who were tweakers. Free knew the look—and this guy had it. Crank gave you so much energy you didn't know what to do with it all. Roy's sunken eyes darted around, and she could hear him grinding his teeth. Meth was famous for keeping its users awake for a hundred hours at a time, and then leaving them sleeping it off so hard they couldn't be awakened. But before they finally crashed came rage, exhaustion and paranoia, as the mind and body began to burn themselves out.

"Look, do you know what I have back at my house? I have about seven hundred thousand dollars in cash. In small, unmarked bills. Take me back there and I'll give it to you. You can have it. All of it. And I promise I won't call the cops." Suddenly, the money had no more importance to Free than scrap paper. Instead of freeing her, the money had gotten her into this mess.

"How'd you get that kind of money? This battered-wives gig must pay better than I thought."

"It doesn't matter where I got it. All that matters is I have it. And if you take me back there, I'll give it all to you."

"Right. Like you would ever give it to me. Like you wouldn't have the cops waiting for me. No way, sister." He looked at her and laughed. "So are you the butch? Is that why you have your hair all cut off? Do you wear that wig so you can pass in public? You know, funny thing, but when I first saw you from the back, I thought you were my crazy bitch of a wife! How'd you get that baby in your belly, with no man around? I've heard about you people, get some gay guy to beat off into a turkey baster. Was that how it was?"

"Yeah, Roy, that's just how it was."

Free had aimed for sarcasm, but he seemed to take it at face value, looking pleased with himself. "I thought so."

Free thought of Lydia's diary, of the dozens of times she had written about this man beating her, kicking her, forcing himself on her. What was Roy planning on doing to Lydia when he got her back? And what would he do to Free when he realized Lydia was never coming?

"How did you know where to find Lydia?" She aimed for a tone a notch below flattery.

Smirking, Roy lifted his chin. "I've got my ways. She got herself a new driver's license with your address. At first I thought it was for the shelter, but then I watched it for two days, and all I saw was you and your girlfriend. So I figured you were a cover for the shelter. After all, you don't want the real address running around, all openlike and everything, do you? And you two are the ones who run the whole scam, hiding women from their legal husbands, when you aren't running crying to the government for handouts. That's probably where you got the money, isn't it?"

It wasn't really a question, so Free didn't answer it. "Could we please go inside now? I'm cold." Not only that, but she was hoping that inside the cabin she might find a potential weapon.

Roy made his voice a high, mocking singsong. " 'Could we please go inside now? I'm cold.' All right, after you, Princess Dyke." He made a gesture with the gun that was a cross between a bow and a threat. "But the first thing I'm going to do is tie you up— and this time you can bet I'll make sure you can't get loose."

The door wasn't locked, so Free turned the handle and went in. Her eyes swept over the inside of the cabin, alert for anything she might be able to use to her advantage. It consisted of only one room, and looked like something the pioneers might have built. The walls were made of yellow logs of peeled pine. Maybe the pioneers *had* built it. The old black woodstove must serve for both cooking and heating. Two windows were covered with limp curtains gray with dust. Along one wall was a counter, cupboards and a sink with a pump handle instead of a faucet. Great. She had wanted to go the bathroom, not just because her bladder was full but on the hope that she might be able to lock the door, or climb out the window, or locate a weapon like a nail file—or all three. Now the best she could hope for was that in the winter the outhouse that must be out back wouldn't smell too bad.

The furnishings were equally plain. An old maroon couch with the cushions mashed flat. It looked like the kind you could pull out to make into the world's most uncomfortable bed. Opposite the couch, next to the stove, was an equally ancient recliner, the black vinyl laced with cracks. Roy must have been living here for at least a while, because there was a crumpled McDonalds' bag on the counter, an afghan and pillow on the couch and an army-green duffel bag in the corner.

"Sit down." Roy waved his gun at her when she went to sit in the chair. "On the couch. That's *my* chair."

Free took a quick inventory of the weapons that presented themselves. The pieces of kindling in a basket next to the stove were heavy. On top of them lay a cast-iron poker. And on the counter was a knife block with two handles jutting from the slots. But what if she managed to grab one of them and only came up with a three-inch paring knife?

293

Roy solved that problem by pulling out the bottom knife, which proved to be the small one. He took some heavy twine from a drawer and sawed off a piece right on the countertop. It wasn't the kind of place where you had to fret about niceties like cutting boards. He tucked the nose of the gun into the waist of his jeans. Then he tied a slipknot in the twine and came over to Free.

"Hold out your wrists." He caught them in the loop of the twine and then tightened it until it bit into the skin of her wrists. "Now don't fuck around or I promise you you'll be very sorry. And don't bother screaming—the nearest house is about seven miles away." He began looping the twine back and forth in a figure eight pattern until each wrist had about six turns on it, then finished it off with a series of knots. Free had a bleak thought. Would there be any chance that Craig would be asked to examine the knots that held together her dead hands?

"What's your name?" he asked while he worked. His tone was oddly conversational.

She was thankful that in his hurry he had left her purse where it fell on the sidewalk. If he had seen the license with her picture on it and Lydia's name, she would probably be dead by now. "Free Meeker," she answered. It felt strange and more than a little bit right to finally be using her own name. She tried to make enough eye contact so that this guy would know she was human, not class her as some animal that could be disposed of like the cat in his car. And she tried not to think about how her belly seemed to be tightening in another contraction, as it had done a few times in the car. Stress, that was all it was. Stress and her uterus picking the worst possible time to practice for what lay three months down the road.

"And I'm Roy. But you already know that, don't you?" Without warning, his tone veered closer to a jeer. He reached inside his jacket and pulled out a cell phone.

"Call," he commanded, thrusting the cell phone at her. "Call that safe house you've got my wife stuck away at. I want to talk to her. I'm going to tell Lydia that she'd better get her butt out here to my grandpa's by nine o'clock tonight." He paused for emphasis, his reddened eyes boring into Free's. "Because if she's not here by nine o'clock, I'm going to kill you."

Afraid her face betrayed her, Free looked down. The sight of her belly bulging with life renewed her determination to somehow make it out of this. "I can't do that."

"Why not?"

Frantically, she searched for a lie he would believe, maybe one that might even help her, too, if she played her cards right. "The safe house doesn't have a phone on site—too easy to trace. I'll have to tell my roommate to find the house manager, and then get him to get Lydia to come here. And that may take a while. Lydia's got a part-time job, so they'll have to track her down. Let me call my roommate and explain it to her."

"Your roommate, huh?" Roy made a rude gesture, wiggling his tongue between the V of his fingers. "Okay. Only you tell her if I see or even think I see a cop, then you're getting it."

Free dialed Lexi's work number, then held the phone as close to her ear as she could with her hands tied together.

"This is Alexis Ashburg."

"Hi, it's me."

"Lydia!" The relief in Lexi's voice turned to worry. "Lydia, where are you? The mailman called and said he found your purse on the sidewalk outside the house. I tried to call you at home, but nobody answered."

Free was grateful the phone she was holding wasn't one of those cell phones with a speaker feature. Or else Roy would be asking her why Lexi was calling her by his wife's name.

"Okay, Lexi, I need you to listen carefully. I've been kidnapped by Lydia's husband. He says he wants Lydia back or he'll kill me. Listen—you've got to tell Craig, the house manager, to get Lydia from the safe house. Tell him Lydia's got to come out to Roy Watkins's grandfather's cabin by nine o'clock tonight, or he'll kill me." Free tried to hold three things in her mind simultaneously— what she was saying, what Roy was hearing, and what she hoped

Lexi was reading between the lines. "By nine o'clock, okay, or I'm dead. And Roy says if he sees any cops, then he'll kill me right away."

Lexi's reply was desperate and sad at the same time. "Lydia, I'm sorry, but I don't understand. I don't understand why you're talking about yourself in the third person. And I thought your husband was dead."

"Please just listen to what I'm telling you. It's very important. Tell Craig to tell Lydia that she's got to go out to the cabin. Roy's grandpa's place." Free sent up a little prayer that Lexi would immediately call Craig and that he could figure out where the place was well before nine o'clock. Roy nudged her neck with the gun, mouthed something in her ear. Twisting her head back so Roy wouldn't hear Lexi's questions floating out of the earpiece, Free repeated his words.

"He says he won't hurt Lydia if she comes, and he'll let me go. But she has to come by nine o'clock tonight, or it's too late."

"But you're Lydia." Lexi's voice was plaintive. "Aren't you?"

"Just do what I ask. Please, Lexi. Tell Craig to get Lydia to come to Roy's grandpa's cabin tonight by nine o'clock. It can't be any later than nine o'clock. And he says she has to come alone."

"You're not making any sense."

Free found a way to say what she was feeling without deviating from what Roy thought to be the truth. "I know, honey. I love you, too." Maybe those words would be the last she uttered to a normal human being. And she realized she did love Lexi. Loved her for the way she had taken Free under her wing, for the way she still took people at face value even after being terribly disappointed.

Roy tore the phone away from her. Oh God, Lexi would surely give the game away now, and Free would be dead.

"No cops," he barked, his words running together. "No cops. I mean it. I'll be watching, and if she's not alone, your lady friend here will get it right in the belly. Then her and the baby will die together. You'd better believe me, because I've killed people before." His boast made Free shiver, and she knew instinctively that it was true. "Tell Lydia all I want is her back. That's all. Tell Lydia that if she comes back, it will be all right."

Free prayed that Lexi had enough sense to agree with Roy's proposition, even if it sounded nonsensical to her. Lexi must have, because the next thing Free knew, Roy was biting off the word "Good," then punching the disconnect button.

She looked at her watch. Lexi had less than seven hours to find Craig, impress upon him the gravity of the situation, overcome whatever puzzlement both of them felt about Free talking about herself in the third person, figure out where she was, round up a rescue party, drive two or more hours, arrive out here and save her without alerting Roy to their presence.

In other words, Free realized, she had better start thinking up Plan B.

Fifty-one

For the past two hours, Roy had been lecturing Free in the flickering light of a single lantern that sat at one end of the counter. A storm had begun to blow in. She was thankful every time the sleet rattled on the tin roof, because it made it hard to hear him. Women didn't know their place. Women tried to make men look stupid. Women took away men's jobs and then couldn't even do them right. Then he moved from the general to the specific, specifically the topic of Lydia, explaining that he had only hit her a few times, when she needed correcting. Lydia, Roy informed Free, was like a stupid dog that had to be kicked a few times before it knew how to behave. Now he asked for the third time, "So who's this Craig guy again?"

Free had known it was a risk to say Craig's name to Lexi, but she hadn't imagined that upon learning of Craig's imaginary occupation, Roy would be consumed with jealousy.

"I told you, he runs the place where your wife is staying. The— the safe house."

"Is Lydia sleeping with him? She is, isn't she? She would lie down with anyone. She won't tell me the truth, but I know her. She's a whore."

"She's not like that," Free said, finally stung into defending poor dead Lydia.

With a feigned weariness, Roy just shook his head. "You don't know her like I do." He was nursing his third sixteen-ounce Budweiser, alternating beers with snorting white lines of meth off the counter in the light of an old oil lantern he had lit. Pushing himself up from the recliner, Roy stuck his face in hers. His eyes were red and when he spoke, flecks of spittle landed on her cheeks and chin. "You don't understand. You don't know, really know her. And you sure as shit don't know me. And you don't know us." The words were an angry, agitated slur. "Things were fine between me and her when she just kept her place. That's the trouble with you dykes. You don't even understand about what it's like between a man and a woman."

Free had stopped listening because she felt it again, a persistent ache low in her abdomen. Under her hands, her belly rose and tightened until it felt as hard as wood. A contraction. But was it the practice kind the doctor at the hospital had talked about? Or was she in labor? She didn't know if this were the second or the third time she had felt a contraction in the past hour. Time kept accordioning, stretching out and then squeezing together again. Sneaking a glance at her watch, visible between strands of twine, Free swore to herself that she would remember better the next time how long it had been since the last one, then realized she was thinking as if a next time were inevitable. It was a few minutes after four. It had been a little over two hours since she had called Lexi, and it had taken Roy, driving on dry roads, two hours to get here from Portland. Now the roads were probably covered with ice. Maybe she could use that idea to buy time when Lydia failed to show by nine P.M.

The room was so cold that every time Roy moved close to the lantern she saw his breath hanging in white clouds. Free was glad she hadn't taken off her coat before he tied her hands up. The stove didn't seem to be putting out much warmth, even though the top was faintly glowing, even though Roy kept getting up to pile wood inside and poke at it with a poker. He was starting to stagger when he got up, and to list farther to one side every time he sat back down on the couch. Earlier, he had told Free he had been awake for more than three days. His eyelids were drooping. She knew if he fell asleep it would take a lot to waken him, and the idea held a kernel of hope. Could she get the poker and swing it like a bat, making any sleep of Roy's permanent? And then what? Could she somehow burn off the rope? Which led to another question—which would burn faster, the rope or her hands? Maybe she could hold a knife between her feet and saw through her bindings. And after that she would take the keys to his car off his body, then just drive away. The plan was so rough she could have used it to file her nails, but it was all Free had.

Roy's head fell forward, then jerked back up again. "Okay, bitch, I'm going to have to go to sleep. Just for an hour. And then you're going to wake me up. In fact, you're going to lie down next to me on the couch so I'll know you're not up to anything. So don't try anything stupid. Because if I feel you try to get up or get away, I'll shoot you right between the eyes. Do you understand me?"

Through a gap in the curtains, Don saw Roy stand, take the Colt from his waistband, and then put it between Free's eyebrows. He was going to kill her now, while Don watched helplessly. And that would spell the death of everything—Free, the baby she carried, his hopes for getting the money back, and eventually Don himself.

He took a few steps back, then launched himself toward the window, his head tucked, his left shoulder leading, and the gun ready in his right hand.

At the cold touch of the gun between her eyebrows, Free closed her eyes. Even though she knew Roy was just threatening her, everything narrowed down to that circular space. The next few minutes were a riot of confusion—the sound of glass shattering, shards pricking her face, a gust of freezing wind, men shouting, and two gunshots, very near. Ears ringing, Free found herself standing with her back against the rough logs without being aware that she had moved. With his hand clapped over his right shoulder, Roy was screaming obscenities. And there was a big bald man lying twisted on the floor between her and Roy, bleeding from the chest, and absolutely still.

Free realized Roy was yelling at her. "I said no cops, you bitch!" He kicked the other man's gun away from his hand until it spun under the couch, then raised his own weapon and pointed it at her.

Until the man on the floor cried out, Free had taken him for dead.

"She didn't lie to you! I'm not a cop!"

Roy hesitated, but only for a fraction of a second. "Shit, yeah, of course you're not!" He raised the gun again, only this time he aimed it at the man on the floor.

"I've been—" he gasped. "—following her—" another pause, his fingers white against the wound. "—because she's got my money." Blood seeped past his fingers and joined a puddle on the floor. "I'm no cop." His words came slower. "Name's . . . Don Cannon. . . . Check my wallet. . . ." And then his eyes rolled up in his head.

Roy took a half-step forward and pointed the gun directly at the man's head. She watched his hand tighten.

Whatever else Don Cannon had done, he had just saved her life, so Free returned the favor. "Don't kill him," she said to Roy, struggling to keep her voice calm and reasonable. "Keep him alive as a bargaining chip. And if the cops do come, you can shoot him to show them you mean business."

Roy tilted his head and squinted. She could tell he was thinking, and she could also tell it was hard going. "Is that true, what he said? About the money?"

"I do have some money that originally belonged to him, yes."

"You mean, you weren't shitting me about that money you said you had?"

"We can still go back and get it." Even knowing Roy probably wouldn't take it, Free felt she still had to make the offer.

"What we're going to do is wait for Lydia. And then we'll see. But first, I need you to take care of my arm." Roy gave Don a hard kick to the head, but the other man didn't move. The pool of blood had grown so much that Free thought he was probably dead. Never taking his eyes off Free, Roy peeled his hand off his right bicep, leaned down, picked up the other man's gun and tucked in the back of his pants.

The cloth of Roy's shirt was torn, but to Free's eyes it looked as if Don had only grazed Roy, leaving a shallow crease and a slow trickle of blood.

"I'm going to need you to bandage me up," he said, picking up the paring knife in his left hand. He still held the gun in his right hand, pointed at her. "I'll cut you free for a little bit. But if you try anything tricky, I'll kill you." For emphasis, he kicked Don again, this time in the ribs. Again, he stayed motionless, seemingly unconscious. But was it Free's imagination, or had the prone man's eyes flickered? She tore her gaze away, not wanting to betray him.

It was then that Free made her move. Roy was as relaxed as he was ever going to get again on this night, with a gun in one hand and a knife in the other and another gun tucked in his waistband, with one captive dead or dying on the floor and another with her hands tied before her.

So she went for it. Not away from Roy, as he might have suspected, but toward Roy and the lantern on the counter behind him. With her left hand, Free pushed up the barrel of Roy's gun, and with her right she groped to turn off the lantern. All she wanted was the cover of darkness and a chance to hide in the woods and wait for Craig. The gun fired into the ceiling, but instead of putting out the lantern, she knocked it over. A spurt of liquid ran the length of the counter. The flame lapped eagerly behind it. In a second, the curtain that had been touching the counter blazed up. Free ran for the door.

With a shout, Roy tore down the curtain and tried to stamp it out. But he was too late. The wall, as dry as kindling, caught. At the doorway, Free risked a look behind her. Roy was aiming the gun toward her. Then he screamed. Fire raced up his legs. He dropped the gun and began ripping at his clothes, shrieking and dancing in the flames blooming across the floor.

Don had somehow gotten to his knees, the fire licking at his shoes. Without making a conscious decision, Free took two steps back and leaned over to take the other man's right hand in both of her still-tied-together ones. By some miracle, he struggled to his feet. Free ran from the cabin, Don lurching behind.

Under the milky spill of the stars, they slid and stumbled on pebbles of ice that carpeted the ground with white and weighed down the branches of the trees. Behind them, the fire popped and crackled, sending out showers of sparks that hissed as they landed. As they staggered away, Free turned to look, but all she could see were flames. No Roy stood silhouetted in the door of the cabin.

Don had to shout to make himself heard over the eager roar of the fire. "My van's behind the trees over there!"

Free fell to her knees as they ran, and when Don helped her up his hands were slick with blood that shone black in the moon-light. Finally they made it to the old white van that she remem-bered seeing from inside the trunk. Leaving bloody handprints on the frame, Don opened the passenger door, then sprawled on the seat. "I can't see very well anymore. You'll have to drive." He reached out and pressed a key ring into her hands. She looked behind her. No Roy, just the cabin burning bright and hot, the flames so fierce that the air rippled.

Free slammed Don's door closed with her knee, then went back around to the driver's side. With her bound hands she opened the door, thankful it wasn't locked. She was busy trying to twist her wrists to fit the key in the ignition when something leaped onto the windshield. She screamed. Roy, his face mashed against the ice-glazed glass, gave them a maniac's cold and terrible grin. Parts of his shirt were burned away. Underneath, it looked like hamburger. And in his blackened right hand, he held a gun.

The van's engine rumbled to life without her being aware that she had turned the key in the ignition. Then she realized Don had done it. "Go!" he shouted. "Go! Run the bastard over!"

She hit the accelerator and the engine roared and then whined, but the van didn't go anywhere. "It's still in park!" Don yelled, then fixed that and released the emergency brake for good measure.

With his left hand, Roy had grabbed on to the top of the van, and with his right he tried to aim the gun at her. It was nearly impossible to hold the wheel, and Free relied on her wrists more than her fingers. The car fishtailed underneath them, the wheels finding no purchase. Suddenly Free felt as if she were back behind the wheel of the Impala, Lydia beside her and horror all around. With one part of her mind, she was aware of Roy taking careful aim, but she felt as if she were falling, as if she were falling and would never touch the ground.

Then the baby kicked her, hard, right in the ribs. Free managed to jerk the wheel to the right and into the low-hanging branches, heavy with ice. Roy was suddenly—gone. As the wheels ran over him, she grunted at the terrible moment of impact and his shriek that was suddenly stilled.

The van shuddered, stalled and died.

And there, ahead of her, the sight she had been longing for. One, two, three squad cars, strobe lights cutting red and blue through the woods, the lights multiplied on the ice that coated the trees.

Don stared down at his chest. So much blood. So much blood. So much blood he could taste it, as if someone had laid an old copper penny on his tongue like a communion wafer. And then he was above his body, floating over it, watching with detached interest as the blood leaked out of his chest and bubbled between his lips, while the girl cried out his name and a cop shone a flashlight on him. Until finally Don was pulled backward and up and inside out. And there beside him was Rachel, her dark eyes smiling. She laid her cheek against his, pressed him close without saying a word. Her warmth gave him the courage to let go of the only life he had ever known.

Gently, Free eased the lifeless body of Don Cannon back on the bench seat, sticky with blood.

Then Craig opened the driver's side door and caught her as she fell backward in a dead faint.

Fifty-Two

"And one more push! Come on! You can do it!"

Lexi shouted encouragement in Free's ear, seeming not to notice that the epidural had worn off quite a long time ago. All the people crowded around the end of the bed began to laugh, crowing that they saw the head crowning. All Free could think about was that she was simultaneously on fire and being ripped apart.

This morning the doctor had induced her, and now after fifteen hours of sometimes boring and sometimes excruciating labor, Free was a few seconds away from giving birth.

Back on the first day of November, Free had spent a day in the hospital being treated for shock and having her own and the baby's health monitored. The exam revealed that her contractions hadn't been labor, but stress induced. Free couldn't argue that she hadn't been under stress. But riding to the hospital beside Craig, the siren cutting through the still night air, she had found that her fear of being inside a car had vanished.

He hadn't talked to her much on the drive, too intent at getting her to the hospital, but the next day he came to visit her. Instead of bringing flowers, he brought questions. "Lydia Watkins was arrested for shoplifting and fingerprinted when she was a senior in high school. I checked your prints against hers. They don't match. So who in the hell are you?" Free told him who she was, and why she had done what she had done, in a telling that took two hours.

What was left of the money—about $730,000—had been swallowed by the United States government, as mandated by federal law for any money that resulted from illegal activity. Neither side argued that a bag containing hundreds of thousands of dollars in cash probably fell into that category. At the same time, the feds didn't ask Free to give back what she had spent. Free didn't know whether Craig had had a hand in that or not.

It hadn't taken Diane and Bob very long to get over their anger that she had let them think her dead. After everything that had happened, Free had decided to accept them on their own terms, just as they seemed to accept what she had done to them.

Free had gone back to using her real name. Upon hearing it, most people smiled or made one of the jokes she had heard a million times before, which she accepted with good grace. For the first time in her life, she felt at peace with herself.

Craig brushed a strand of hair out of Free's eyes. "Just one more push," he urged, squeezing her hand. Suddenly the pain and pressure were gone. Free felt the baby's long body go sliding out of her. And a new world began.